Michael Wood is a freelance journalist and proofreader living in Newcastle. As a journalist he covered many crime stories throughout Sheffield, gaining first-hand knowledge of police procedure. He also reviews books for CrimeSquad, a website dedicated to crime fiction.

www.michaelwoodbooks.co.uk

x.com/MichaelHWood
facebook.com/MichaelWoodBooks
instagram.com/MichaelWoodBooks
bookbub.com/authors/MichaelWood

CW01507790

Also by Michael Wood

DCI Matilda Darke series
For Reasons Unknown
Outside Looking In
A Room Full of Killers
The Hangman's Hold
The Murder House
Stolen Children
Time Is Running Out
Survivor's Guilt
The Lost Children
Silent Victim
Below Ground
Last One Left Alive
Worse Than Murder

Dr Olivia Winter series
The Mind of a Murderer
The Devil's Code

Standalones
The Seventh Victim
Vengeance is Mine
Chapter One

DCI Matilda Darke short stories
The Fallen
Victim of Innocence
Making of a Murderer

CHAPTER ONE

MICHAEL WOOD

One More Chapter
a division of HarperCollins*Publishers*
1 London Bridge Street
London SE1 9GF
www.harpercollins.co.uk
HarperCollins*Publishers*
Macken House, 39/40 Mayor Street Upper,
Dublin 1, D01 C9W8, Ireland

This paperback edition 2025

1

First published in Great Britain in ebook format
by HarperCollins*Publishers* 2025

A catalogue record of this book is available from the British Library

ISBN: 978-0-00-861858-2

This novel is entirely a work of fiction. The names, characters and incidents
portrayed in it are the work of the author's imagination. Any resemblance to actual
persons, living or dead, events or localities is entirely coincidental.

Printed and bound in the UK using 100% Renewable Electricity
by CPI Group (UK) Ltd

To the real Luke Jackson.
(wherever he is)

Chapter One

LIVERPOOL, ENGLAND

Out of Darkness by Aidan Cullen.

It seemed strange after all these years of rejections, setbacks, and hurtful criticism to finally see a physical hardback in his hands. Although it was his first published novel, it was actually the fourth he had written.

Looking back, the first two were complete rubbish. The first he was now even embarrassed to admit he'd written. It was terrible. It was beyond terrible, it was … no, it needed forgetting. There was no first book.

The second showed promise. His style of writing had improved but the plot was thin and full of gaping holes. He could understand why it had been rejected time and time again. It deserved to be shredded.

The third book was different. He liked his third novel. It had heart. The central character was dangerous and intriguing and was purposely written so the reader couldn't quite decide if she was good or bad. The story had a twist he was proud of, and he was convinced this would make it to publication. He was wrong. Publishers didn't like the protagonist. She was flaky, annoying, and readers wouldn't root for her. Another one for the shredder.

Ten years of writing and he was getting nowhere.

He was ready to give up when the idea for *Out of Darkness* came to him in his sleep. The story – of a blind woman who murders her husband but manages to convince the police, her lawyer, the judge and jury that she is innocent – was inspired. He wrote the first draft in a month. He wrote the second in a fortnight. He didn't bother with a third. It didn't need it.

The first agent he sent it out to snapped it up. There was very little editing to be done and soon there was a bidding war between the top publishing houses in the country.

A healthy five-figure sum was offered. He was happy with that. He could buy a new car outright, maybe have a holiday somewhere hot and sunny. He'd have signed the contract there and then, but he had an agent to do his bidding now, and she knew which buttons to press.

A low six-figure sum came next. His agent was thrilled. She was practically singing down the phone to him.

'Do you have ideas for future books?' she asked him.

'Yes. I'm working on the second now and I have an idea for a third, which I'm quite excited about.'

'Write a synopsis. A page each and email them over to me by the end of the day,' she said.

So he did.

Within a week, on the basis of *Out of Darkness* and two further psychological thrillers, three huge publishing houses had offered high six-figure deals.

'This is nuts. I can't believe any of this,' he said in a Skype call with his agent. 'It's a lot of money for three books. It's just … well, it's bonkers,' he said, his soft Irish accent getting stronger with every exclamation.

'Normally, for a debut author, I'd agree with you,' she said calmingly. 'But *Out of Darkness* is a stunning example of the thriller genre. It has noir written all over it. When Beth is attacked in the first chapter and left blind, I was ready to stop reading. I was expecting another cheap story written by a man who enjoys putting female characters in unnecessary peril with gratuitous violence, but there was something in your prose that drew me in and by page twenty, I couldn't stop reading. Your writing is sublime. Your characters are unique and authentic. You know exactly what the reader is crying out for.'

'Thank—'

'I'm sending over an email right now,' she interrupted. 'It's the best offer. Sign.'

He signed.

———

He had his complimentary hardbacks for three weeks before he showed anyone. It didn't feel real. He kept expecting his agent to call and say there had been a massive mistake, that his book was too similar to another book written by an established author and his would have to be pulped. The call never came. This was real. This was happening. It was time to tell the world.

A party was arranged for Friday night. Well, not really a party, more of a small gathering of some of his oldest friends. He'd hired a room above the Bucket of Blood, a pub he and his friends had frequented in their university days. He didn't tell any of them why they were meeting; it was going to be a surprise.

Every time he stopped at the traffic lights and glanced over at the box on the front seat beside him, he grinned. He could just see the jagged letters of the title beneath the flaps of the cardboard. *Out of Darkness* by Aidan Cullen. This was his book. His creation. Finally, at thirty-three years old, he knew what happiness was.

He pulled up in the rear car park of the bizarrely named pub in his battered VW Polo and turned off the ignition.

The Bucket of Blood was in the middle of nowhere, the wrong

side of the M57 to be classed as Liverpool. The hum of the motorway was all that could be heard, and the pub's uneven stone walls were blackened from years of pollution from passing traffic. The windows of the eighteenth-century building were small and leaded, the chimney stacks tall and broken, reaching into the sky like gnarled fingers.

It was a dark night in late October and the temperature was dropping. A mild autumn was releasing its warm grip and the ominous sign of a long, bitter winter was making itself known.

There was one other car in the car park, which belonged to the landlord, Ken. It never moved, as Ken never went anywhere.

He carried the heavy box of books to the back door and struggled to open it under the weight of his load. He didn't want to put the box on the ground, as it was wet. A gust of wind whistled around the building, and he stopped in his tracks, convinced he heard his name being called. He must have been mistaken; there was nobody else around.

He entered the pub, stepping in out of the darkness.

The main bar was dull, even with all the lights on. The stone floor was a health and safety nightmare, even if you were wearing sensible shoes. Dark oak beams covered the ceiling and walls; horse brasses and cartwheels, and prints depicting barren landscapes of centuries gone by, were the only decoration. Had the pub always been this depressing? Where had the pool table and quiz machine from his student days gone?

'Good evening, Ken,' he said. 'Is everything set up?'

'As per your instructions, my good man,' the landlord said, bowing his head. Ken was the only person who knew what this evening was all about, and that was only because he'd wheedled it out of him when he was booking the room.

'Is anyone else here yet?'

'No. You're the first. I thought you'd have been here sooner.'

'The bloody car wouldn't start.'

'Are you still driving that Polo? I thought you'd have traded up by now.'

'I still can't bring myself to say goodbye,' he said, smiling.

'Sentimental old fool. Mind you, I'm the same with the wife. I keep meaning to trade up for a better model, but we've been together that long she's like part of the family,' Ken said, grinning a broken-toothed smile.

There was a cough from behind him and he quickly turned.

'Oh, hello precious,' he said.

'Don't you "precious" me. And who'd have you?' Ken's wife, Jan, looked him up and down. 'When he sends his Polo to the knacker's yard, maybe you should ask for a lift.'

'Are them pies cooked? I'm sure I can hear the timer,' Ken said, pushing past Jan and disappearing into the back room.

There were three other drinkers in the pub, who all jeered after the embarrassed husband.

'I'll just go upstairs then.'

'Want a hand?' Jan asked, rolling up her sleeves, and showing off her thick, muscular arms.

'No thanks. I can manage,' he said, slightly frightened of the formidable woman.

The room above the pub, available for parties, wedding receptions and work dos, according to the faded poster behind the bar, wasn't exactly inviting. It was large enough to comfortably hold a group of fifty people, but, like downstairs, it was dated; the carpet was faded, its original colour a complete mystery, and the walls were crying out for a fresh lick of paint. There was an underlying fusty smell emanating from somewhere. It could have been from lack of use and the fact that no fresh air had passed through for months, or maybe something, or someone, had died in here and was yet to be detected.

This was not the ideal place to tell your oldest friends that you were about to become a literary sensation, yet this pub had a special meaning to them all, and when he had invited them there, they'd all replied in a similar vein:

'Oh my God, we haven't been there for years. I thought they'd pulled that place down.'

'We had some great nights in there when we were students.'

'Remember when Grey drank that yard of ale and it came out of his nose?'

'I hope Ken's still there. He made great pies. I can taste them just thinking about them.'

'The best dive in the North West, if you ask me.'

The room was set. The heavy curtains were drawn, the lights were on, the table laid out with a dozen bottles of Moët and Chandon champagne and a near complete set of matching glasses. Next to those was the box of hardback novels. *Out of Darkness* by Aidan Cullen. He still couldn't believe it. The only thing missing was the guests. It was three minutes past nine. They were only three minutes late. And traffic was always dodgy on a Friday night. Three minutes turned into ten and then into almost twenty before the first people arrived.

'I. Am. So. Sorry. We're. Late,' Clare declared as she whirled into the room, arms outstretched for a hug. 'We would have been on time if this knobhead I married had remembered the one job I asked him to do and called the babysitter. Ooh, is that champagne?'

'I thought she said we were doing this on Saturday night. It really is my fault. I'm sorry,' Martin said, holding out a hand to shake.

'Don't worry. You're the first to arrive anyway.'

Clare and Martin had been a couple since the dawn of time: well, since the first week of university. They'd met at the freshers' ball, slept together on the first night and had been a sickeningly happy couple ever since. Usually. Clare was an administrator in the NHS. Martin was a purchaser for a steel manufacturer. They had two children, two cats, two cars, two holidays every year, and Martin had two kidney stones.

'So, what's the big news?' Clare said, pouring herself a glass of bubbly and tentatively sitting down on a rickety chair, after wiping it clean.

'Not until everyone's here.'

She stuck out her bottom lip. 'Spoilsport. I'm guessing you're not announcing you're getting married, otherwise you wouldn't be here on your own. Unless she's hiding in that box.' She laughed.

'No. I'm not getting married,' he said, blushing.

'Of course, he isn't. He's got more sense.' Martin smirked. 'You know, I can't believe this place is still standing,' he said, looking around him.

'Yes, Martin, you've said that practically every hour for the last week,' Clare said, rolling her eyes.

'Well, I can't. Remember that time when I got my foot stuck in the pocket of the pool table and they had to call the fire brigade?' He laughed.

'Unfortunately, yes we do. Just one of many embarrassing stories that make up your highly unfunny repertoire,' she said, a hint of bitterness in her tone.

The door opened, revealing the second couple to arrive: Grey and Floella. Another two graduates from the University of Liverpool. Like Clare and Martin, they were full of apologies.

'I was all set to leave work at four when a call came through; one of my patients had internal bleeding and we had to whip out her gall bladder. Very nasty,' Floella said.

'It doesn't matter. You're here now. That's the main thing.'

'I must say, we were surprised when you asked to meet here. We didn't think … Clare, what have you done to your hair? It's gorgeous.'

'Thank you,' Clare said, running her hands through her hair. 'I decided to be daring and go for a complete change. Martin hates it, of course.'

'I didn't say I hated it. I said it'll take some getting used to.'

'Champagne, eh? Won the lottery?' Grey asked, helping himself to a glass.

'Something like that. I…'

'Only one glass for you, you're driving,' Floella called out.

'You're the one on call. You could drive,' Grey said.

'And if I get called out, how are you going to get home?'

'I'll get a taxi.'

'And leave the Merc around here? I don't think so.'

Grey gave a weak smile, took a sip of his drink and headed over to Martin, his hand held out.

His heart sank. This wasn't going to be the happy evening he'd had in mind. Everyone was so preoccupied with their own lives and not one of them had engaged him in any meaningful conversation. He stood and watched four people chatting animatedly. They felt like strangers to him. He didn't feel a part of their social circle anymore. Who were these people?

The third couple to arrive was Sara and Lynne. Sara had been at university with them all, but Lynne was a new addition to the group. She hadn't come along until Sara divorced her husband, Daniel, after three months of marriage, and decided she'd rather date his sister. It was an interesting piece of gossip that had kept them all entertained when they met for their monthly curry nights. Well, they'd started off being monthly, but soon dropped to every now and again, and then to whenever anyone had anything special to announce.

'Can you believe I got lost?' Sara said. 'How long have I been coming to this pub? And I got lost. I should be ashamed of myself.

It's lovely to see you. I was only … ah, is that champagne? I'm not drinking at the moment; I'm trying to get pregnant. I'll just go and get an orange juice or something.'

He turned to look at his box of books. They no longer made him smile. The background chatter was noise from the mouths of people he used to know. They'd all gone their separate ways and made lives for themselves.

They were drifting apart, and it was only now that he could see that. They wouldn't care about his book. They probably wouldn't even read it.

'I hate to be a wet blanket,' Clare said. 'But we've only got the sitter until eleven.' She tapped her watch as she spoke.

'Luke isn't here yet,' he said. Luke needed to be here. They were best mates. They'd been through a lot together. He knew Luke would get such a kick out of his news, even if everyone else didn't.

'I know, but, well, you know what Luke's like with his timekeeping. He's never been the most reliable bloke, has he? Can't you just make your little announcement and Luke can catch up when he gets here?'

Little announcement. That hurt. He wanted to go home.

He gave a weak smile and cleared his throat. He reluctantly nodded in agreement.

Everyone took their seats. Everyone? That was a joke. Only six friends. And he doubted they really were his friends. He didn't even know Lynne's surname, and had Clare always been so … bitchy?

'Right, well,' he began nervously. 'First of all, thank you for coming. I know you're all very busy people, and have your own lives and everything, but I do appreciate you coming out all this way tonight.' He suddenly felt self-conscious standing at the top of the room in his fitted navy suit and white shirt, open at the collar. He ran his hand through his black hair and then held onto his glass with both hands. He didn't know what else to do with them.

'As you know, when we were all at university together, I was reading English and I wrote a few short stories, nothing amazing, but they were published in magazines. Well, some of them were, not all, of course.' He felt himself turn red as the eyes of six people burned holes into him.

'When I said we only had the babysitter until eleven, I meant eleven o'clock tonight,' Clare said icily. A ripple of awkward laughter drifted around the room.

'OK, sorry, I'm rambling. Anyway, since leaving uni, I've been working on various novels, in between working in libraries and Waterstones, and, to cut a long story short…'

'Too late,' Clare sniggered.

'I'm published,' he concluded, and gave a gauche smile. 'Well, I'm not published yet. It doesn't come out until January, but I've made it. I'm an author.'

He hadn't expected them to shower him with kisses and squirt him with champagne like the winner of a Formula One race, but he had expected more than the blank faces that stared back at him.

'Oh, sorry, I haven't shown you. This is it.' He turned to the box, pulled open the flaps and grabbed a copy of the hardback novel. He held it aloft, showing them the cover.

'Congratulations, mate,' Grey said, jumping up and stepping forward. He shook his hand and took the book from him, opening the cover and reading the synopsis inside.

'Thank you.'

'That's excellent news. I'm so pleased for you,' Sara said, kissing him on the cheek and helping herself to a book. 'Who's it dedicated to? I'm always interested by dedications in books,' she said with a huge grin – which slowly fell as she opened the front cover. 'Ah. That's lovely,' she said, a catch in her throat. 'She'd have liked that. And I'm pretty certain your mum would have been incredibly proud of you.' She reached up and kissed him on the cheek again.

One by one, they approached the table, offered their congratulations and took a book. It wasn't a fanfare and, although they claimed to be pleased for him, there was something holding them back. Jealousy, perhaps?

'This sounds familiar…' Clare said upon reading the blurb. 'I'm sure I've…'

The door opened and Luke breezed in. 'I'm so sorry I'm late,' he declared.

The atmosphere of the room lifted as Luke entered; he always had that effect on people. As he came fully into the room, he brought with him a stylish blonde woman. She was slim and pretty, with bright blue eyes and a beaming smile.

'I would have been here sooner but it's Daisy's birthday today. I took the day off to take her out and we were in Bakewell and … one thing led to another, and we're engaged!'

Daisy lifted up her left hand to show off the antique engagement ring.

The room erupted. The books were slammed down on the table and everyone ran to Luke and his fiancée to express their congratulations.

Out of Darkness by Aidan Cullen was forgotten.

———

'Aren't you going with them?' Ken asked as he stood in the doorway, his arms folded against his massive chest.

'No. I'm not in a celebratory mood,' he said.

'What are you going to do with all that champagne?'

He looked at the box. Only one bottle had been removed and opened. 'You have it. Sell it on. Make a profit.'

'But you bought it. It's yours.'

'You know something? I've never liked champagne,' he said.

He began packing away all of the hardback books he'd brought with him. None of them had taken one when they'd all decided to go on somewhere to celebrate Luke finally settling down with someone. Clare hadn't mentioned the eleven o'clock deadline once. In fact, it had been her idea for them all to go for a curry.

'Do you and your wife read?'

'Not really.'

'I can't even give them away. Let's hope it's not an omen.'

The wind had picked up while he'd been in the Bucket of Blood. The back door almost slammed back in his face as he pushed it open. He made his way over to the VW Polo, head down, dragging his feet on the broken tarmac, his head full of dark thoughts. The box of books in his hands felt like they weighed a tonne.

He placed the box on the roof of the car, struggled to get his keys out of his trouser pocket and unlocked the boot.

'Mate, have you got the time?'

He hadn't realised there was anyone around. He turned and saw a young man, probably not even twenty, in front of him. He wore a black Adidas tracksuit, matching cap, peak pulled down, with a whisper of blond fluff on his chin.

'No. I haven't. Sorry,' he said, turning back to his car.

'What about any cash? Can you give us a tenner or something?'

He turned back. 'No. I don't have any money on me, sorry.'

'I don't believe you,' the kid said, stepping forward.

From around the front of his car, two other young men, similarly dressed, came towards him. He looked back to the first guy, who reached into his pocket and took out a flick knife. He pressed the handle and the silver blade glistened as the light from his car caught it.

'Wallet, mobile phone, watch, and whatever you've got in that box.'

'Look, I don't have a watch and I've no cash on me, honestly,' he said, holding up his hands.

'I don't believe you,' the man said again, softly, stepping even closer. Their noses were almost touching.

'Jez, check his car. Ben, do the box.'

'No. Please. Leave the box alone. There's nothing worth stealing in there.' His voice was shaking.

'You won't mind us taking a look then, will you?'

He closed his eyes tightly shut. He couldn't believe this was happening. Today was supposed to be a good day.

'It's books.'

'What?'

'In the box. It's a load of fucking books.'

'Nothing in the car, Will.'

'Fuck me!'

Will patted him down. He found something hard against his breast pocket, reached inside and grabbed his wallet. He opened it up. There was a single ten-pound note inside.

'Is that it?' Will's face reddened in rage.

'They're all the same,' Ben said.

'What are?'

'All these books. They're all the same.'

'Gi' us it here.' Will pulled the box off the roof of the car. It landed on the ground. He tore it open and spilled the books onto the wet tarmac. '*Out of Darkness* by Aidan Cullen. What the fuck are you doing with all these?'

'They're mine,' he said, his voice hardly above a whisper. He had an overwhelming urge to cry and struggled to maintain control of his emotions.

'Yours? You mean you wrote them?'

He nodded.

'Here, he's not wrong, that's his mug in the back,' Ben said, showing his photo to the ringleader.

'You must be fucking minted, mate,' Will spat.

'I'm not. Honestly, I'm not. It's all based on sales. It's not even released yet.'

'Fuck off. You think I'm thick? Look at that bird who wrote *Harry Potter*. She's got her own island or something.'

'I'm not rich. I don't have money. Honestly,' he cried.

'We've struck gold here, lads,' Will said with a brown-toothed grin.

Behind them, the car park was lit up by the headlights of a passing car.

'Come on, Will, he's nothing on him, let's just do one.'

'Nah. He's seen us. He's a big fucking author. He'll tell the papers.'

'Then slice him and let's go.'

Will stepped close once again. They were toe to toe, noses touching. 'I don't like you,' he said quietly. 'You think you're better than me because you've written a fucking book. You need to share the money out, mate. We're all supposed to be equal, ain't we?'

A light came on in an upstairs room of the pub. The brightness shining out across the dark night caused the men to turn. He saw this as his chance to escape. He turned and started to run back to the pub, but was quickly caught by his collar and dragged to the ground.

'Why are you running?' Will said, standing over him, knife in hand, cruel smile on his lips. 'You scared?'

His mouth was dry. He didn't dare open it to speak in case it unleashed a torrent of fear. Instead, he nodded.

Will laughed and looked up at his mates. 'He's scared, lads. We've got a famous author here, and he's scared.'

'Will, come on, it's risky. We should go,' Ben called out.

'Let me ask you a question. This book, is it crime?'

He nodded.

'You'll have done research, won't you?'

He nodded again. He felt tears roll down his cheeks.

'Well, here's some early research for your next book.'

He pulled him up off the wet ground and slammed him against the back of his car before stabbing him in the stomach.

He took a sharp intake of breath as he felt the steel blade cut through his clothing and skin with ease, then enter his body. At first, he didn't feel any pain. It was only when he looked down, saw the knife inserted into him and blood leaking out around the entry wound that his brain registered what had happened. He looked up at Will, saw the sneering grin on his young face before the knife was pulled out. It was like a release, and the life began to ooze out of him. He clamped both hands firmly to his stomach. His fingers were cold, but the leaking blood was warming them up.

Will stabbed him again.

'Feel the pain,' he hissed through gritted teeth. 'What's going through your head right now? Do you feel like you're sinking? That's life slowly fading away from you, mate. *Out of Darkness*, by Aidan fucking Cullen. Chuck us your lighter, Jez.'

Will caught the lighter with his left hand. Ben held a book open and Will set fire to the pages. Once it was fully alight, he dropped the book on top of the pile of the remaining nine hardbacks. The flames engulfed them all.

'I fucking hate books,' Will spat.

He felt tears stream down his face as he watched his books burn, his dreams going up in smoke. His legs shook and he dropped to the ground. His hands were slippery and were struggling to keep the blood from flowing out of his wounds. He dragged himself along the tarmac towards his burning books. With every movement, the pain intensified, and more blood seeped out of him. He could feel the heat from the fire growing hotter, the closer he got to the pyre.

He didn't feel the third stab as the blade of the flick knife was plunged into his lower back. And then he was left alone, to bleed out in the car park of the Bucket of Blood.

He heard a voice, but he had no idea where it was coming from. He felt someone grab him and pull him away from the burning books. He looked up and saw Luke standing in front of him, a concerned expression on his usually happy face.

'Luke,' he said, his voice barely above a whisper.

'Don't worry, mate, I'm here. Everything's going to be fine. I've got you. I've always got you.'

SIX YEARS LATER

Chapter Two

GALLOWSFIELD, DERBYSHIRE

I open my eyes and for a split second I have no idea who I am or where I am. It's a split second of bliss until my memory wakes and fills my mind with the miasma of dark thoughts. They are the same dark thoughts that were there yesterday and the day before and the week, month and year before. I've survived another night. I let out a heavy sigh as I stare at the white ceiling.

There's movement on my bed. I look down and see a friendly face staring at me, ears pricked, tongue lolling. A smile spreads across my face.

'Come here,' I say.

My dog. Nanook. He's a two-year-old pure white German Shepherd. He jumps up and pads over to me. I don't think he realises how big and heavy he is, as I'm often squeezed into the corner of the bed while he takes up the rest of the space. He plonks himself down next to me and licks my face. One of these days, I'll lick him back and see how he likes it.

'I don't need to ask if you slept well because your snoring woke me up at 2 a.m. I don't know what you were dreaming about but I bet my legs are covered in bruises with all that kicking you were doing.'

A few minutes with Nanook is more than enough to convince me I can get out of bed and face the day ahead. He gives me the strength to push back the duvet, grab my crutch, and go downstairs.

I take my time on the stairs and Nanook goes down ahead of me, waiting impatiently at the bottom.

After I received the money from the book deal, I decided to move out of my pokey flat in Liverpool. I had been thinking of a bungalow, but nothing piqued my interest. When I saw Gallows View House for sale in the tiny village of Gallowsfield in Derbyshire, I fell in love. I actually felt my heart skip a beat. I had to have it. I called the estate agent and made a provisional offer for the asking price before even seeing it. I didn't want anyone else getting their hands on it.

It's a five-bedroom eighteenth-century property on three floors, though the top floor is rarely used. There's a snug off the living room which I converted into an office, and the dining room was turned into a library to house my ever-growing book collection; the kitchen is more than big enough for me to eat my meals in. I'd feel lonely sitting at a table for six to eat a cheese sandwich. The master bedroom has an en suite that is bigger than my entire flat was in Liverpool.

The moment I stepped over the threshold I knew this was going to be my forever home. I could relax here. I could be comfortable here. I could be safe here.

I moved in almost a year to the day after I'd been stabbed. Once the furniture was inside and the removal men drove away, I closed the front door and it was like a weight was lifted from me. I could feel contentment rise up through my body. I was home.

The décor was dated but I saw past that. The same carpet throughout the entire ground floor was an assault of colour and the busy wallpapers were divided by a dado rail around the middle. It was ugly, but I knew it had the potential to be so beautiful.

Even before the ink was dry on the contract, I set about making this my home. The carpets were ripped up, the kitchen and bathrooms torn out, the wallpaper stripped, and the walls plastered. Hiding beneath the gaudy carpets were solid oak floorboards. It was criminal for them to be hidden for so long. I had them sanded and stained. The walls were all coated in the same mid-grey, or Manor House Grey, as the colour chart called it. Luke thought it might be a tad dark, but that was what I wanted. The carpet on the stairs and in all the bedrooms was the same light grey and I found curtains in a similar shade. I had a slate floor laid in the kitchen with pure white minimalist units and granite worktops. The bathrooms were simple yet elegant, and rugs were laid in the living room and library. The heavy curtains were always half closed, and the lighting was dim in every room. It was a warm and cosy home. It was my home.

Despite being in the middle of the stunning Derbyshire countryside, I had no intention of exploring it. I didn't move here for that. There were no close neighbours; sometimes days could go by without me seeing anyone pass on the lane at the top of the drive, and that was precisely the point. If I can't see other people, then other people can't see me. And if they can't see me, they can't attack me.

Nanook runs through the kitchen into the conservatory, and sits by the door leading out to the sprawling back garden. I fish the keys out of my dressing gown pocket, remove the Patlock from the handles, unlock the double doors and watch, with a smile on my face, as my large puppy charges onto the grass. Whenever I feel low, all I need to do is look at Nanook, and whether he's sleeping, chewing a toy or gazing out of the window, my heart is lifted. He's my whole life.

I decide to step out and join my dog. I take in a lungful of fresh air. Although it feels good to breathe in the cold winter air, I do feel exposed. I should be able to enjoy this. But I can't. The trees are bare; meaning the view of my surroundings is open. If I can see further into the countryside, then it gives others a view into my garden and home. I don't like that. I quickly go back into the house.

I limp into the kitchen, plug in the kettle and flick it on. Breakfast first, then a shower. I tackle each task one at a time and don't move on to the next one until I'm ready. It's all about taking things slowly. Baby steps.

I spend my days writing and reading. I'm at my desk no later than eight o'clock and I make sure I've written a couple of thousand words before I stop for a break. I need to have something positive to look back on or it will be a wasted day, and that would cause me more anxiety. I'm around halfway through my seventh novel. There's a long way to go, but there's no rush. I'm ahead of schedule.

My office is an eleven-by-seven-foot rectangle and it's the room I spend most of my time in. This is the room in which I devise new and ingenious ways to kill people. My mind is at its most active here and, when I'm sitting in front of the computer, the rest of the world ceases to exist. I have a solid oak desk in the middle of the room, with a padded seat at the small window. There are shelves on two of the walls running from floor to ceiling, all of them packed with copies of my own books in various languages, as well as research books on psychology, criminology and pathology. The fourth wall has framed images of my books. It's the only room in the house with something on the walls. I have no interest in having framed paintings and I have no family photographs to display. However, in my office, my work is celebrated. I'm incredibly proud of what I've achieved. Here, in this room, I can forget about who I am – the plethora of problems I have – and concentrate on my protagonists. I become them. I live their lives, breathe their air and talk their language. I'm someone else, a character, and my writing and Nanook are the only things that make me truly happy. Well, happy may be too strong a word. We'll go with satisfied.

The launch of *Out of Darkness*, three months after I was stabbed, was a huge success. I told my agent about my attack. She wanted to use it to get me on the chat show circuit and boost the novel's publicity, but I refused, point blank, to discuss it. It was private. I had no intention of opening myself up for the world to see me as a victim.

'But your life is imitating your fiction. Like Beth in *Out of Darkness*, you're using your attack to grow stronger and prove you're able to live a life in the face of adversity. Let the world throw whatever it wants at you. You're a survivor,' she stated with all the enthusiasm she could muster.

'You seem to be forgetting, Lucy, that Beth went on to murder her husband and manipulate the courts into thinking she was the victim.'

'Potato, potahto,' she said, waving me off.

I had to smile at that. There was something about Lucy that always made me laugh. She wanted the best for me and my career, but I couldn't use my attack to sell more copies of my book. It was exploitative. Eventually and reluctantly, she relented, and my attack was never mentioned between us again.

Out of Darkness peaked at number two in the *Sunday Times* hardback bestsellers list and made it to number one when the paperback was released nine months later. My second, *The Loudest Scream*, delayed slightly due to unforeseen circumstances (as Lucy teased in a press release), was received to critical acclaim. It told the story of a killer couple who stalk their victims, unnoticed for months before striking, mercilessly killing them simply for the enjoyment of ending a life. It was a dark and brutal story, but the violence was merely hinted at through subtle prose, and when the twist was revealed in the final chapter, it turned the entire novel on its head. It won the CWA Gold Dagger award for best crime novel of the year. The award sits to the right of my computer and is inspiration for me to continue on the darker days when the words don't flow quite as freely.

I wasn't at the ceremony to collect my award, for obvious reasons. I blamed a lingering flu for my absence.

Since then, three further novels have been published, with another due out in a couple of weeks. They've all hit the top spot in the bestseller lists and have won awards in Britain and around the globe.

I appear to be a literary success, and my lack of a public persona seems to have added to my mystique and made my books even more enticing to readers. You could say I'm the Banksy of the literary world.

Nanook has a bed in my office; he has a bed in most rooms of the house and spends every minute of every day by my side. While I hammer away at the keyboard, he curls up in his bed, rising occasionally for a drink of water, or nuzzling me for a treat he knows I have hidden away in my desk drawer.

A loud buzz from the intercom makes me jump. I look at the time in the corner of the computer screen. It's a little after eleven o'clock. I bring up the camera feed and select the camera pointing at the gate at the end of the drive. It shows a red Royal Mail van and the postman standing by it, a large cardboard box in his hands. It's not my usual postman, Jim, though. It's not even the replacement man who comes when Jim is on holiday. I've never seen this man before in my life.

This is where my overactive mind kicks in. Is he a real postman or an imposter? If he's an intruder, he's certainly well organised. He has the van, the uniform, the bag over his shoulder. Full marks for ingenuity. Something dark is going to happen. I can sense it. I can feel the dread crawling up inside me.

I take a deep breath and open the microphone.

'Yes?' I say, sounding scared.

'Parcel for Mr Cullen,' he says into the speaker. It's a local accent.

'Do I need to sign for it?'

'No.'

'Can you leave it on the doorstep? I've just got out of the shower.' I tell so many lies to people who come calling that they drip off my tongue with ease.

'No problem.'

I click the release to unlock the gate and watch as the postman pushes it open and walks up the gravel driveway. I change the camera to the one above the front door and watch him approach. He places the parcel on the ground with a few letters on top of it, takes a photo of it in situ, then returns to his van, pulling the gate behind him.

The gate should have automatically locked but the postman hasn't closed it fully and the iron latch clangs against its housing.

'You haven't closed the gate properly,' I say into the microphone. 'Can you close it fully please?'

He doesn't hear and jumps into his van. He drives away, kicking up gravel with his back tyres.

'Shit.'

I lean back in my chair and chew on my bottom lip. I watch the screen as the gate sways in the stiff breeze. I know what I have to do. It's finding the courage to do it that's the hardest part. I can leave the house and go into the back garden, that's fine, no problem at all. It's going out the front door, the entrance to the world, that causes the most distress.

'Why can't people do what they're supposed to do?' I ask Nanook.

I leave my office and go to the cupboard under the stairs to get my shoes and jacket. Luke always laughs at the state of my cupboard. Most people use it for storing their junk, but mine is neatly arranged: shoes lined up, jackets in seasonal order, fire extinguisher facing forward and a first aid box fully stocked for every eventuality. I like to be organised.

As I rarely leave the house, the jackets and shoes are hardly worn. They're mostly used for when I'm playing in the back garden with Nanook, or when I have to put the bins out on a Wednesday evening. I venture out into the back garden quite often to play with Nanook, maybe hang out a bit of washing, or to read a book with a glass of whiskey when the weather is fair. It feels safe to be in the back garden. There are no houses or roads visible from there. And I plan for those events. I can build up to them. This is an unexpected outing and I can already feel the sweat dripping down my back.

I remove the BuddyBar door jammer from beneath the door handle and struggle to bend down to the floor to unlock the barricade. There are two locks on the door, a cylinder lock I open with a key and a Yale latch lock. The door is now unguarded. There is nothing to stop anyone rushing in and pushing it open. I look down at Nanook, faithfully by my side. He has no idea of the internal struggle I'm going through and looks excited about going out of the front door for a change.

I pull the heavy door towards me and feel the blast of cold winter air like a hard slap in the face. I recoil and squeeze my eyes tightly closed.

Nanook bounds out into the front garden like it's the most natural thing in the world. I wish I had the inner strength of a German Shepherd.

I bend down and pick up the parcel and letters. I recognise the postmark on the box. It's the complimentary copies of my new book, *The Confession of Billy McLean*. I usually can't wait to open these boxes and hold a copy in my hands, but right now, I really don't care. I push them into the house, close the door behind me, lock it with the key and place it deep into my pocket.

It seems alien to be out in the front of the house. The gravel drive curves around to the gate and the road beyond. Up the hillside in the distance, I can see farm buildings, cottages, vehicles on the roads. Life is unfolding beyond the confines of the safety of the gate, and I don't want any part of it. My world is enclosed. Nobody is allowed in. And I want to keep it that way.

Nanook is enjoying the front garden. A bird lands on the wall by the gate. He charges towards it, barks, and it flies away. He continues to bound around, sniffing new smells, leaving his own scent and trotting on the gravel pathway, revelling in the sound his paws make. Why can't I be more like Nanook?

I close my eyes and try to block out everything around me. The sound of nature. Birds tweeting, bare branches thrashing together in the breeze, the lowing of distant cattle, the chug of a tractor somewhere. I can hear it all. It's thundering through my head as loud as if it's in my own garden.

I feel sick and take a deep breath. I open my eyes, see the gate straight ahead and charge for it as fast as I can, using my crutch for stability over the gravel.

I fix my eyes on my destination. The gate is clanging against its housing, swinging in the wind. My crutch scrapes through the gravel, and I stumble twice. I reach the gate, slam it closed, and make sure it's secure before turning back. I see my house, my sanctuary. It seems like a thousand miles away.

'Shit, shit, shit,' I mutter to myself and I run as fast as I can for the front door, shouting to Nanook to follow me.

I scramble in my pocket for the keys, unlock the door, and

push, but it won't open. I push harder, slam my shoulder against the wood, but it won't move.

'Fuck!' I scream.

The keyless Yale has locked. I type in the six-digit security code (Nanook's date of birth) and it still doesn't open.

'Jesus Christ!'

I must have pressed a different number in my panic. I take a breath and try to calm down. It's useless. Another breath. An internal chat with myself.

Calm down. Take your time. Breathe. A few more seconds and you'll be inside. Relax. Six digits. It's easy. You can do it. Go.

I type in the code. I hear the mechanism release and the door opens. I practically fall inside the house. Nanook bounds in after me and I slam the door closed, securing it with the key and the bolts at the top and bottom of the door. I lean against it, breathe a sigh of relief and slide down onto the floor.

I'm physically drained. My breathing is unstable, and sweat is pouring down my face, mixing with my tears. My rapid breaths resound off the walls of the empty hallway.

Nanook walks slowly up to me and sits beside me, resting his head on my lap. I place a hand on his warm head and begin to stroke him. I can feel his soothing presence wash over me.

'I'm so pleased you're with me. I don't know what I'd do without you.'

Pathetic. All that drama just to close a gate. Look at the state of you.

'Go away,' I say to myself.

Chapter Three

It's Nanook nudging me that wakes me up. I sit up on the sofa and look around me. I'm in almost total darkness and wonder how long I've been asleep.

After I managed to summon the energy to drag myself up off the hallway floor, I stumbled into the living room and flopped on the sofa. I intended to rest for a few minutes, get my breath back and return to work. I must have fallen asleep because now it's practically dark outside. I've lost a whole day, more or less, thanks to my neuroses.

I've never been a big fan of crowds and open spaces. I'd have locked myself away years ago, but I always had to leave the house for work, at least. Being stabbed and my writing career taking off came at roughly the same time and I spent time indoors recovering and writing. The longer I was inside, the harder it was to leave. Whenever I was asked out, I made an excuse that I was busy with my next book, or I was still feeling the effects of the stabbing. No great effort was made to get me out. I faded into the background of my own life, and nobody tried to stop me.

Why didn't anybody try to stop me?

I limp over to the curtains and pull them to, bringing the

29

barrier between me and the outside world just that little bit closer. I turn on the standard lamps. The dull bulbs cast long shadows across the room. It's cold in here. A fire should have been lit hours ago. It's a quarter past six. I look down at Nanook and he's looking back at me with those large brown eyes. He knows something is wrong.

'We've missed snack time, have we? And you've missed your dinner time.'

I squat down to his level, take his head in my hands and give him a hug. His eyes seem to sparkle at the attention.

'You're so good to me. Let's make you something special to eat. You can have that leftover chicken I was going to have, and I'll give you extra biscuits.'

I make up his dinner while he's outside relieving himself. It's a while before he comes running into the house so he must have had a full bladder. I feel bad that I've neglected him so much today.

While he's eating, I sit at the island in the kitchen and take out my mobile phone. There are no emails or texts waiting for me, not that I was expecting there to be, but I decide to give Luke a ring, see how he's getting on.

On the night of the attack six years ago, Luke had returned to the pub to apologise for stealing my thunder, as he later put it. He hadn't known I was going to announce the launch of my literary career and that news of his engagement would usurp everything. While everyone was heading for the nearest Indian restaurant, Luke decided to come back and try to convince me to join them for a double celebration. But instead he found me…

'Hi Aidan. How are you?' Luke answers, his Liverpudlian accent thick and loud. He always sounds like he's smiling.

'I'm fine thanks. A bit tired.'

'Been writing all day?'

'Something like that. How are things with you?' I always want to deflect attention away from myself.

'Don't ask.'

'Problems?'

'You could say that. The carpets arrived today and there's nowhere near enough to cover the floors. I said as soon as they started unloading the van that we needed more but I was told they'd been measured, and this is what had been ordered. An hour later, I was proved right.'

'What are you going to do?' I ask.

'I've been on the phone for hours trying to find that out.'

'It sounds like a nightmare.'

'You could say that. I'll be having a few drinks tonight.'

'So you won't be coming back home at the weekend then?'

'It doesn't look like it. You'll be OK, won't you?'

'Yes. Fine. I've got Nanook.'

'How is he?'

'Fine. I'm surprised you can't hear him eating his tea from there,' I say with a laugh.

'He's eating late, isn't he?'

'Yes. I fell asleep on the sofa.'

'You'll not sleep tonight.'

'I never sleep at night. I have to grab it where I can.'

'Look, I've got to go. I haven't eaten myself, yet. Me and some of the lads are going out for a Chinese. Take care of yourself. If you need me, give me a call.'

'I will.'

'Promise me, Aidan.'

'I promise.'

'Good.'

I don't know if Luke felt guilty after my stabbing, but he stayed with me at the hospital that night and visited me every day throughout my recovery. When I was discharged, he wouldn't let me go back home. As with all his previous relationships, the one with Daisy didn't last, and I moved in with him while I got my strength back. When I moved to Gallows

View House, he decided to come with me. Not that he's here much.

Luke Jackson is the kind of man who can turn his hand to anything. He's a qualified builder, plumber, plasterer and electrician. He can paint, hang wallpaper, level a garden, plant and uproot trees, retile a roof and repoint brickwork. He's a jack of all trades and, unlike the saying, he's a master of them all, too. There is nothing Luke cannot do.

When his engagement got called off, Daisy disappeared from his life as quickly as she had entered it. He didn't seem to mind. Luke is a free spirit, and he soon grows restless. He can't sit through a whole film without getting up and moving about. He's always on the go.

Luke can change the atmosphere of a room simply by walking through the door. His boundless energy and permanent smile are infectious, and he doesn't allow anything to get him down. Right now, he's working away in Newcastle, laying the carpet in a new department store. Had he been running it himself, he would have measured each room perfectly; the carpet would have been delivered and laid in record time. Two days maximum. I'm sad that his time away is being extended. He rarely spends more than three nights in a row at home, but I miss him when he's not here. He leaves a massive hole.

I let Nanook back out into the garden and turn on the security lights, which glow across the lawn like an alien invasion. While he's out, I make my own tea. I'm not hungry, so a cheese and pickle sandwich will do.

Nanook comes running back in and I lock the conservatory doors and secure the house. I look out into the brightness of the garden to see if there is anyone lurking in the shadows or behind a tree. I don't think there is, but I can never be one hundred per cent sure. I turn off the outside light and change the setting on the LCD display to 'sensor'. If anyone does approach, the lights will come on and I'll get an alert by a notification on my tablet. I'm as secure as I can be without actually having an armed officer standing sentry at each door.

It's still only early evening and there are a lot of empty hours left before the day is out. I'm not one of those people who can sit in front of the television for hours. I often go to bed early with a good book and a mug of tea, or a large glass of whiskey. After the exertions of the day, I decide to give alcohol a miss and settle for a large mug of Yorkshire Tea and a handful of biscuits. While the kettle is boiling, I go around the house making sure all the doors and windows are locked and the curtains are closed.

I pause at the top of the stairs to catch my breath and lean against the crutch before entering Luke's bedroom. Luke's scent is still here, a mixture of whatever fragrance he sprays on himself and his own natural odour. It's earthy, peaty, masculine and heady. It tickles my nostrils and makes me sneeze. I run my fingers along the headboard and let them fall onto the pillowcase, where they lightly dance over the place Luke rests his head. I'm about to lean down when something outside the window catches my eye.

Ahead, in the distance, above the trees in the valley, on a road in the hillside, a series of flashing blue lights pierces the darkness. I go over to the window and half close my eyes, but I can't make out what's happening. Nanook jumps up to the windowsill and looks out.

'Do you see that as well, or is it just me? What do you think it is, eh? Shall we go upstairs and have a better look?'

The roof space of Gallows View House had been converted long before I bought it. Two large bedrooms and a spacious landing.

In one of the rooms, I've positioned a telescope. On clear nights, when I can't sleep, I like coming up here and looking at the stars. Whenever the planets align or the moon is turned red by its position to the sun, I can spend hours staring through the lens into the blackness above and marvel at the wonder that is outer space.

It's calming and gives me a serene sense of peace. Unfortunately, the feeling rarely lasts long.

Nanook also has a bed in this room. As soon as we enter, he runs over to it and digs around in it to make it comfortable.

The room is lit only by the light from the full moon coming through the angled windows. It casts long shadows onto the plain carpet. I perch on the edge of the stool, resting my crutch against the tripod, and look through the telescope. It's aimed at the sky, so I lower it and bring it into focus.

On the road up the hillside, an ambulance and three police cars have their emergency lights flashing. Something has happened. Suddenly, I'm pleased I had that nap earlier. There's no chance of me getting any sleep tonight with a drama taking place right on my doorstep.

'Maybe I should have a kettle and a mini fridge up here,' I say to Nanook. He barks. 'Yes, and a box of Bonios.'

Chapter Four

It's after midnight when I end up prising myself away from the telescope and going to bed. There's nothing left to see anyway. I watched as the last of the police cars drove away slowly up the winding road, without its lights flashing, and that was the end of the drama. I've been perched on that stool for over five hours and my leg is stiff and my back aches. My own fault. I have to keep moving about or I seize up, and that's precisely what's happened.

'I'm going to be in agony in the morning,' I say to Nanook as I limp down the stairs to my bedroom.

I've got one of those plastic box things on my bedside cabinet to put the tablets in that I have to take each day. I hate it. It makes me feel like I'm elderly. I'm on several different types of medication – something for the pain, something for anxiety, something to settle my stomach because the medication for the pain makes me bring up my meals. I know I shouldn't, but I take two extra small white pills for the pain and an additional one to stop the dark thoughts racing around my head. They don't work. I've no idea why I take them. Habit? A sense that I'm actually doing something to improve myself?

As I lie in bed, I wonder what happened on the hill to call out an ambulance and a fleet of police cars. I watched teams of uniformed police officers standing around and the white-suited forensic investigators popping in and out of a white tent for hours. A white tent usually means a body. A hit and run, most likely. It's a very narrow road, and some of those corners are very tight. Drivers don't seem to realise you can't see what's upon you until you start to turn, and by then it's often too late.

I'm uncomfortable and it takes me a while to find a position I think I'll be able to sleep in. I'm disturbing Nanook, and he lets me know by sighing heavily.

Just before I nod off, I wonder about who might have died up there. A retired businessman enjoying his freedom after forty years behind a desk; a woman in her seventies, recently widowed, taking a walk on her own without her husband of thirty years by her side; a pair of foreign tourists, visiting an England they'd only seen in period dramas and wanting to see the history and landscape for themselves; or perhaps a dog walker, a regular from the village, and both walker and dog killed by a boy racer in a car he couldn't handle.

I reach out a hand in the darkness and find Nanook. I don't know what I'd do if I lost him. I've had him since he was a puppy, a present from Luke, and although he's only been with me for two years, it feels like we've been together our whole lives.

When I wake up, the first thing I want to do is scream. I have a sharp pain shooting from my lower back down my right leg. It's my fault. I know I shouldn't sit in one position for too long. I know I have to keep movement in my muscles, but I was hooked by the human drama, which, looking back, was actually mind-numbingly boring.

I take my pills, and an extra one for luck, and rub a good dollop of Deep Heat into my back. I'm not sure if it'll do any good but it'll make me feel better for having done something, and, strangely, I quite like the smell.

Before heading downstairs, I pop up to the attic room and have another nosy through the telescope. I don't know why I do this. I doubt there's going to be a huge neon sign announcing someone has been hideously murdered, but I'm a crime writer: I'm curious by profession. As expected, there's nothing there and, momentarily, I wonder if I imagined it. Were they really police officers or, like the postman, were they in disguise and watching me?

Pull yourself together, you eejit.

Nanook barks. He wants his breakfast. So do I.

I'm about to start work when I notice the unopened box with complimentary copies of my latest book, *The Confession of Billy McLean*, that was delivered yesterday. I get out the box cutter and slice through the tape, pull open the flaps and grab the first copy. I know what the cover looks like as I had to approve the design. I know what the words inside say as I wrote them, rewrote them, edited them and read them more than a dozen times, yet there's something special about holding a copy of your own work in your hands. There's no other feeling like it in the world. I don't know how many books I'll write in my life, but this elation of holding a physical copy will never get old. I sit and stare at it, caress it, smell it. I love this book.

There's a special place for it on my shelves with a copy of all my others. I'm building up quite the collection.

Before I begin writing, I check my emails. I have fourteen that have been redirected from my author website from readers around the world, one of which is from Rebecca Charlesworth: obviously. I quickly scan them. They all seem positive, and they make me smile. I'll reply later while I'm having a lunch break.

I check my notes and read what I wrote yesterday: which is not much. I've barely written a sentence when the intercom buzzer sounds, making me jump and Nanook bark.

I bring up the camera feed over the front gate and zoom in for a closer look. There's a dark blue Astra parked haphazardly, and two women stand in front of it. They're both conservatively dressed in professional suits, but, judging by how they hang, I doubt they're designer, probably bought from a supermarket – functional and cheap. They're not smiling or chatting while waiting to see if there's anyone at home. They look harassed and cold. And they don't seem friendly towards each other.

They buzz again. Something tells me not to let them in. So I don't.

Nanook barks again.

'They're Jehovah's Witnesses, Nanook,' I tell him, even though I don't think they are. 'I'd send you out to bite them, but then they'd know there was someone in.'

They don't buzz a third time; they just stand there. Eventually, they start chatting to each other. I'd love to know what they're saying. I'd open the microphone, but I don't want Nanook to bark and give us away. After a while longer they give up, head for the Astra and drive away.

'Maybe I should put one of those signs up that says no religious groups, no utility suppliers and no charity collectors,' I say to Nanook. 'I'll ask Luke when he gets back.'

I keep my eyes fixed on the computer and the view from the camera above the gate. Nothing else happens. No cars come down the road, no people walk by. It's as quiet as the grave; just how I like it.

Lunch today is a cheese-and-onion-crisp sandwich and a mug of tea. I reply to my emails between mouthfuls, but I ignore a second one from Rebecca Charlesworth. When I've finished, I have a walk around the ground floor to keep the blood circulating. I'd pop out into the back garden, but it looks cold out there today. I sit back down at my desk and return to work. The words are flowing freely this afternoon and I'm pleased with what I've written.

The buzz from the intercom stops me mid-flow, fingers hovering above the keyboard. Nanook barks. I bring up the camera feed. It's the same two women from this morning.

Who the hell are they?

I chew my bottom lip as I think. They're persistent and they obviously want to speak to me about something. If I don't answer now, they may come back again, and it might be dark then. I'm definitely not letting strangers into my home after dark.

'Shit! I get the feeling I might need your protection, Nanook.'

I look down at him and he looks back, head tilted, tongue lolling. He's a large dog, his ears permanently pricked, and his bark is deep and vicious-sounding. But really, he's a big softie. He's anyone's for a Bonio and a belly scratch.

The second buzz is louder and longer. The taller of the two women has her finger depressed on the button.

'Yes?' I say, testily, through the microphone.

'Mr Cullen?'

How do they know my name?

My mouth dries. 'Yes?' My reply isn't as strong this time.

The taller one leans into the mouthpiece. 'I'm DS Marshall. This is DC Graves from Derbyshire Police. Could we have a word?'

The police?

'What about?'

'An incident took place in the area yesterday. We're seeking witnesses.'

'I didn't see anything.'

'Mr Cullen, could we come in for a moment? We just want to

ask you a few questions, simply routine. We won't take up more than five minutes of your time and it's very cold out here.'

I don't want these women in my house. I get the feeling that, by the time they leave, I'm going to be reaching for either my anxiety pills or the whiskey. I've already taken one Lithium today; I can't risk taking another. Either way, I won't be in a very good place, mentally.

'Mr Cullen?'

I must have zoned out, because the tall one calling my name makes me jump. I can hear my heart thundering in my chest. This has been such a good day up until now. Why did they have to come here and ruin it?

'Can you hold your ID up to the camera please?'

They exchange a glance and the tall one rolls her eyes. So much for the police wanting members of the public to question those who come to their door. It's obviously fine to question a bogus plumber or electrician, but the police themselves don't want their identity questioned. Double standards. I don't like these women.

They hold their IDs up in turn and I take a screenshot of each. Just in case. Reluctantly, I press the release button and unlock the gate.

'Let's go and meet our guests then,' I say to Nanook as I straighten my hair.

As I stand up, I get a sharp bolt of pain down my right leg. I grip the crutch tighter, and my limp is more pronounced as I head for the front door.

'Mr Cullen?' the tall one asks with a fake smile on her face.

'Yes.'

'This is a nice house you have.'

'Thank you.' I wasn't expecting a compliment. 'Please, come in.'

I step to one side and allow them both to enter. They wipe their feet on the mat and stand in the hallway while I close and lock the door. They're respectful of my home and I can feel myself softening towards them slightly.

Nanook makes a fuss. We rarely get visitors. In fact, thinking back, I don't think we've ever had a visitor we don't already know. This is new territory for Nanook.

'What a gorgeous dog,' the shorter one says. She drops to her knees and begins stroking him.

Naturally, the tough, dangerous dog that he is, he rolls onto his back with his legs in the air.

'What's his name?'

'Nanook.'

'As in Nanook of the North?'

'Yes.'

'I'd love a dog, but we're only in a small cottage. It's not big enough. Besides, we're both out all day.' She turns her attention to Nanook. 'But you are gorgeous,' she says in a sickly, childish voice. 'Yes, you are. You're a beauty.'

'You said you wanted to ask me something.'

'Yes. Is there…?' The taller one looks around her. I'm pretty sure she's DS Marshall.

'Of course, yes, sorry.' I head for the kitchen, and they follow. 'Can I get you a tea or coffee or something?'

'Tea would be nice, thank you,' DS Marshall says.

Their shoes clack loudly on the slate floor and the stools at the island scrape across it as they pull them out to sit down. Years of being alone must have made me ultra-sensitive to noise, as I recoil at the sound.

I set about making them tea. While the kettle is boiling, I turn to look at them and offer a nervous smile. DS Marshall has dark brown hair cut into an untidy bob. Her face is free of make-up and is red where the chill of the winter breeze has nipped at her skin. Her fingernails are bitten to the quick and there's no ring on her wedding finger. I can't decide if she's divorced or never married. I make a snap decision that she's never been married but has a string of failed relationships behind her, possibly because her main focus is her job. She's a DS but she's probably itching to be a DI. She has a depth to her eyes, but they look sad, as if she's already defeated by what life has thrown at her, even though I guess she's only in her mid-thirties. I bet she goes home to a cold, empty house every night, a microwave meal for one and the TV on in the background just for the company.

DC Graves, on the other hand, is a complete contrast. She sits on the stool with her back straight, eyes sparkling, and a smile on her lips. When she's not making a fuss over Nanook, she's gazing at the kitchen like she's never seen such a beautiful room. She's younger than Marshall and is wearing a touch of make-up and a layer of light red lipstick. Her hair is tied back in a neat ponytail and recently dyed. She's wearing an engagement ring on her perfectly manicured hands. They're chalk and cheese detectives. I almost baulk at the cliché. I don't think I'd use either of these women as characters in one of my books.

'This is a great kitchen,' Graves marvels. 'We've just moved into a cottage. It's a bit of a wreck, we're doing it up room by room, but I'd love a worktop like this in the kitchen. Do you mind me asking where you got it from?'

I have to think about that, as Luke did all of the decoration. 'I'm not entirely sure. I think it was from a company in Nottingham.'

She strokes the granite with one hand and with the other she strokes Nanook. 'It's so smooth. It'll last a lifetime, I'm sure.'

'How long have you lived here, Mr Cullen?' Marshall says, obviously wanting to bring the conversation back to the point.

'Five years. More or less.' The kettle boils and I turn my back to them as I make the tea.

'You're not from around here?'

'No.' I don't know why I don't tell them I'm from Ireland. I mean, they can probably guess from my accent, but I could have elaborated.

I hand them a mug one at a time and present them with a matching milk jug and sugar bowl and ask them to help themselves. I've not made a cup of tea for me. I'll have one later, when I can relax.

'Do you live here alone?' Marshall asks.

'No. I have Nanook.'

'Wife, husband, girlfriend, boyfriend?' she asks, pouring milk into her tea.

'A friend lives with me.' I pull out a stool to sit down. I'm in a lot of pain but I try not to let it show.

'Is he here?'

'He's working away at the moment.'

'When did he go away?'

'What's this about?' I ask harshly. I'm losing patience now.

DS Marshall takes a dog-eared notebook from an inside jacket pocket and flips it open. 'There was an incident up on the Leigh Road yesterday late afternoon. I don't suppose you saw anything?'

'No.' My answer is a little too quick.

Marshall doesn't say anything. She takes a sip of her tea and looks at Graves, who's still mentally cataloguing my kitchen.

'Don't you want to know what the incident was?' Marshall asks.

'I'm not interested in gossip. I'm guessing it doesn't directly involve me.'

'How do you know it doesn't directly involve you?'

'If it did, I'm sure I would already have known about it.'

There's a twitch of an eyebrow on Marshall's face. 'A woman was killed yesterday, on Leigh Road.'

'Oh. A hit and run?'

'Why do you say that?'

'I've lived here for five years. In that time there have been seven fatal incidents involving careless driving on that road.'

'I didn't think you were interested in gossip.' There's a smug little smile on Marshall's chapped lips.

'It's not gossip if it's a fact.'

She looks down quickly at her notebook.

Her voice changes. It's deeper, sterner. 'This woman wasn't killed in a hit and run. She was murdered while she was out for a jog. It was a savage and brutal attack. She was beaten to death with a rock.'

'Good grief.'

Whenever I hear of anything like this, my mind goes straight back to the stabbing. Strangely, when I'm writing about murders, I don't think of what happened to me, probably because I know it's all made up. But knowing that a woman was brutally killed not far from my own home makes me think of when I was alone in the car park on that cold, damp October night. I was scared and in so much pain. This poor woman must have felt exactly the same. I wonder if she hoped death would come quickly, just like I had done.

'She had to be identified by fingerprints and a tattoo. There was nothing for her parents to look at,' Marshall adds.

'That's awful.'

I get down from the stool and wince at the shooting pain in my leg. I turn my back on them and look out of the small kitchen window.

'Are you all right?' DC Graves asks.

'I'm fine. It's just … you don't expect something so violent to happen so close to home, do you?'

'Do you want to know who the victim was?' Marshall asks.

I turn back to look at her. 'OK.'

'She was called Melanie Burton. Do you know her?'

I shake my head. 'No.'

'Do you know the Burton family?'

'No.'

'You have a good view of Leigh Road from here. Did you see anything yesterday?'

'No. Well, I noticed the blue flashing lights from the police cars when I was closing the curtains. I thought it had been a hit and run.'

'Have you noticed anything unusual lately?'

'In what way?' I try to sit back down on the stool, but my leg just won't work properly. I notice DC Graves frown at my attempts, but she doesn't say anything.

'Strange cars? People you haven't seen before?'

'No.'

'How about when you've gone into the village?'

'I don't go into the village.'

They exchange a look that I can't read.

'I meant for shopping, milk, things like that,' Marshall says.

'I don't go into the village,' I repeat, more firmly this time. I look down and I can feel both their gazes burning into the top of my head.

'What do you do for work, Mr Cullen?' Graves asks.

'I'm a writer. Crime fiction. I have everything I need here in the house. I don't need to go out.'

Nanook leaves the detective and pads over to me, his nails tip-tapping on the slate. He presses himself against me. His presence helps a great deal.

'Mr Cullen, is everything all right?' Graves asks. There's a severity to her question this time.

'Everything is fine.' I can feel myself smiling at this reply and I hope it's not showing on my face. 'Everything is fine' is my mantra. Whenever anyone asks, Luke or my agent, I tell them 'Everything is fine', even when it most definitely isn't. Right now, nothing is fine, but I'm not going to tell two complete strangers that. I want them out of my house. It's starting to feel claustrophobic having them here.

'Is there something you want to tell us?' Marshall asks.

I shake my head.

Marshall clears her throat. 'Purely for elimination purposes, can you tell us where you were yesterday afternoon from around four o'clock onwards?'

'I was here,' I answer, my voice barely above a whisper.

'Here in the house?'

I nod.

'You didn't go out?'

'No.' I look at Marshall.

'Was anyone here with you?'

'No.'

Marshall holds my stare and gets up from her stool. She fishes around in her pocket again and brings out a business card, placing it carefully on the worktop. 'Well, we'll leave you to it. If you think of anything, or remember anything, please, give me a call. We'll see ourselves out.'

'I'll need to unlock the gate for you. It locks automatically when it closes.'

I limp towards the front door. I can feel them close behind me. I unlock the mortice and, using the screen by the door, I enter a code to unlock the gate at the top of the drive.

'That's quite a security system you have,' Marshall says.

'You can't be too careful these days,' I say with a smile, but I can feel my lips twitching.

'No. I suppose you can't.'

I open the door for them. A breeze blows into the house and, despite it being icy cold, it's good to feel fresh air on my skin.

'You'll call us if you remember anything?' Marshall asks.

'I will.'

Graves gives Nanook a final stroke. When she looks at me, her smile falls slightly.

They leave the house and I close the door quickly behind them, locking it back up again. I watch on the screen as they walk through the gate and I make sure it's locked, the button turning from green to red, before I allow myself to relax. I can see the two detectives talking animatedly to each other as they head for their car. I know they're talking about me, and it's bound to be something negative. They've probably already got me down as their number one suspect. I won't be surprised if they come back in a couple of days and ask for my fingerprints. I'm not sure if they're allowed to demand them or not. I'll have to email my police contact and check: but when they search my computer, they'll see my email and wonder why I was asking soon after they'd left.

'Shit,' I say under my breath.

Once the car has disappeared out of the frame, I turn away from the screen and head for the living room. I'm sweating. I'm damp under my armpits and I've a prickling sensation creeping up my neck. I feel sick.

'I don't feel like working any more today, Nanook.'

I slump onto the sofa. Nanook places his head on my lap. A wave of depression has swept over me.

'Did you hear what they said about what happened to that woman? Her head was smashed in. She had to be identified by fingerprints and a tattoo. Does that sound familiar to you?'

Nanook tilts his head to the left and then to the right, as if he understands every word I'm saying.

'It's almost exactly like what happened to Laurie.'

'An instant classic'
DAILY MAIL
'Genuinely chilling'
THE SUN
THE LOUDEST
SCREAM
AIDAN CULLEN
THE SUNDAY TIMES BESTSELLER

Chapter One

Laurie Bateman was running in anger.

Her fists were clenched tight as her arms pumped through the air. Her feet pounded the uneven ground with all the intensity of someone running for their life. And that wasn't far from the truth.

Laurie's life had been turned upside down in recent weeks. It was only March, but she was already wishing the year was over. In the past three months she had thrown out her boyfriend, lost the promotion she had been guaranteed to someone under-qualified who was related to the managing director, buried her last surviving grandparent who died from injuries following a mugging, and the builder who promised to fix her leaking roof had done a runner with her deposit. That was a great deal to absorb in such a short space of time.

When Laurie was angry, bitter or enraged, she channelled her frustration into running. Right now, she was furious, and the fact that her new running shoes were rubbing against a blister on her big toe didn't bother her in the slightest. Pain was the cleanser.

A keen runner from a young age, Laurie had medals for long distance and marathon running. She'd raised thousands of pounds for several local cancer charities and had been in the newspaper many times for winning races. Her last marathon was something she would rather forget. Hoping to beat her personal best time, she set off brimming with confidence, but eight miles in she was knocked by someone passing her wearing an impractical fancy dress costume, and she went over on her ankle. She hit the tarmac with a painful thud.

Fortunately, no bones were broken and after a few

weeks of taking things easy with a sprained ankle she was back in the woods, bounding through them like a cheetah in the Serengeti.

Following the heartbreaking announcement of the promotion, Laurie felt physically sick. It was hearing the gossip in the canteen at lunchtime that was the final straw. She faked a migraine and decided to leave work early: screw the Zoom meeting with HR. She went home to change into her Lycra. She wanted to run fast, run hard, run far, and maybe never come back.

As Laurie turned a corner, she stopped abruptly. A woman in pink running gear was sitting on the ground, leaning against a tree. Laurie thought back to the day of the marathon when she was in agony, and the people who had helped her.

'Is everything all right?' Laurie asked, pulling out her earbuds as she approached, struggling to talk as she tried to catch her breath.

'I tripped on a root and twisted my knee. I think I'm going to be sick.'

Laurie squatted beside her. Her running trousers were torn, her knee grazed and bloody. Laurie wasn't trained but she was pretty sure her knee might be dislocated. She didn't want to touch it and quickly looked away. She wasn't good with blood.

'Do you think you can stand up?'

'I've tried three times. I can't put any weight on my leg. Oh God,' she said, as she dry-heaved.

Laurie looked around for a kindly stranger. There was no one there. She checked her phone but in this part of the woods she knew she wouldn't get a signal. She thought for a moment. 'OK. I'm going to help you up. I want you to put your arm around me, put all your weight on me, and I'll help you home. Where do you live?'

'Not far. Are you sure?'

'I'm positive. Come on.'

Carefully, the woman put her left arm around Laurie's neck and after a few deep breaths from both, Laurie stood up.

The woman tried her best not to scream, but once she was upright, she let out a violent exclamation that caused the birds to flee from the trees.

'Sorry,' she said with half a smile.

'That's OK. I find swearing helps, too.'

'This is worse than childbirth.'

'I wouldn't know about that.'

'I've had two. Trust me, it is. At least you get drugs when you're in labour. Please tell me you have an epidural in your bum bag.'

'Only a packet of Jelly Babies, sorry. As soon as we're clear of the woods, I'll get an Uber or something.'

'Thanks. You're a lifesaver. I'm Ally, by the way.'

'Laurie.'

'Nice to meet you. So, do you come here often?' She laughed through her pain.

Laurie laughed back. 'Most days.'

'I'm new to running. Not sure it's my thing.'

'It takes time. Don't let this put you off.'

They stumbled and Ally bit her bottom lip to stifle a scream. Laurie increased her grip on her, keeping Ally upright.

'You need to distract yourself from the pain,' Laurie said. 'Tell me about yourself. Tell me about your kids.'

Ally filled her in on her two sons, how they were a whirlwind of noise and mess, but she loved them with all her heart. Then, it was Laurie's turn. Five minutes later, the exit of the woods in sight, Laurie had told her all about her cheating bastard of an ex-boyfriend and the promotion she'd been promised at work going to someone else.

'Men!' Ally seethed. 'They're only useful for one thing. And most of the time they're useless at that.'

As they reached the clearing, Ally collapsed in pain and let out a scream.

'I'm sorry. I really think I'm going to vomit or pass out.'

'Do you want me to call your husband or something? Get him to come and pick you up?' Laurie asked.

'If the gormless lump could drive, that would be ideal.'

Laurie looked around. Parked in a layby was a red Ford Focus. She squinted and could see someone sitting in the front driver's seat.

'OK, wait here. I'm going to go and see if there's a good Samaritan in that car,' she said, and smiled.

'Be careful. He could be a descendant of Jack the Ripper,' Ally said, smiling back through the pain.

'I do Krav Maga. Anyone who tries to touch me where I don't want to be touched will be spending the night in A & E.'

Laurie made sure Ally was as comfortable as she could be, sitting on the cold, wet ground and leaning against a tree, before jogging off towards the Ford Focus. As she approached, she could hear a loud conversation from inside the car. She leaned down and saw there was only the one person in there. The driver had obviously pulled over to take a call.

She tapped on the window and smiled as the man looked up at her. He told his caller to hang on and lowered the glass.

'Yes?'

'Sorry to disturb you. My friend has fallen while jogging. I think she's dislocated her knee and is in a great deal of pain. I know it's a cheek, but you couldn't give her a lift home, could you? She's literally five minutes away from her house.'

'I don't know. I'm late home as it is.' He mouthed 'the wife' and pointed at the phone.

'Trust me, I wouldn't ask if it wasn't important. Her husband doesn't drive and I don't have my car with me. Please. I'm sure your wife will understand. I'll explain to her. I don't mind,' Laurie pleaded.

The man looked at his phone. 'Ah. She's hung up.'

'Oh. I'm sorry.'

'No worries. She'll shout at me if I'm five minutes late home, what's another ten?' He smiled, unbuckled his seatbelt, opened the door and climbed out. He stood tall over Laurie and looked lean in his fitted suit. 'Where's your friend?'

'She's right over…'

Laurie turned to the woods and stopped. Ally was standing in front of her, a smirk on her lips.

Before she could react, a hand was placed over Laurie's mouth from behind and she was pulled back into the man's tight embrace. She could smell his sweat, and his hot breath was in her ear.

'One sound out of you and your death will be painful,' he hissed.

Ally stepped forward. She showed no sign of a limp. 'Forgotten your Krav Maga moves?' she asked.

It was two days before Laurie Bateman was found. It was surprising, really, as she was left in plain sight. What her attackers had done to her could only be imagined by detectives, but her injuries were extensive and the postmortem examination took almost six hours. It was a further three days before she was formally identified, through fingerprints taken from around her home and matched to the body. Despite cries from her mother saying she wanted to see her only child one last time, investigating officers managed to dissuade her. There was nothing for her to see. Laurie's face was a broken mess. The murder weapon, found next to her body, was a broken chunk of rock that was used to pummel and obliterate her.

Her killers knew exactly what they were doing and had inflicted maximum torture before Laurie had succumbed to her death. The attack had been lengthy and sustained but she had clung on to life until all hope was lost, and she had died, alone, frightened and in agony. A tragic end to a good life.

Chapter Five

I open my eyes and know straight away that something is wrong.

Nanook is not on the bed where he usually is, and the door is ajar. He's never been able to open the bedroom door, despite several past attempts. Someone must have opened it for him. There is someone in the house.

I struggle to sit up and I listen intently for any sound. I can't hear anything.

Where's Nanook? What have they done to him?

I push back the duvet and swing my legs out of bed. I grab my crutch and struggle to put on my dressing gown as I stand in the doorway, listening for something, anything, that tells me where my intruders are. I have no idea what I'd do if they hurt Nanook. I don't think I'd ever get over something like that.

Stepping out onto the landing, I look around. All is silent. There's no sign of Nanook. During the summer, when the nights are hot, I leave the bedroom door ajar so he can walk out onto the landing where it's cooler. I half expect to see him out here, sprawled under the windowsill, but the space is empty.

'Shit,' I mutter to myself.

Then a smell tickles my nostrils. It's only faint, but it's enough to stop me in my tracks. I sniff harder. Bacon. That can only mean one thing. Luke is home.

Luke Jackson is sitting at the island in the kitchen enjoying a bacon sandwich, with Nanook by his side hoping some will be left over for him.

'What are you doing here?' I ask from the doorway, slightly out of breath from rushing down the stairs. I try to fight the grin from spreading across my face, but I can't. I'm so happy to see him home.

Luke turns. He's the same age as me, thirty-nine, but looks like he hasn't aged a day since his early thirties. He's taller, fitter, and better-looking than me, too. His dark blond hair is thick and short, almost military in its length. There isn't a hint of grey or any sign of balding. His eyes are piercing and icy blue. They twinkle when he smiles, and when he does, his whole face lights up.

'I thought I'd surprise you,' he says in his thick Liverpudlian accent.

'You certainly did that.'

'I had to pick something up from Sheffield so thought I'd drive the extra few miles to see how you are.'

'I'm glad you did. It's great to see you. Do you want another coffee?'

'Please.'

I go over to the kettle and flick it on.

'How's the new book going?' he asks.

'It's going very well. I wrote a tense interrogation scene in a hospital yesterday. I'm going to need to do some research into sedatives and anaesthetics today to make sure I'm using the right doses. I don't want a repeat of the complaints I got after I incorrectly used that angina medication in *The Science of Silence*.'

Luke laughs at the memory. I've missed that guttural giggle.

'What's happened on Leigh Road?' Luke asks. 'There are flowers by the roadside and one of those police signs asking for witnesses.'

The kettle boils and I pour the water into the cafetière.

'A woman was murdered. The police came here and asked if I'd seen anything.'

'Were you OK? With people coming into the house, I mean?'

'Yes, fine,' I say, shrugging.

'Did you see anything?'

'No. Well, only the flashing lights from the police cars when I went around closing the curtains. I didn't see the murder happen.'

'Did they say who she was?'

'They did, but I can't remember her name. They said she had to be identified by fingerprints so I'm guessing whoever killed her did a number on her.'

I hand Luke his coffee, which he takes in his large, calloused hands.

'Poor woman,' Luke says, wistfully.

'Hmm. Probably a jealous husband or something.'

'Or something.'

I perch on the edge of a stool at the island and look over at Luke, who seems to be staring somewhere far into the distance.

'Has the problem with the carpets been sorted out?' I say to change the subject.

'More or less. It's going to cost the company a lot of money to put right, but they made the mistake in the first place, so they've no one to blame but themselves. Listen, I had some good news yesterday.' He smiles and the temperature in the room rises by several degrees from the warmth that radiates from him. I find myself smiling back, something I rarely do. 'Me and a few of the lads were in this Chinese having a moan. There weren't many people in, and we weren't exactly quiet so, next thing I know, this bloke comes over and asks if I know any decorating firms. I tell him I'm a decorator, and he tells me about this student apartment block that's just finished being built. One hundred and twenty flats across twelve floors and they all need decorating.' He beams.

'You're doing them?'

He nods rapidly, a child-like grin on his face. 'I showed him a few of the projects I'd done on my phone. I showed him your living room and office, hope you don't mind. I also gave him your number to call for a reference. Just don't tell him we're mates.'

'I won't.'

'Anyway, I popped round to the building, gave him a quote, knocked off a bit for cash, and we shook on it. I'm getting that dodgy solicitor bloke I know to draw up some kind of a mates' agreement so neither of us gets ripped off, but it's worth a packet.'

'Isn't it going to be a bit boring, though, decorating one hundred and twenty flats on your own?'

'I'm going to have to hire some temp lads because he wants them finished quickly. I've been on to the job centre in Newcastle and I'm setting up interviews for early next week. I thought I'd decorate one on the ground floor while I'm doing this carpet job, and I can live in there while doing the rest. I'll only need a sleeping bag, microwave and a kettle.' The excitement in his voice is evident.

'How long are you going to be away?' I say, my face souring.

'A good few months.' He looks guilty. 'I'll come back at the weekends, don't worry.'

'I'm not worried,' I lie. 'I just don't want you getting bored or lonely up there, that's all.'

'You've never been to Newcastle, have you? The block of flats is right on the edge of the city centre and that place is full of pubs and clubs. There's a hen party visiting practically every weekend. I'm laughing, mate.'

I can feel my smile wavering slightly. I admire Luke's carefree attitude and fun approach to life. I often wish we could change places, but maybe I'd find Luke's lifestyle exhausting after a while.

'Are you OK?' Luke asks.

'I'm fine.'

'You look tired.'

'Bad night,' I lie.

'Are you taking your medication?'

'Religiously.'

'I worry about you,' Luke says.

'There's no need.' I smile, but it doesn't reach my eyes and I can feel my lips quiver.

'I tell you what, before I go back, why don't I take Nanook out for a long run in the woods?'

Upon hearing his name, Nanook sits up from the floor, ears pricked.

'I think he'd like that,' I say.

'I'll just go for a piss and get my walking boots. Fancy coming with us?'

I wince at the offer. 'I need to start work.'

Nanook isn't a noisy dog, but while he was out with Luke the house was deathly silent. This must be what life was like before Nanook arrived. It seems like such a long time ago, but it's not a time I want to return to. There will come a time when Nanook is no longer with me. It's a shame dogs don't live as long as humans. They should. They deserve to. I don't want to even think about that day right now.

I can't settle at my desk. I try to work, but the words won't come. I need my canine companion by my side. Instead, I log on to my author website and open the messages file. My agent, Lucy Graham, understands my anxiety and agoraphobia. She accepts I won't be able to go to writers' events, meet readers in person or sit on a panel being interviewed. But she made it clear I need to connect with readers if I want a strong readership, and that means having a website. Reluctantly, I agreed. Luke knew someone who could design me something impressive and I was pleased with the result. I don't like the window it opens, however. I can connect with readers, but they can also connect with me. There are dozens waiting for a reply. I let out a heavy sigh. They all say the same sort of thing and I reply using the same words but in a different order to make it sound sincere each time.

Dear Mr Cullen,

I finished reading The Loudest Scream over a week ago and I can't stop thinking about it. It gave me chills, and a few nightmares too. The relationship between the two killers was so intense I could actually feel the energy coming off the page. I wanted them to get caught for the horrible things they did, but at the same time, I didn't want them to be separated from each other as I knew they wouldn't survive alone. You're a truly gifted author. I don't usually read two books in a row by the same writer but I'm going to start reading My Wife tonight.

Keep writing.
Julianne Clower

Aidan Cullen,

My Wife was one of the most frustrating books I've ever read. Not because it was poorly written or anything like that, but because of how true to life it was. Gill knew she was being stalked. The police knew she was being stalked but because Tom knew the law backwards, he was able to do just enough to avoid being arrested yet still make Gill's life a misery. I loved the open ending, too. I hate the way some writers tie everything up in a neat bow. You don't do that.

You treat your characters like real people, like their lives will continue after the final page. Can't wait for your next book.

Best wishes,
Celia Pratt

Then there is the inevitable daily message from Rebecca Charlesworth. I sigh as I click the mouse to open and read.

Aidan,

I hope you're well. You'll never guess where I was at the weekend. Me and my sister were at a loose end so decided to go for a drive and we ended up on Tawney Street. There was a house up for sale, so we called the estate agent and booked an appointment to have a look around. Obviously, I don't know if it's the same house you chose that Beth from Out of Darkness lived in, but it was nice to be in a house that was like you described. As soon as I entered, I felt like I knew the place. As you know, I've read Out of Darkness several times. It's a brilliant novel, so I felt like I knew Beth's home, but to be actually standing inside the house, to walk through the living room into the dining room, walking up the winding staircase and seeing the en suite just off the master bedroom where Beth killed her husband, it was ... well, it was an experience I'll never forget. I'm going to read Out of Darkness again this weekend. I know it'll feel even more real now that I've been in 'her' house.

Bye for now,
Rebecca

I can't remember the last time I replied to one of Rebecca Charlesworth's emails. She messages me a great deal. At one point it was once a day, occasionally more than once. She has all my novels, in hardback and paperback, signed copies, and she bought a first edition of *Out of Darkness* from a seller on eBay for more than a thousand pounds.

Rebecca is a fan, of that I'm in no doubt, but she seems to consider me as a friend. Some of her emails are incredibly detailed and she's told me all about the breakdown of her marriage and her breast cancer scare. There was one email in particular that went into a great deal of detail where she told me about her mental health and her struggle with depression and loneliness. I couldn't reply to that one. It hit too close to home.

At first, I replied in my usual polite way to Rebecca, but the more she began to intrude, the shorter my replies became, hoping she would take the hint that I wasn't someone she could confide in. And, although it pains me to do so, some of her messages are deleted without a reply. I don't want to invite her into my life more than I have to. As far as I'm concerned, she's one of the many readers I have around the world. She's no different to the others, despite what she herself might think.

'Aidan, you there?'

Luke's call from the back of the house snaps my mind back from its flight of fancy. I turn off the computer and leave the office, closing the door firmly behind me.

Nanook is filthy. But what else would you expect from a white German Shepherd running in the woods in the middle of a wet winter? His legs are brown and mud-splatter is all over his body and face. Luke doesn't look much better. He's stroking Nanook, who's so out of breath his panting tongue almost reaches the floor. He looks happy, so I don't mind.

'Look at the state of you two,' I say. 'You know, when Nanook bounds into the river to fetch a stick, you don't have to follow him.'

'Funny! I didn't. If you must know, I slipped and fell on my arse.'

I raise an eyebrow. 'I bet you wouldn't have slipped if you'd been walking sensibly. What were you doing?'

Luke thinks before he replies. His cheeks redden slightly. 'Well … actually, I was wrestling Nanook.'

A natural laugh erupts from the pit of my stomach. 'I don't mind hosing down a dog, but I'm not cleaning you up.'

'Don't worry, I'll give Nanook a wash out here then I'll go for a shower.'

'Maybe I should have one of those outdoor showers installed, like they have at beaches for surfers to use.'

'Good idea. It wouldn't take much to install. You could run a pipe from the utility…'

'I was joking.'

'Oh. Shame.'

Luke takes Nanook out into the back garden while I find the items needed to give the dog a bath. I watch from the conservatory window as a soaking wet Nanook shakes off the excess water. Luke's unable to jump out of the way in time and is sprinkled with soap suds. He turns on the hose and begins rinsing the German Shepherd, getting himself more and more wet in the process, but loving every minute of it.

I can feel myself relaxing. This is what I want: a life with fun and action in it. A life that stops me thinking of the darkness of my past, the mental anguish I'm still struggling to make sense of, even with regular therapy sessions. Why can't I be more like Luke? Why can't I see the world as one giant playground? Why is everything so fucking serious all the time?

'I've been calling you,' Luke says from the doorway.

I break out of my daydream. 'Sorry?'

'What were you thinking about?'

'I … I don't know. My work. My book,' I say, stumbling. 'I've written myself into a corner and I'm not sure how to get out of it,' I lie.

'You'll think of something. Listen, you couldn't make me something to eat while I have a quick shower, could you?'

'I could probably roast you a chicken in the time you'll need to wash all that off.'

'Very funny,' he says as he squelches through the kitchen, leaving dirty footprints behind him. 'You don't know where my camping gear is, do you?' he asks over his shoulder.

'You're moving up to Newcastle today?' The concern in my voice is clear.

'Yeah. I need to get started on those student apartments. Listen, can I raid the cupboards, take a few canned goods with me?' He grins.

'Sure. I've got a Sainsbury's delivery coming later. Take what you want.'

'You're a star.'

He leaves the room, taking the air of happiness in the atmosphere with him. I turn and see a soggy and tired Nanook glaring at me from the doorway.

'A fleeting visit, then. Just you and me again.'

I'm sure I can see disappointment in Nanook's eyes.

Chapter Six

JOGGER MURDERED ON COUNTRY ROAD

Police are hunting for a killer after a woman was brutally murdered on a countryside road in Derbyshire.

Melanie Burton, 22, was found by a family friend who had gone to look for her after she failed to return home from an afternoon run.

Ms Burton, from Ashford-in-the-Water, had a regular jogging route which took her along Leigh Road in the small village of Gallowsfield. She was found at the side of the road with extensive injuries.

'The 999 call came through saying they believed Ms Burton had been the victim of a hit and run,' Detective Inspector Victor Finch of Derbyshire CID said. 'Officers quickly attended the scene and soon discovered the extent of the incident. A post-mortem examination revealed Ms Burton suffered at the hands of a brutal and senseless attacker. A murder enquiry has now been launched.'

Detectives were seen in and around Gallowsfield yesterday, conducting house-to-house enquiries, and the search for the perpetrator of this seemingly motiveless crime will continue in the days ahead.

A statement from Ms Burton's family released by Derbyshire Police last night said: 'Melanie was a true star in our family. She was intelligent, fun and always had a smile on her face. She meant so much to so many people. To have her torn away from us so cruelly is too painful to contemplate. This family will never be the same again.'

DI Finch said: 'We believe this to be an isolated incident. However, caution should be taken when people are out alone in isolated areas.'

Anyone who has information about this crime should call 101 quoting reference: RZ89.

I'm not sure why, but I've made notes. I know the police aren't going to release all the gory information about how Melanie was killed to the press and, even if they did, they wouldn't print it in glorious technicolour. However, I can't help feeling this murder is something that is going to haunt me.

There are three photographs accompanying the article. The first is of Melanie Burton, taken when she was alive, smiling to the camera. Her arm is around someone just out of shot, and she has a glass of white wine in one hand. Her nose wrinkles as she smiles, her eyes are half closed. She's beautiful. It's so sad to think of her young life so tragically cut short. The second photo has obviously been supplied to the media by the police, as it's of the crime scene. A forensic tent is hiding the body from view and white-suited forensic officers are milling around, collecting evidence. The third picture shows the aftermath. The tent has gone, the body removed, and bunches of flowers lie at the side of the road.

I log on to Google and type in Melanie Burton's name. A couple of news stories come up about her murder, but there's very little to add to my notes from what I've already read on the BBC News website. There are links to her social media accounts, which

I click on but, as I'm not a member of these sites and Melanie had set her privacy settings so only her friends could view her posts, I'm not able to access her profiles or look at any photographs. I'd like to have known what she was like as a person. There's something about her death that's niggling me. I think I'm trying to figure out how much like Laurie Bateman she is.

I heave myself out of my chair. I've been sitting in a position that's comfortable but, when I try to move, I'm in a great deal of pain. I have to brace myself for a couple of minutes before I attempt the stairs. By the time I reach the top floor, Nanook is impatiently waiting for me and I have a sheen of sweat on my forehead. I can even feel it dripping down my back.

Looking through the telescope, I point it towards Leigh Road and the spot where Melanie Burton lost her life. The raw elements of a Derbyshire winter's night have devastated the tributes. A strong easterly wind has torn apart the bunches of flowers and scattered them across the road. Vehicles have run over them, crushing the stems and petals into the tarmac.

'I hate to see roadside tributes,' I say to Nanook. 'You never see people lay the flowers, do you? They just seem to appear, as if by magic. The body is taken away to the mortuary and is replaced by bunches of flowers and teddy bears. And why flowers? You pull them out of the ground, wrap them up in polythene, and without water they die within a few days. That's not a tribute, is it? Before you know it, the site of where a loved one was killed is marked by decaying flowers.'

I look down at Nanook and he's looking up at me with hopeful eyes. People are really quite strange in their behaviour, when you think about it. I'd much rather be a dog. The wind has picked up since yesterday and the bare branches of the trees are swaying gently, as if they're waving to me. I smile. I find nature to be an interesting phenomenon. It's relaxing to watch rain run down the window or snow fall silently from the sky. In the summer, the warmth of the sun beats down and everything seems to come alive. The sky is bluer, the grass greener; everything is magnified and radiant. Even in the winter, when the leaves have been plucked from the trees and the ground is dulled by a lack of colour, there's something calming about the countryside sleeping, hiding from the harshness of the weather, readying itself for the spring.

At the other end of the scale, nature can be cruel, and the past couple of winters have brought devastating storms to the area. I've spent many a sleepless night listening to the sounds of gale-force winds rattling around outside, wondering if a chimney stack is going to fall through the roof or a tree smash into the conservatory.

It's not an exaggeration to say that my home is my fortress and I live in fear of it being violated in some way. And it's not just people I'm scared of coming in without permission. I have to try and keep nature at bay, too.

I shake my head to try to force out the unwanted thoughts. There is so much running around in there – my dark imaginings, my paranoias, my past – all of it trying to shout the loudest.

In the distance, the village church clock chimes. It's two o'clock. The day seems to have passed by in a blur, for which I am grateful.

'Shit,' I say to myself.

It's two o'clock. It's Thursday. I'm late.

Chapter Seven

I started seeing my first therapist when I was twenty. I had a lot going on in my life at that time and I was struggling to cope with it all. My parents had gone and my only remaining relative, my grandmother, was showing signs of dementia. I had nobody to turn to. Despite having severe trust issues with strangers, I made an appointment with someone I didn't know to open up about my deepest and darkest secrets. Talk about a contradiction.

I'm not against therapy. I like to think I'm open and receptive to new ideas and thinking. But there's something about revealing all to a total stranger that doesn't sit well with me. It's a one-sided process. There I was, a frightened twenty-year-old, in a consulting room that somehow managed to smell both fusty and of furniture polish, disclosing intimate details of my past to someone who I only knew the name of. Annette Del Mar sat week after week, with her head tilted to one side and a Montblanc fountain pen poised to scribble down the meanings of my darkest nightmares, and all I knew about her was that she was a fan of *The Simpsons*, because there was a Homer Simpson keyring attached to the key in the filing cabinet. It was hardly a balanced relationship built on mutual trust and respect.

I didn't see her for very long. I cancelled one appointment and didn't bother to book another. She didn't call to see how I was or if I was still alive. I could have thrown myself from the top of the Liver Building and she wouldn't have known about it.

Not long after I moved to Derbyshire, Luke noticed I'd not left the house and made every suggestion he could think of to try to get me to go out. I turned them all down. He even suggested booking a box at Twickenham, which would have been cool, but I couldn't face it. It was then he suggested I should talk to someone professional. Luke said that he couldn't blame me for wanting to live in isolation after the stabbing, but I needed to try to be happy. The dark thoughts needed to go. He was right. He's always right. Unfortunately, how could I be happy when I didn't know what being happy meant?

So, every Thursday at two o'clock, I sit in front of my computer for an hour and speak, via Skype, to Dr Charlotte Wood. It took a great deal of research to find someone I felt comfortable speaking to. I had no idea how many therapists there actually are until I started looking, and they all seem to specialise in something different. Charlotte has written books on self-torment, the subconscious id, childhood trauma, repressed memory, and nightmare incarnations. It's like she was tailor-made to help me.

Charlotte doesn't believe in simply listening to me talk. She has engineered a relationship that is open, and she doesn't hold back on sharing the horrors of her own life. In the five years we've been talking, I know as much about her as she knows about me. She was sexually abused by her father for six years until she was twelve, when he died of a heart attack at the wheel of his car. But it was years before she told me she had a child. There was a sadness about her that day and I wondered if he was dead, but she opened up to me. That was a real reversal of roles. I didn't mind. I actually came away from the session feeling better about myself because I'd been able to help her. It turned out it was her son's birthday. She hadn't seen him for years. She loved him. She told me that several times, but ... there was something there, something underlying she wasn't telling me. I don't want to push her for information, like she doesn't push me. I am curious, though. I sometimes get the impression she's as unhappy as I am. She has this look about her, occasionally.

Yes, she's been through a level of hell even Dante couldn't have conjured up, but she's survived, and it's her mission to help her clients become survivors too.

It's two minutes past two when I throw myself into my chair and the familiar jingle from an incoming Skype call fills the room. I accept and Charlotte's face fills the screen. I smile instantly, and it's not a forced smile. She's wearing a cream-coloured cardigan over a navy shirt, open at the collar. Her hair cascades around her head and shoulders, like a lion's mane. It's thick and dark red. Her face is subtly made up, because, as she said in our first meeting all those years ago, 'I'm the wrong side of fifty and high definition is a cruel bitch.'

'Good afternoon, Aidan,' she says in her usual bright tone as if she's genuinely delighted to see me. Her voice is soft and almost lyrical. I love her accent.

I suddenly feel relaxed. It's a joy to be in the presence of someone I like and admire.

'Good afternoon.'

'How are you?'

'I'm well, thank you.'

'And how's that gorgeous dog of yours?'

'Sleeping.'

'Lucky for some. It was gone two before I nodded off this morning, thanks to the pillock next door drilling into the small hours.'

'That's not fair.'

'He's had insomnia ever since his wife died. We're detached but I can still hear the noise. People don't seem to realise how much sound travels in the dead of night.'

'Maybe you should offer him some therapy,' I say, smiling.

'I'm not getting involved with any of my neighbours. Not again. Not after last time. Anyway, how's your week been?'

'Good. It's been a productive week.'

'Excellent. I finally got around to reading your latest last weekend, *The Science of Silence*. It was bloody good.'

'Thank you. My next one is due out in a few weeks.'

'I'm way behind with my reading. Thank you for the mention in the acknowledgements.'

'Well, credit where it's due. I'd have never come up with the parallels between the immediate aftermath of a disaster and wanting to relive the trauma. It was inspired.'

Charlotte sits back in her chair. She's studying me. 'I've noticed that about you over the years.'

'What?'

'Whenever you talk about your work, your face lights up. You seem happy.'

'Do I?'

'But whenever we talk about your personal life, your past, there's a sadness about you. I can sometimes feel it coming through the screen.'

'I don't like talking about me,' I say, taking a long sip from the glass of water on my desk. I always get a dry mouth when I'm talking for a long period of time and talking to Charlotte once a week for an hour is the longest I talk to anyone. I'll need a sit down after this conversation. Not to absorb what we've talked about but to try and dissolve the tension headache.

'Yet, here we are, every Thursday at two o'clock,' she says with her usual warm smile.

'I know I have to talk about me, about things, to make sense of them, to silence them. It's just … it's not easy.'

'Have you had any wobbles this week?' she asks.

'Only one. The postman came and didn't close the gate properly. I had to go out and do it.'

'How did you cope?'

'Well, I did it. I was knackered afterwards and lost the rest of the day to sleep, but I did it.'

'That's good. At least you didn't wait for Luke to come home like you've done in the past.'

'He's working away at the moment.'

'How do you feel about being alone in the house?'

'I'm fine. As long as I'm left alone, I'm fine.' I turn and look out of the window. I can't see the floral tributes on Leigh Road from here.

'Aidan, the last time we spoke, you mentioned that it's coming up to the anniversary of the death of your mother. I asked if you wanted to talk about it and you said you would. Do you?'

I take a deep breath. It's a while before I answer because I don't know what to say. 'I'm not sure.'

Charlotte leans closer to the computer. 'One of your main issues is survivor's guilt. You survived the car crash whereas your mother didn't. But she was the one driving, you were just a child. You also survived the knife attack. You don't think you're worthy of being alive.'

'I've cheated death twice,' I say. There's a catch in my throat.

'Some people would have embraced that, seen it as a sign of how short and fragile life is and decided to live life to the full. You've retreated.'

I look away from my computer towards the window again. I often sit on the padded seat in the window and look out at the front garden and the view of the sprawling Derbyshire countryside. It's comforting.

'Do you want to talk about your mother?' Charlotte asks after a long silence.

I shake my head.

'Why not?'

'Because every time I think about her, I hear the sound of

smashing glass. I smell the…' My voice shakes and I can feel my bottom lip wobbling. I don't want to cry.

'Tell me a happy story about her.'

I wasn't expecting her to say that. I stare at her blankly for a few long moments while I search my memory. There are lots of happy memories to choose from, but I can't let myself go there.

'Are you all right?' Charlotte asks me.

I'm fine.

I nod. I'm not all right. I'm worried that, if I open my mouth to speak, I'll burst into tears.

I take another sip of water, longer this time, and clear my throat.

'I remember my mum reading to me,' I begin. 'I'd sit on her knee, and she'd read me stories from those old children's Penguin books. At night, when I went to bed, she'd tuck me in, and she'd read to me until after I fell asleep. She said she'd carry on reading so that the story would go on in my dreams.'

'That's lovely.'

I'm smiling at the memory, but I feel incredibly sad. 'Mum enjoyed reading.'

'She'd be very proud of your achievements.'

'She'd hate the fact I'm writing crime.' I laugh. 'She liked happy, uplifting stories. Or a good romance.'

'She'd be proud of you.'

'Yes, I think she would. She always said I should find what I was passionate about and do that for a job. She was a hard worker, my mum. With my dad gone, it was always just the two of us. Well, it was until the accident. Then my gran took over.'

'The accident was only one part of your mum's story. Yes, she died far too young, but if you dwell on that, the pain, the torment, it will eat away at you. You should remember the happiness.'

I hear what she's saying. I understand it, but they're just words. It's not easy to remember a happy Christmas or a fun birthday when you've witnessed a scene of horror that eclipses everything that went before it.

'You can take your memories wherever you go. All you need to do is close your eyes and picture your mum by your bed, reading to you. Your memory is better than any photograph album.'

I can't decide if she's right about that, or not. I used to love looking at old photographs when I was young.

'What are you thinking?' Charlotte asks. 'Be honest.'

I don't make eye contact with her. 'I should have died with her.'

It's a shocking revelation but her face doesn't react.

'But you didn't. You survived. You're still here. You should honour her memory by living the best life you can.'

'We had a murder here the other day,' I say suddenly. If we keep talking about my mum, then the dark thoughts will creep in and I'm running low on my Lithium.

'A murder? Who?'

'I don't know. A young woman. She was out jogging and was killed. The police came to the house.'

'Did you let them in?'

'I didn't have any choice.'

'What did they want?'

'To know if I'd seen anything.'

'So, it was close to your house then?'

'Yes. I can see the road from here.'

'*Did* you see anything?' she asks, interested.

'No.'

'How did you feel about having strangers in the house?'

'Unsettled. They seemed nice enough, but I was relieved when they left.'

'Are you worried?'

'About what?'

'A murder being committed on your doorstep.'

'I surround myself with murderers on a daily basis,' I say with a smile.

'But that's fiction. You control the narrative. So, you're not frightened of being on your own?'

'No. I've got Nanook. I've got good security.'

'That's good. Remember just after you moved in and there were three burglaries in the next village, you were a nervous wreck.'

'I was,' I say. I smile at the memory.

'You may not think it, but you've come on a great deal in the past five years.'

'But I still can't leave the house,' I say, almost forlorn. 'I still can't be around people. I still can't look in a mirror.'

'You can do all of those things; you simply choose not to.'

Simply?

'I...' I stop myself, just in time.

'Go on.'

'No.'

'Are you sure?'

'I'm sure.'

'OK. Aidan, let me ask: do you want to leave the house?'

'No,' I say without pausing to think.

'So you're happy to stay in that house for the rest of your life?'

'I think "happy" is a strong word.'

'Content?'

'Better. Yes, I'm content here.'

Charlotte takes a deep breath. 'We need to get you out of that house,' she says with a smile on her lips. 'I want you to enjoy your success. I want to see you at a book event. I want to see you interviewed for magazines and newspapers. I want you on a stage reading from your latest bestseller to a sell-out crowd sitting on the edge of their seat, hanging on your every word.'

I shudder at the thought. I honestly cannot think of anything worse.

'I'm getting ahead of myself. We can build up to that. Let's just get you past the garden gate first.' She smiles.

'That's doable.'

'See, leaps and bounds. That would have been a firm no-no a year ago.'

I laugh. I love chatting to Charlotte. It doesn't feel like chatting to a therapist.

'Have some faith and believe in yourself. You're still young. Enjoy life. Do something wild and dangerous, like playing with Nanook in the front garden rather than the back.'

I let out a guffaw of laughter.

She sits back in her seat. 'You look so happy when you laugh. You should do it more often.'

'I'll try,' I say.

'Same time next week?'

'Same time next week.'

'Take care of yourself, Aidan.'

'You too. Thanks, Charlotte.'

We say our goodbyes and Charlotte disappears from my screen. I lean back in my chair and allow the silence to envelop me. It was a useful session, but I can't help but feel guilty. I really shouldn't be lying to my therapist, should I?

Chapter Eight

I take out the empty shoeboxes and push aside the vacuum-packed blankets and duvets at the bottom of the wardrobe. I disturb the dust and it makes me sneeze. A few seconds later, Nanook, comfortable on my bed, sneezes. I find what I'm looking for. It wasn't exactly hidden but it was out of sight, and obviously out of mind, too.

When my gran died, it was the first time I'd returned to Ireland since I left to go to university. I was sorting through her house with a friend of hers. He was a strange bloke. He had this intense stare that felt like it was burning into my skin. He's probably dead now, too.

Everyone's dead.

Anyway, as we were bagging up her things to either throw away or send to a charity shop, I found a photo album in the drawer beneath her bed.

The first time I looked through it, I had no idea who any of the people in the photos were. The strange bloke had to identify them for me. Apparently, my gran had lived quite the full life. She'd had a rich circle of friends, and a few exciting lovers. Good for her. The further we went through the album, the black-and-white photographs changed to colour, and I didn't need the strange bloke to point out who was who anymore. I recognised my mum straight away.

I nudge Nanook up the bed and make myself comfortable. He sniffs at the mustiness of the album and looks at me, as if for an explanation.

'I've no idea who most of these people are,' I say. 'It's fun to make up stories about them, though. They all seem so happy, despite their dodgy haircuts and criminal dress sense,' I say with a laugh. 'Now, this one here is definitely my gran when she was younger. Same eyes. They never change, Nanook. I'm pretty sure the man with his arm around her was my grandfather. He died long before I was born and he was never really spoken about, so I'm not a hundred per cent sure. There are a few pictures of my mum when she was young, but there's only one of my mum and dad together.'

I rifle through the pages of the album, glancing at the photos as I go. I really should spend more time looking at these one day. They're snapshots of history.

I find the photo I'm looking for and my heart misses a beat. Despite everything, it's warming to see my mum and dad together.

The picture has dulled with age and shows a young couple standing in front of a brick wall. The man is tall and thin, with a shock of dark, wavy hair and an oversized jacket and matching flares. He has his arm around a much shorter woman. She has long, wavy, dark red hair flowing freely down her back, a white cardigan over a light-pink blouse with a huge bow tied loosely around her neck. They're both smiling at the camera.

I take the picture out and look at the back. In faded handwriting I recognise immediately as my mum's, it reads: 'Me and Mick, Wexford. 21st birthday weekend.'

I'm smiling, and tears are filling my eyes.

'Don't they look happy? Shame he didn't stick around. I never even got to meet him.' I angle the album and show the photo to Nanook, who doesn't seem the least bit interested. 'This is the only photo I have of him. And the only photo of them together in existence. Maybe I should have it framed and on display?' I look around the room as if trying to find the perfect place to put it.

But none of my surfaces have picture frames or ornaments on them. I don't like anything on show. A photo would stand out. I'm not sure I'd like that.

'I'm in here somewhere,' I say, smiling as I look back at the album. I flick through the pages; more snapshots of my gran with her friends. She seemed to enjoy life more once she was widowed. 'There are two photos of me. Look. There I am, fast asleep in my cot, and there I am on my mum's lap, wide-eyed and smiling, not a care in the world.'

I lean back on the bed, my head resting on the pillow. 'It's a shame there were no other albums in my gran's house. There should have been loads. The camera was always brought out when we went on holiday or for big occasions, and I know for a fact Mum always sent Gran a copy of the photo I had taken at school every year. Where have all those gone? You don't throw photos away, do you? It's strange how things get misplaced over the years: photos, letters, memories.'

I feel a kick, look down and see Nanook has nodded off. He's twitching in his sleep. Tales of my past are obviously fascinating to him.

I don't have many photographs of Nanook. That will have to change. I'll start in the morning.

I close the album and place it on the bedside table next to the book I'm currently reading. I'm not in the mood to read tonight, so I turn out the light, plunging the room into darkness. It's not long before I join Nanook in sleep.

I'm shocked awake by something. I wake, literally, with a gasp. I rarely remember my dreams, which, if my bedding in the morning is anything to go by, is just as well. I must really thrash about while I'm sleeping.

But I've remembered something.

It must be talking to Charlotte yesterday, then looking through the photo album, bringing the past to the front of my mind. I remember a conversation between my mum and my gran. I'm looking at them between the railings of the staircase. I'm on the landing. It's night. It's cold and I should be sleeping. They're sitting in the living room. The door is open and a warm glow from inside lights up the hallway.

'He came to my work again today, Mum. He says he won't leave me alone until I agree.' That's my mum. She sounds frightened.

'Then tell him you'll bring the police in if he keeps going on. That'll scare him off.' My gran's voice is firmer, more severe. Nobody messes with my gran.

'I don't want to get the police involved.' My mum's crying now.

'You may have to if he doesn't leave you alone.'

'But it'll all come out. I don't want Aidan finding out about his father,' she says, her voice a loud whisper.

'He won't find out.'

'Are you kidding? They love a bit of gossip around here. It'll spread like wildfire. I will not have Aidan finding out how he was conceived. No child should hear that.'

I reach out and hold onto Nanook. My memory faded as soon as my eyes snapped open. I've no idea what my dream was about but, judging by the sweat pouring off my brow, the fitted sheet no longer doing its job, and the feeling of fear in the pit of my stomach, I'm pleased I don't remember.

Chapter Nine

My sleep was fitful after last night's dream. I woke up several times in a tangle of bedclothes and had to kick myself free. Nanook soon tired of me waking up and jumped off the bed with a heavy sigh to sleep on the floor, bless him. I can't remember what I was dreaming about, but I have a dark feeling it was something bad, and it involved my parents. I often wonder why I haven't tried to track my father down. I've no idea if he's still alive, but he would be my last surviving relative. I wonder if he's ever tried to look for me.

By four o'clock, I decide to give up on sleep and get out of bed. By half past, I'm working at my desk with a steaming cup of strong coffee by my side. It's pitch dark and silent outside. Nanook's fast asleep. I've done half a day's work before it even becomes light. Any normal person would reward themselves with the rest of the day off and do something fun. But I think it's patently obvious by now that I'm far from normal.

Sitting at the island in the kitchen eating breakfast, the conservatory doors wide open and Nanook leaping about outside chasing birds, I shiver as the cold air blows in. I can feel the goosebumps on my arms. I like being cold. I'm trying to work out what it is I'm feeling. I've written three very good chapters this morning so I should be buoyed, but my mum is at the forefront of my mind. Even though it's been years since her death, I miss her.

I push my porridge to one side and reach for my tablet.

A news alert has come through. I set one up to notify me of any local stories in the hope there'll be more information about Melanie Burton. I log on to the BBC News app and go to the local news page. There's something about a lorry crashing into a bridge in Bakewell and almost falling into the river below. The headline of the next article catches my attention.

COUPLE FOUND MURDERED AFTER FOUR WEEKS

The murdered remains of an elderly couple have been found in their home.

James and Millicent Hargreaves lived in the small village of Over Haddon near Bakewell. Millicent was last seen around Christmas in the village shops and James had been housebound for two years following a severe stroke. Their bodies were discovered by a neighbour.

Detective Inspector Victor Finch said in a statement outside the detached home: 'The deaths of Mr and Mrs Hargreaves are a chilling reminder of how some elderly members of our community are forgotten. They had lain dead in their bed for a month, and nobody had missed them. This should not have been allowed to happen to two people in their nineties.'

Alluding to the cause of their deaths, DI Finch continued: 'We are treating this as a murder inquiry due to the nature of the condition their bodies were found in, and I ask anyone with information to come forward. Cast your minds back four weeks. Did you see anyone suspicious hanging around? Were there any unusual vehicles around? Please, think. We owe it as a community to make sure the killer of James and Millicent is caught, and they are able to rest in peace.'

Next-door neighbour Julia Fitzherbert said: 'I cannot believe I didn't know anything was wrong. I've lived here for six years and knew the Hargreaveses well. After James suffered his stroke, he was housebound, and Millicent looked after them both. I often went shopping for them, but Millicent was very independent and liked to do as much as she could herself. I think she was often offended when I tried to help. I told her to call me whenever she needed anything. When she didn't, I just assumed everything was fine. I'll never forgive myself.'

DI Finch hasn't given any motive for the apparent murder and hasn't said if it was a burglary gone wrong. Anyone with information should call 101 and quote reference number RZ97.

I limp into my office, leaving Nanook outside and the conservatory doors wide open. My home is exposed, but I don't have time. I need to check that I'm right, but I'm praying to anyone who'll listen that I'm wrong.

It seems darker in the house. The walls of the hallway seem closer, and I can almost feel them moving, pressing me in, squeezing me. I need air. I can hardly breathe.

I pull a book from the shelf. It's my fourth book, *When the Barking Stops*. The cover shows the silhouette of two barking wolves on a hillside against a backdrop of a clear sky. It's not my favourite cover and I'm not overly fond of the cartoonish image, but it's the sense of isolation and loneliness that makes it work. With shaking fingers, I get to the first chapter and skim read, even though I know exactly what it's going to say.

'I'm right,' I say to myself, softly. 'I'm fucking right.'

WHEN THE BARKING STOPS

AIDAN CULLEN

Chapter One

It was the fact the rear bedroom curtains hadn't been opened that first alerted Sylvia Price that something was wrong next door.

She was in the back garden tending to her beloved roses when she looked up at a cloud blocking the sun. The weather forecast had said it was going to be sunny all day, which was why she changed into her gardening clothes straight after breakfast. The deepening grey clouds were putting her plans in serious jeopardy. When her eyes fell on the main bedroom of the house next door, she frowned. It was a little after ten o'clock, and Edie was always up before sunrise. On tiptoe, she peered into the back garden. The curtains in the living room were drawn, too. If it was any of her other neighbours, she wouldn't have batted an eyelid. The fact it was Edie gave her cause for concern. Edie was a creature of habit.

Sylvia walked slowly up the incline of the garden and entered the conservatory, where she'd left her husband struggling with a crossword an hour ago. He was still there, wearing his dressing gown and slippers, dried egg yolk on his chin and a painful expression on his craggy face as he attempted to access parts of his brain he hadn't used since leaving work. She hated him coming into the conservatory in his nightclothes where the neighbours might catch sight of him. She'd brought it up many times and he always gave the same reply: 'I'm retired for crying out loud.'

'Nocturnal bird hides in hollow log,' he read out when he sensed her presence.

'Jack, have you seen them from next door lately?' Sylvia asked from the doorway, trowel in hand.

'Which side?' he asked, not looking up from his paper.

'Frank and Edie.'

He looked up as he thought and blew out his cheeks. 'Nope. Can't say I have.' He returned to the newspaper.

'Me neither. Don't you think that's a bit strange?'

'No. They're not going to go out much, are they? She can hardly walk, and he's started losing it.'

'I know, but Edie always has washing on the line when it's a nice day, and their bedroom curtains aren't open.'

'Maybe they're having a lie-in.'

'Hmm. I think I might pop round. Where have we put their key?' Sylvia said.

'On the hook. You can't just let yourself in.'

'Why not?'

'What if they're in bed?'

'And what if they're … you know…?'

'What?'

'You know.'

'I don't.'

'Oh, come on, Jack, do I have to spell it out for you? What if they're dead?'

'You've been watching too many soap operas.'

'I'm going round.' She placed the trowel on the sill, took off her gardening gloves and walked into the house.

'If you're so concerned, why don't you call their daughter, whatshername?' Jack shouted through to the kitchen.

'Melissa. What can she do from Chester? That's why we've got a key.'

'I mean, maybe she's spoken to them recently. She'll know how they are.'

'You know she only calls when she feels she has to. Are you coming with me?' Sylvia asked, leaning back into the conservatory.

'I'm in my dressing gown.'

She rolled her eyes and walked away. 'You're always in your sodding dressing gown,' she said to herself.

'I'm retired for crying out loud.'

'Owl,' she called out.

'Sorry?'

'Nocturnal bird hides in hollow log. Owl.'

'So it is,' he said, a smile on his face. 'Do you want another?'

He didn't receive an answer as the front door slammed closed.

It was a stifling summer morning, but the grey clouds rolling in had taken an edge off the heat and a breeze was beginning to pick up. Sylvia looked up at the sky; there would be rain within the hour, she didn't doubt. So much for a day in the garden.

She approached Frank and Edie's house, not as well kept as their own, a sign of Edie's decline. She had always been so house proud. All the curtains in the downstairs rooms were closed so Sylvia was unable to see inside. She hesitated at the front door and decided to ring the bell before letting herself in. She leaned closer, listening for any sign of life. Nothing. She rang the bell again. Nothing.

She looked around her and took in the street. It was quiet. After the hurly-burly rush of kids going to school and adults reversing out of their drives and heading to work, silence had fallen. Sylvia didn't like it. There was something ominous about this silence that worried her. It was a harbinger of something sinister to come.

She fished the key out of the pocket of her gardening trousers and unlocked the door. She pushed it open and stepped inside.

'Frank? Edie? It's me, Sylvia. I've just popped round to see if you're all right,' she called out from the doorway.

The house was cold and there was an underlying musty smell. A glass-topped table by the door held a landline phone and an address book. Sylvia swiped a finger across the top and looked at it. A layer of dust came away. It was not like Edie to allow dust to settle.

'Oh, dear Lord,' she said under her breath.

Frank and Edie's house hadn't been decorated for a long time. The carpet was a headache of gaudy colours. The anaglypta wallpaper had been painted over many times and was in need of a fresh coat. The prints on the wall were cheap and generic and the furniture dated back to the 1970s and 80s.

There were three doors leading off from the hallway, to the lounge, the dining room and the kitchen. They were all closed. Sylvia remained in the hall, not knowing where to look first. Something was drawing her to the stairs. She placed a hand on the banister and slowly started to ascend.

With each creak of the floorboards, Sylvia's sense of unease deepened. It wasn't like Frank and Edie to sleep in late. It certainly wasn't like Edie to keep all the curtains and windows closed, especially during the summer. She was embarrassed about the house smelling, especially since Frank had become incontinent, so she liked to get fresh air to whip through the house on a daily basis. The windows were always open.

When Sylvia reached the landing, she stopped and listened intently for any noise. Again, nothing, apart from the distant tick of a clock from somewhere. Three doors led off the landing; all of them were closed.

There was a smell. She'd detected it coming up the stairs but couldn't put her finger on what it was. It was a nasty smell and caused her to wrinkle her nose. She had never smelled anything like it before.

She placed her hand on the black plastic handle of the bedroom door, gripping it hard. With her other hand, she knocked lightly on the door.

'Frank. Edie. Are you awake?' she asked with a shaking voice. She waited for a reply that didn't come.

She depressed the handle and pushed open the door.

The smell hit her before her eyes had a chance to adjust and her brain register what she was seeing. She buckled, bent over and was almost sick. She clamped a hand to her mouth and nose, looked up and saw the decaying bodies of her neighbours, lying in bed as if they'd both gone to sleep and simply died. If only that had been true.

The bedsheets were awash with dried blood. Flies buzzed around the room and maggots were crawling over the gaping wounds of the elderly couple, feeding on what flesh was still left.

Sylvia remained in the open doorway, mouth open, breathing in the putrefied air. She tried to scream but couldn't. She was frozen and couldn't take her eyes from the maggots that were crawling in and out of the mouths of the people she had lived next door to for the last ten years. Something was moving beneath the duvet. She saw it rising up and down. She couldn't take her eyes from it. The lump, whatever it was, was crawling, slowly, up the bodies towards their heads.

It was a rat. A small brown rat with a long tail crept out from under the duvet and up Frank's neck. Its nose and whiskers were twitching. It crawled up his face, clawed at his lips and pulled them open before squeezing itself through the gap and into his mouth.

Sylvia felt sick. She suddenly realised she was standing

in the midst of a nightmare. She found her voice and she used it.

Chapter Ten

I scramble to the conservatory as fast as I can and shout for Nanook. The panic in my voice causes him to charge into the house. As soon as he's inside, I slam the conservatory doors closed, lock them, fit the Patlock, and alarm the entire building using the LCD display. If anyone approaches or tries to get in, I'll know about it. The whole of Derbyshire will know about it.

I grab my mobile from the island. It takes a while to unlock as my fingers are shaking and my eyes won't focus. I select Luke's name from the contacts list and call him. It rings for ages before the voicemail kicks in. I don't leave a message.

'Shit. Answer your phone, for crying out loud,' I scream.

I can't settle. I'm pacing up and down the house, my crutch clacking on the hardwood floor, moving from room to room. My mind is a mess. I try to take deep breaths to calm myself down, but it's not working.

The house is secure. The doors are all locked. The windows are closed. There is no way someone can get in here without me knowing it. There's no fresh air, either. It's all stale. The grey walls are closing in.

My phone rings in my hand, making me jump. It's Luke. I swipe to answer.

'Luke.'

'Aidan, is something wrong?'

'Yes. Something is wrong. Something is *very* wrong. Can you do me a favour? Are you near a computer?'

'I've got my tablet with me. What's up?'

'Can you look on the local news for me?'

'Erm, sure. Why?'

'I need you to check something for me.'

'Can't you do that? Is your internet down?'

'No. Nothing like that. Just … let me know when you're on the news site,' I say, running my fingers carefully through my hair. They come away damp. I'm sweating.

Something has moved outside. I look up at the large window in the living room. There's someone out there. Someone has just walked past my window. I know it.

'OK, what am I looking for?' he asks.

I don't answer. My eyes are fixed firmly on the window. I saw a shadow, someone, something.

'Aidan. Are you there?'

'What? Yes. Sorry. Look, is there a story about an elderly couple found dead in their bed?'

'Let me see … yes, there is. Why? Do you know them?'

'No. It's just … doesn't it remind you of something?'

'No.'

I turn my back on the window. 'It's exactly like the opening chapter of *When the Barking Stops*.'

'Is it?'

'Yes!' I snap. It frustrates me how my closest friend, my only friend, doesn't read my books. 'And the woman who was killed the other day on Leigh Road while jogging, that was like the beginning of *The Loudest Scream*.'

'Was it?'

'Yes!' I spit.

'What are you saying, Aidan?'

I take a deep breath. 'I think someone's killing people based on my books.'

'Oh, Aidan, I hardly think that's likely,' he says, a hint of laughter in his voice.

'Isn't it? How many murders do you think we get in Derbyshire? Not very many. All of a sudden, there's three deaths within a matter of weeks and within a few miles of where I live, and both incidents are very similar to what I've written. That's too much of a coincidence; can't you see?' I'm gripping the phone firmly in my hand. I can feel the sinews tightening in my wrist.

'Aidan, are you taking your medication?' Luke asks. There's genuine concern in his voice.

I turn to look back out of the window. There's nobody there. But there is. I know there is.

'Of course, I am,' I say.

'Have you been drinking?'

'It's not even nine o'clock in the morning yet. Luke, I'm not making this up.'

'I know you're not, it's just … well, coincidences do happen.'

'I think I should call the police.'

'What? Why?'

'To tell them someone is copying my books.'

'Aidan, I wouldn't. They'll think you're … I don't want them thinking bad things about you.'

'What do you mean?'

'Look at it from their point of view – a writer of crime fiction, living in a big house in the middle of nowhere, reclusive – they might make fun of you. I don't want you feeling more despondent than you already do,' he says.

'You call them, then.'

'What?'

'You phone them. Tell them you've seen the two items on the news and that you think they resemble my books.'

'Then they'll think *I'm* a crank.'

'I can't not call them, Luke. What if there's a third incident? I'd never forgive myself.'

Luke sighs. A silence grows between us as he's obviously trying to think of the right words to say.

'OK. Do you still have the card of the detective who came to the house the other day?' he asks.

'Erm, yes, I think so.'

'Right. Phone her and tell her your theory, but don't make it sound too serious. Just let her know you've noticed a similarity and you think she should be aware of it. Almost make light of it.'

'Won't that make me sound even weirder if I'm making jokes about murder?'

'I'm not saying make jokes, be more matter of fact than that, but don't make it sound like it's a life-or-death situation.'

'OK. I can do that,' I say. I can feel myself begin to relax.

'Phone me back, Aidan. Let me know what she says.'

'I will.'

'And Aidan, make sure you're taking your tablets when you're supposed to.'

'I am doing.'

I think.

———

I hang up on him. I know Luke's just concerned, but does he think I'm crazy? He mentioned taking my medication twice and scoffed at my theory as if it was the ramblings of a madman. Is that how he sees me?

I look back out of the window. I'm sure there's someone out there watching me.

'What do you think, Nanook? Am I mad?' I ask him. He's

followed me into the living room and jumped up onto the sofa. He doesn't give me an answer. I don't care even if he does think I'm cuckoo. I know he'll still love me, no matter what.

All my life, I've preferred to be in the background and not stand out. All I want is to keep my head down, write books, and have the world leave me alone. Is that too much to ask? However, three people are dead and it may be all my fault.

'Hello. Hi. Yes. Sorry. Is this … is this Detective Sergeant Marshall?' I ask. My voice sounds high-pitched and nervous, despite the few glasses of Bushmills whiskey I downed for courage to make the call. I don't usually drink this early in the day, but this is hardly a normal day.

I've rehearsed this conversation over and over. I've pictured DS Marshall laughing at me, taking me seriously, shouting at me for wasting police time, arguing with me, keeping me on hold: every scenario I can think of.

'Speaking.'

Suddenly, I can't remember what I'm supposed to say next. The last couple of hours have been for nothing. I take another sip of Bushmills.

'I'm not sure if you remember me. My name is Aidan Cullen. You came to my house after the body of Melanie Burton was found on Leigh Road.'

'The writer?' Marshall asks.

'That's right,' I say, smiling. 'The thing is … I really don't know how to say this, but I may have some information.'

'About Melanie Burton?'

'Well, yes, and also about … oh God, I've forgotten their

names. An elderly couple who were found dead in their home at Over Haddon. Are you working on that case as well?'

'I am. Mr Cullen, what is it you're trying to say?' She sounds in a hurry, as if she's got better things to do.

I take a deep breath. 'Their deaths. Melanie Burton's and the elderly couple. I've written about them in my books. Well, the murders I wrote are very similar to what's happened. I'm not sure if it's a coincidence or what, but I just thought you should know.'

'Sorry. You're saying that you wrote about their deaths before they happened?'

'Yes.'

'Are you trying to tell me you're psychic?'

'What? No. Of course I'm not.' *Jesus Christ, she's going to think I'm a loon. She's going to send the men in white coats round to lock me up.* 'All I'm saying is that … perhaps … well, maybe someone is copying the murders from my books.'

DS Marshall doesn't say anything. I know the line hasn't been disconnected because I can hear people talking in the background.

'DS Marshall, are you still there?'

'Yes. I was just making some notes. Thank you for letting me know.'

'Oh. OK. Well, I thought I should tell you so you could…'

'Yes. Thank you very much, Mr Cullen. We'll be in touch. Goodbye.'

I sit on the sofa, facing the television with my phone in my hand. I can see my silhouette reflected in the blank screen, staring back at me. My shoulders are slumped. I look dejected. I feel it. So DS Marshall doesn't take my comments seriously and probably thinks I'm crazy. I can almost picture her telling the rest of her colleagues. I'm surprised I can't hear their taunts and guffaws all the way out here.

I look at Nanook, sprawled out on the opposite sofa, watching me.

'At least I've actually said something about it and, if another murder does happen, I won't feel guilty. But we both know that's a big fat lie, don't we? If there's another murder and it's similar to one of my books, I'm going to feel terrible. But there's nothing I can do about it, is there? I can hardly go all Jessica Fletcher and investigate the murders myself.'

My books are sold all over the world and translated into more than a dozen different languages, but these murders have happened right here, in my own backyard. Who knows I live here in Derbyshire? Apart from my therapist and agent, my researcher and Luke, nobody knows I'm here. But that's not strictly true. Royal Mail delivers on a daily basis. How many Aidan Cullens are there in the world? Utility bills, internet subscription, mobile phone bill, television licence: they're all in my name. People in call centres will be able to see my name on the screen, remember it from a paperback they've read and suddenly have my address. Hundreds of people could know where I live.

But then, if someone is using my books to commit murders, why now? Why in Derbyshire?

I know the answer. Someone is taunting me.

I really am cut off here in Gallows View House. If someone is taunting me, then soon it won't be enough for them. They'll up their game and, if they approach, make contact, attack, not a single person will hear me scream. I look out of the window. There's someone out there. I know it.

Chapter Eleven

I had to look at the calendar this morning to work out what day it was. It doesn't feel like a Saturday. Weekends don't really mean much to me. When you're a recluse, every day is exactly the same. I work no matter what day of the week it is, even if it's just for a couple of hours. I even worked on Christmas Day last year; something Luke chastised me for.

I don't want to work today, though. I'm not in the mood. My mind keeps returning to that poor couple lying dead in their bed, undiscovered for four weeks. And poor Melanie Burton. They'd all still be alive if it wasn't for my books. I'm sure of it.

Nanook wants to go out. I unlock the conservatory doors and he bursts out into the garden. I put on a pair of battered Converses and follow him into the fresh air. It's very fresh this morning. The wind has picked up and the clouds have thickened and darkened since yesterday. I close my eyes and listen. Apart from birdsong, branches rubbing against each other in the wind and four paws pounding the lawn, there isn't a sound. Leaning with my back against the stone wall, I feel my whole body relax and my mind empty itself of its dark thoughts. I can feel a hint of a smile appear on my lips. Then I hear a thud at my feet.

I open my eyes and see that Nanook has found a tennis ball and dropped it next to me. I carefully bend down, pick up the drool-covered ball and throw it as far as I can down the garden. I watch as the white German Shepherd charges after it.

'Come on then, bring it back,' I say.

Nanook returns, drops the ball and waits, impatiently, for me to throw it again.

The more I throw the ball, the more I feel myself start to loosen up. I have exercises to do to ease the muscular tension in my back and legs, but most days I forget, or simply can't be bothered. Playing with Nanook helps to take my mind off the pain and is the best form of exercise for me. I lob the ball again; this time it goes further, and I follow.

As I approach the shed halfway down the garden, just before the neat lawn turns into an unkempt area with wild grass and trees, I notice one of its windows is broken: a hole, no bigger than a golf ball, right in the centre of the small glass pane. I look at the ground. There's no glass outside the shed, so nothing could have fallen inside against the window, which means something must have been thrown into it. But what? And how?

———

I return to the house and retrieve the key to the shed from a drawer in the kitchen. I go back down the garden, unlock the shed and wait for my eyes to adjust to the darkness before stepping inside. I rarely come in here. With my disability there's little I can do in the garden, so Luke takes care of mowing the lawn, trimming the bushes and trees and cleaning the patio. Cobwebs hang from the ceiling. I can feel them in my hair and on my face. Broken glass is on the floor beneath the broken pane. I tell Nanook to keep out. On the ground, next to the glass, is a small, jagged piece of stone. I bend and pick it up, look at it in the palm of my hand with a frown. Where has it come from?

My house is at the end of a small village. There are no other houses close by. I rarely see or hear children playing. I'm surrounded by farmland, an expanse of fields stretching as far as my telescope in the attic can see. The question remains, where has the stone come from? And why? A third question needs answering: how close was the person to the shed before the stone was thrown? The garden is surrounded by trees and tall bushes. Whoever threw it must have been in the garden. When? Why? And are they watching now? I knew there was someone outside the other day. I *knew* it.

Chapter Twelve

After a shower, I'm sitting on the bed wearing only my dressing gown when my mobile rings. Nanook is snoozing on my bed and doesn't move. It takes more than a ringing phone to disturb him.

I'm relieved to see Luke's face fill the screen.

'Aidan, is everything all right?' he asks as a greeting.

'Yes. Fine.'

'Did you call the police?'

'I did. Yes. You were right. She was polite, but she more or less dismissed what I said.'

'I thought as much, but, well, you've covered all the bases, haven't you? Like you said, if something else does happen, at least you've said something.'

'I suppose.'

'You sound a bit down.'

'I am.'

'Do you want to talk about it?'

I take a deep breath. 'There's a broken window in the shed. Someone threw a stone at it.'

'Who?'

'I don't know. The thing is, they had to have been pretty close to throw it, and you can only do that by being in the garden.'

'You think someone's been in the garden?'

'I don't … Yes.'

'When?'

'I don't know. Tell me I'm being paranoid, Luke.'

There's a long pause before he speaks. 'I'm not sure what to say.'

'I'm not sure what to think.' I half laugh. 'About the shed *or* the murders. I mean, anything can be a trigger to a killer. Maybe a murderer read my book and thought he'd like to kill someone in the same way. It sounds far-fetched, but it happens. Look how people are influenced by horror films and video games. But, if someone purposely came into my garden and broke a window in the shed, well, that sounds like a stalker to me.'

'Hmm,' Luke muses. 'I can't see how anyone could have thrown a stone at the shed without coming into the garden.'

'Neither can I.'

'But why risk coming into the garden just to break a window? I suppose it could have been a dare.'

'A dare?'

'Yes, you know how kids dare each other.'

'What kids? When was the last time you saw a child around here?'

'There's bound to be some in the village.'

'I assume there are, but it's a long way to walk from the village for a dare.'

'Unless they had bikes.'

'I'd have heard them, surely. Or Nanook would have done.'

'I suppose. Look, I doubt it will, but you'll let me know if something else happens, won't you?' Luke asks.

'Like what?'

'I don't know.'

'You think something else is going to happen?' I can hear the panic in my voice.

'No. I mean, not necessarily. It's just … if something does, you'll tell me, won't you?'

'Of course.'

'Don't let things bottle up.'

'I won't.'

'Good. I'm going to have to go. I'm rushed off my feet with these apartments. And I'll fill you in on the carpet drama later.'

'OK, thanks for phoning.'

I end the call and lean back on the bed. It's started to rain outside, and I can hear it lashing against the windows. I'm starting to feel better. I've always known I have an overactive imagination; I need one for my job. And really, the thought of someone using my books as manuals for committing their own murders is laughable. As for the stone through the shed window, well, I can't explain it at the moment, but I'm pretty sure there's a logical explanation for it happening. There's bound to be one.

I get dressed and limp downstairs. The fire is burning in the living room. It's cosy and warm. I pour myself a glass of Bushmills and sit on the sofa, patting the seat next to me for Nanook to jump up, not that he needs an invitation. I'm less than a page into a new book when my phone starts to ring. I hope it's Luke again. It would be nice to have a good long conversation, maybe even a few laughs.

'Hello,' I answer tentatively.

'Mr Cullen?'

It's not Luke. It's Detective Sergeant Katherine Marshall. My heart sinks.

'Yes.'

'It's DS Marshall from Derbyshire Police. Is there any chance I can pop over for a word?'

'A word? What about?' I ask, sitting up.

'It's about what you said when you called. I'd like to ask you a few questions.'

'Can't you ask me over the phone?'

'I'd rather do this face to face.'

'Oh. Erm, well, I suppose … sure.'

'Shall we say seven o'clock?'

'This evening?'

'Yes. Is that a good time for you?'

No time is a good time for me.

'That's … yes, that's fine.'

I don't hear DS Marshall say goodbye. Blood is thundering through my head like a tsunami. I feel hot and the room blurs around me. A detective is coming into my house to question me.

———

It's four hours between DS Marshall phoning and her arriving at the gate of Gallows View House. In that time, I've worked myself up into a bit of a state. What does she want? Has another murder been committed? Is it similar to one of my books? Has the killer been caught? Have the police received a message from the killer saying they're coming after me? Do they want to move me to a safe house?

As the minutes tick by, my thoughts become more outlandish. I can't settle, and Nanook notices something is wrong. I'm up and down, looking out of the window as the dark grey clouds grow thicker and the rain lashes down on the countryside, concealing any signs of a stalker in the bushes watching my house.

'Shut up, Aidan, for fuck's sake!' I shout. I actually scare myself by how forceful my voice sounds.

There are so many questions, voices, running around my mind.

When I mentioned it to my therapist once, I likened it to being at a rugby match, sitting in the centre of the crowd, surrounded by thousands of chanting fans and trying to make out each and every voice. It's an impossible task, but that's what it's like in my head twenty-four hours a day.

The buzz from the intercom makes me jump. DS Marshall is here.

Slowly, I go into the study and look at the computer screen. She's at the gate, soaking wet in the rain, her car parked behind her. She's on her own.

I unlock the gate. She pushes it open and swings it back behind her, running to the front door.

I open the door and recoil at the wind and rain that blows in. DS Marshall enters without being asked and I close the door behind her.

'Horrible weather,' she says. 'I usually have a decent coat in my car, but I must have left it at home.'

Her hair is plastered to her head, droplets run down her face and her thin navy jacket is saturated.

'There's a bathroom through there for you to dry off in,' I say, pointing to the door to the left of the kitchen. 'I'll make you a mug of tea to warm you up.'

'That would be lovely. Thank you.'

I watch as she enters the small bathroom, closes and locks the door behind her. Satisfied she's gone where she said she would, I go to the kitchen.

The kettle's almost boiled when I hear the toilet door unlock and Katherine Marshall comes through to join me. She carries the damp jacket over one arm. Her hair is drier and sticking up in various directions.

'Can I put this somewhere to dry?' She holds out the jacket.

'Put it over the back of a chair and place it in front of the Aga. It'll be dry in no time.'

'Thank you. Is there somewhere else I can freshen up? There's no mirror in that bathroom,' she says, flattening her hair.

I turn to look at her. My lips twitch as I try to form a smile, but it's awkward. 'I don't have a mirror.'

She frowns. 'You don't have a mirror? How's that possible?'

'There isn't one in the entire house.'

'Oh. How do you know your hair isn't sticking up all over the place when you go out?' she says, smiling.

My free hand instinctively goes to my hair. I know it's in perfect condition. It always is. 'I don't go out.'

'Oh yes.'

'Not for five years.'

'Why?'

'Shall we take the drinks through to the living room? The fire's on in there. Would you carry them through for me?' I ask, indicating my crutch.

'Sure.'

Nanook and I follow DS Marshall as I tell her where to find the living room. There are two floor lamps lit, but the dim bulbs are emanating very little light. We sit on opposite sofas, the dog curled up by my feet.

DS Marshall picks up her mug of tea, wraps her hands around it, and takes a long sip. Her face relaxes. A cup of tea in front of a real log fire is exactly what she seems to need right now.

'This is a lovely room. Very cosy,' she says.

'Thank you.' I feel uneasy with her here and want to cut to the chase. 'Why did you want to come and see me?' I ask.

'When you called and mentioned the two murders being similar to what you'd written in your books, I'm afraid I dismissed it as being … I don't know…' She struggles to find the right words.

'The overactive imagination of a writer?' I finish for her.

She smiles. 'Something like that.'

114

Her face softens when she smiles, and dimples appear on her cheeks. She's not the stern detective she was the last time she visited, with her neat hair and her pursed, thin lips. Her eyes are twinkling in the light from the fire. She seems to be glowing. She doesn't need to put on an act in front of her junior colleague. She can be who she wants to be when she's alone.

I return her smile. 'I understand.' I'm saying what she needs to hear to hurry this up.

'I kept thinking about what you said, though. You wouldn't believe some of the motives people give for killing someone,' she says, rolling her eyes. 'So I decided to look into it, and I downloaded your books.' She roots around in her handbag and pulls out a tablet and a notepad. 'I'm sorry, but I'm not much of a reader, and if I was, I wouldn't read crime fiction. I spend far too much time around criminals to have them in my relaxation time, too.' She smiles again.

'That's fair enough.'

'Anyway, the thing is, you're right. Melanie Burton's murder is exactly as you wrote it in … what was it called?' She flicks through her tablet.

'*The Loudest Scream.*'

'That's right. Obviously, we don't know how Melanie was intercepted, but the crime scene you wrote about could have been Melanie's. The similarity is uncanny.'

This is not what I want to hear, but, somehow, it's a relief to know it.

'What about the elderly couple?'

'Again, you were spot on.'

I squeeze my eyes tightly shut. 'The crime scene…'

'I'm afraid so. I've never seen anything so graphic. They were both stabbed multiple times and didn't put up any resistance. The heating was left on in the bedroom and how we found them was exactly how you'd written them.'

'Oh my God.' I look down.

'I went to my boss, DI Victor Finch. He's a good man. He listens to every idea and is very fair. He asked me to come to you.'

'Why? Do you think I'm right?'

'We're exploring many angles. At the moment, we have no suspects for Melanie's murder, or for Mr and Mrs Hargreaves. On the face of it, they're completely separate incidents, but both seemingly motiveless…' She trails off and takes a sip of her tea.

'Am I allowed to ask you something?' I ask hesitantly.

'Of course.'

'Was anything taken from Mr and Mrs Hargreaves' home?'

'No, and believe me, they had a lot that could have been taken.'

'In my book, Frank and Edie were a wealthy couple. There was expensive jewellery on display in the room they were killed in, and the house was full of antique ornaments and pictures.'

DS Marshall nods. 'Mr and Mrs Hargreaves lived in a beautiful cottage. They also had expensive things. Mrs Hargreaves was wearing pearl earrings when she died. There was a Cartier watch on her bedside table, and she had a few hundred pounds in her purse. None of it was taken. It was not a burglary gone wrong.'

'A random act of murder.'

'Seemingly so.'

'Does anyone stand to inherit?'

'They have a son. He lives in Dorset and he's a wealthy man in his own right.'

I chew the inside of my mouth while I think, my eyes darting rapidly left and right.

DS Marshall sits forward. 'Mr Cullen, I have to ask, do you have any enemies?'

'Enemies? How do you mean?'

'Is there anyone in your life who … I don't know, you've recently fallen out with or someone who would delight in seeing you go through such turmoil?'

'You think someone killed those people to make me feel bad about it?'

'It's another theory we have to look at.'

'No. No, of course there isn't anyone like that in my life. I know very few people, and all of them are decent, honest people,' I say. I can feel myself getting angry, and I don't know why. I only know Luke. To even think he might possibly be a suspect is laughable. Besides, he's a hundred and fifty miles away in Newcastle.

'I'm sorry. I didn't mean to upset you.'

I take another deep breath to calm down. 'No. I'm sorry. I didn't mean to snap like that. I have one good friend in my life. Luke. Well, we're more like family, really, brothers. He'd never do anything like that.'

DS Marshall adjusts herself on the sofa, clearly looking uncomfortable. 'Have you received any silent phone calls, disturbing letters or emails?'

'No,' I answer quickly.

'I looked on Amazon at your books and read a few of the reviews. The majority are excellent, you must be very pleased, but you have received the odd one-star review that isn't very complimentary. Do readers ever contact you personally?'

'Yes, they do. I have a website with a page where readers can contact me.'

'And do the messages come direct to you?'

'Yes.'

'Are any of them ever negative?'

'Some are.'

'Are any threatening or hurtful?'

'The odd one is hurtful, but I wouldn't say any of them are threatening.'

'Hurtful in what way?'

I blow out my cheeks. 'Well, just, you know. You can't please everyone. You're going to offend someone with what you write.

My third book, *My Wife*, is about a man obsessed with a married woman and he stalks her. He's a criminal lawyer and he stays within the confines of the law yet still makes her life uncomfortable. I received loads of emails saying how infuriating it was that he wasn't reprimanded for what he was doing. The thing was, I purposely wrote that book to highlight how someone with knowledge of the law can work around it to achieve their goals.'

'But you didn't feel as though the emails were threatening you in any way?'

'No. I don't even reply to messages like that. I read them and delete them.'

'Would you mind if I sent someone out to take a look at them at some point in the next few days?'

'You want someone to read my emails?' I ask. I can feel my chest tightening at the thought of a stranger going through my computer.

She clears her throat. 'I'm not being alarmist here, but we all interpret things in different ways. You may have received a threatening email that you may not have realised was a threat.'

I swallow hard. 'I hadn't thought of that. OK. I don't mind someone else reading them.' I do, but I can hardly refuse.

A huge gust of wind seems to shake the whole house and rain hits the windows hard, like a handful of grit has been thrown.

'Do you mind living out here with nobody close by?'

I give a weak smile. 'No. I prefer it.'

'Your friend – Luke, is it? He's working away, you said?'

'Yes. He came back the other day to collect some things, but he'll be in Newcastle for the foreseeable future.'

'I see. Well, I've taken up enough of your time. I should probably leave you to enjoy your evening in peace,' DS Marshall says, slapping her hands down on her knees and standing up. 'I may need to talk to you again.'

'I'm always here,' I say, proffering another forced smile.

DS Marshall heads for the kitchen to collect her jacket from in front of the Aga. It's completely dry now. She puts it on and zips it up.

'May I ask you a personal question?' DS Marshall asks.

Here we go.

'What happened to your leg?'

'It's not my leg. I was stabbed a few years ago in the lower back. It's nerve damage.'

'Oh. I'm sorry.' She looks away.

'That's OK. It was a long time ago.'

'Did the police get the person who did it?'

'No,' I reply quickly.

'Oh. I'm sure the force did everything they could,' she says, floundering.

'I couldn't give a very good description. I didn't actually see my attacker.'

Liar.

'Well, it's not stopped you from achieving your goals. Six books published, all to critical acclaim,' she says, beaming.

'I refuse to be a victim.'

LIAR.

'Good for you. Well, I'd better be off.'

'I'll show you out.'

When I open the front door, the wind is buffeting the trees and the rain is almost biblical. It's as if the end of the world is happening right on my doorstep.

'Take care driving,' I say.

'I will. Thanks for seeing me again, Mr Cullen.'

She smiles, lifts her jacket over her head and charges out into the storm.

I remain on the doorstep. I watch her open the gate and slam it closed. I wait until she's in the car and driven up the gravel driveway to the road before I step back into the house, close the solid door behind me and lock it with the bolts at the top and bottom.

All that stands between me and whoever is out there senselessly killing people is an oak door that can easily be broken down by someone determined enough.

Chapter Thirteen

I passed out from exhaustion rather than fell asleep last night. Actually, it was the early hours of this morning rather than last night. I had been sitting up in bed listening intently as the winter storm raged outside.

The wind was howling, the branches were creaking and snapping, the rain lashed hard on the windows. I don't mind admitting that I was genuinely frightened. I've never known a storm like it. If someone had driven a car through my conservatory or used a battering ram to break down my front door, I wouldn't have heard it.

Nanook was no use. He slept through it all. Occasionally he opened his eyes, looked up, sighed, changed position, and nodded back off again. I've never given reincarnation much thought, but if it does exist, I definitely want to come back as a German Shepherd.

I wake at seven o'clock, still sitting up in bed. I'm in an awkward position and I ache straight away. The storm has passed, and I stare at my closed bedroom door and wonder what horror awaits me on the other side.

Nanook wakes. He gives a loud yawn, stretches his legs and jumps off the bed. He looks from the door to me and back again, tail wagging. He needs a pee. I'm shattered. I've managed three hours' sleep, if that. I want to turn over, pull the duvet over my head and sleep until spring. Not possible with a dog. Not possible with a book to write. Not possible with a killer tormenting me.

I didn't take all my medication yesterday. I thought I had. I always tip the box up into my palm. But there's a single white pill in the box. I know I shouldn't, but I take it this morning along with the others.

I don't look out of the window on the landing. I head straight downstairs, through the kitchen and into the conservatory, where I disable the alarm, remove the Patlock and open the doors. Nanook charges out and I follow. There's still a stiff wind blowing, and it feels much colder, too. I pull my jacket tighter around me as I look up at the house and survey the damage. Surprisingly, there isn't any. The chimney stacks are still in place and the tree closest to my bedroom window is still standing, albeit minus a few small branches. On the lawn there is a huge branch which looks like it narrowly missed destroying my shed. Nanook seems to be enjoying jumping back and forth over it; just as well, as I'm going to have to wait for Luke to return to give me a hand moving it.

In the kitchen, I plug in the kettle and switch it on. Nothing happens. I try another socket. Still nothing. I look around. The clock is off on the microwave and the fridge isn't making its usual humming sound. The power is out. Obviously, there *was* some damage in the storm. Fortunately, I have an oil-based Aga, so I'll still be able to have my morning mug of coffee. Caffeine, to a writer, is a lifeline. It's what gets us started in the morning and keeps us going throughout the day. I'm pouring the coffee when the thought hits me – if the power is out, then so is my security system.

Chapter One

I limp as fast as I can into the hallway and press the LCD screen. That usually wakes it up. It remains blank. I tap it again, harder. Nothing. I head into my office and turn on my laptop. I immediately look at how much battery life is remaining – less than fifty per cent. I can't log on to the security site, as the internet is down. I bring up the camera and the images are black squares. This is bad. My home is exposed. I have no protection, and there's nothing I can do.

I go back into the kitchen. I'm scared. I'm genuinely frightened. I know any potential stalker couldn't have manufactured last night's storm, but they could use its aftermath to their advantage and make an attack.

I grab a carving knife from the block on the side. The sound of the stainless-steel swishing echoes around the room. I can see my reflection in the shiny blade. I can't use this to defend myself. It's ridiculous. I'm not Sidney Prescott and this is not a *Scream* movie. I look up and see Nanook running about, chasing fallen leaves. He's my protection.

I have no idea how long the power is going to be out, and I don't know how long fifty per cent of battery life on my laptop will last, so there's no point in working today. Instead, I retreat to my living room, coffee in hand, and treat myself to a rare day off with a good book. I pull the curtains open halfway and turn on the standard lamp to light the room. I never have the curtains fully open; you never know who might be looking in. I curl up on the sofa and begin an advanced reader's copy of the new novel by Elly Griffiths. If there's one thing to help me calm down and relax, it's escaping through fiction. It silences the panic, the anxiety, and dark thoughts. I know my problems will still be there when I'm finished, but I need the respite, or I'll go mad. Or should I say, even madder?

When I glance up, I see the clock on the wall. Three hours have passed. How has that happened? It only seems like two minutes since I started reading. I limp into the kitchen. I can't remember the last time I did my exercises and, after sitting up in bed all night, I'm feeling a great deal of pain.

The time on the microwave is flashing and the fridge is humming again. The power is back on. My home is protected once more. Thank goodness for that. And just in time for lunch.

While dipping bread into a bowl of vegetable soup, I send a text to DS Marshall to see if she managed to get home all right in the storm. I also send an email to my therapist asking for an impromptu session. Recent events are getting to me and I'm not sure what's real and what my paranoid mind is making up. I need a voice of reason to explain things to me.

Charlotte emails back almost straight away saying she can fit me in at three o'clock. I feel better just knowing I'll be able to voice my concerns aloud and not feel judged. I continue to eat my lunch. It goes down much easier now.

The problem is, when I have an appointment, I can't relax. I'm forever looking at the time, wondering how much longer I have to wait. Two hours, ninety minutes, seventy minutes, an hour. I annoy myself.

In the attic, I sit on the stool in front of the telescope and look out at the view beneath the bright blue sky. The wind has subsided; it's barely a breeze now, and the landscape is battered and bruised by the storm. Trees have been uprooted and fences blown down. In the distance, on one of the farms, a tractor is parked by a flattened barn. I hope no animals were injured. On Leigh Road, where Melanie Burton was killed, a blue car is tipped into a ditch.

'It looks like we got off lightly,' I say to Nanook, who is in his bed, chewing on a Kong. I climb down from the stool and sit on the floor beside him. Nanook rolls onto his back and assumes the position for a belly rub. Naturally, I comply.

'I'm glad you were with me last night,' I tell him. 'I know you slept through it all, but the fact you were there means more to me than I can ever say.'

There's a lump at the back of my throat, but it's not emotion, it's frustration. I feel like I'm screaming inside, as if I'm banging my fists on a locked door, shouting, pleading to be let out but nobody can hear me.

'I'm so tired. Why can't I be like Luke? Why am I a prisoner inside my own home, my own mind? Luke sees the world differently to how I see it. Everything is fun for him. Yes, he's got a lot of work on in Newcastle and he's busy, but he's having the time of his life. He has no worries, nobody to answer to, he can go out drinking every night and meet women. Me? I have trouble picking up the post from the doorstep. Luke looks at the world and sees all the potential for adventure. I look at the world and see a scary pit of hell. Because that's what it is. That's what it's always been for me. It doesn't matter where I go – Ireland, Liverpool, Derbyshire – the evil seems to follow me. Why is that?'

I look at Nanook. He looks at me. I nod. I know exactly why the evil follows me. Because it's inside me.

Chapter Fourteen

'**G**ood afternoon, Aidan,' Charlotte says with a smile.

'Good afternoon.'

'Something's troubling you.' It isn't a question.

'Yes. I think so.'

'Go on.'

'I don't know if I'm going mad or if it's real.'

'OK. Tell me what's worrying you and we'll go from there.' She pushes her dark red hair away from her face and looks down the lens at me with concern.

'I think someone's watching me,' I say without thinking. I just open my mouth and the words fall out.

'What evidence do you have?'

'Well, I'm not sure really. It's just … someone's been in my garden. A stone was thrown through my shed window and the only way they could have done that is by being *in* the garden.'

'You don't have neighbours, do you?'

'No. The closest house is a good mile away.'

'Do they have children?'

'I've no idea.'

'It could have been a childish prank, Aidan. I'm not sure how you've gone from a stone through a shed window to being watched,' she says with a frown.

'There have been a couple of murders around here, and they're very similar to what I've written about in my books. I told you about that jogger who was killed up the road? Melanie Burton?'

'Yes. I remember.'

'And an elderly couple were found dead in their bed. They'd been murdered and weren't found for a few weeks. I've written those exact scenarios. The detective even said Melanie's murder is almost exactly like the one I wrote.'

I look down and I'm picking at my fingers, scratching hard with the nail. I've drawn blood on my thumb.

'You've mentioned this to the detectives?'

'Yes. I felt I needed to.'

'And what did they say?'

'It's another angle to their investigations. I wasn't laughed at, so that's a bonus.' I give a smile, but it's awkward. I can feel the sweat prickling at my armpits.

'So why do you think someone is watching you?' she asks, adjusting her position on her chair, her frown growing deeper.

'If someone is out there copying my books, my murders, maybe they're doing it to taunt me.'

'Who would do that?'

'I don't know.' A vague answer, I know, but it's an honest one. I know very few people, and I've discounted all of them. Well, I've discounted Luke.

'Have you received any specific threats?'

'No.'

'Aidan, I think you're allowing your imagination to get the better of you. You need to think rationally and take a step back. There have been two murders *similar* to some that have appeared in your books. Yes, someone may be out there copying what you've written, but that has nothing to do with you. If they are, it's *their* psychological make-up that's making them do this, not yours. You cannot carry the burden of responsibility on your shoulders.'

'I can't just ignore it, though.'

'No, you can't. And you shouldn't. But you're not to blame. Your work is fictional. Do you think the creators of horror films blame themselves when a real-life killer uses their films as inspiration to commit a crime? No. The simple matter is many killers are unintelligent people. They don't have the mental capacity to come up with something original, so they have to look for a source. Is it possible a killer has chosen your books? Yes, it is. But that has nothing to do with you.'

'I don't like the fact people are dying and it's because of my work.' I can feel I'm on the verge of tears, and it hurts when I swallow my emotions.

'But you don't even know if the murders *are* linked to your work, and, even if they are, these people are dying because of a disturbed individual.'

I take a deep breath. 'Am I going mad?'

Her face softens. 'No. You're not. The problem is, your reality is contained within your four walls. Your only snapshot of what is happening in the outside world is through Luke and reading the news, occasionally, online. The mind needs stimulation, and because yours isn't getting it through natural interaction, it's having to create drama where there isn't any. Your brain needs to feel alive.'

I can feel myself frowning. 'I'm not to blame?' I ask, quietly.

'Of course you're not.'

I sigh. 'Why couldn't he have chosen someone else's books?'

Charlotte smiles and shrugs. 'I don't suppose you can look upon this as a form of flattery?' Her eyes twinkle. She's obviously joking.

'I'm afraid not. And what about this business with the stone?'

She blows out her cheeks. 'There'll be a very logical explanation. Maybe … I don't know … maybe when Nanook had a crap and scraped his paws on the garden like a lot of dogs do, he kicked up a stone and it flew through the window. Is that possible?'

I run the scenario through my mind, my eyes darting back and forth. I feel a smile growing on my lips. 'Yes. Yes, it is. That's exactly what could have happened.' I can feel myself physically soften – my shoulders unhunch, my heavy brow lifts.

'There you are then. You need to think rationally about things, Aidan. Look at things from alternative angles. The simplest explanation is nearly always the correct one.'

'Thank you,' I say, genuinely meaning it. 'My goodness, I was going mad this morning thinking there was a killer after me or I had some kind of stalker. You've set my mind at rest. Thank you so much.'

'It's my pleasure. Is there anything else you'd like to discuss?'

'No. I don't think so.'

'I'm always here for you, Aidan, whenever you need to talk.'

I sigh. 'I was doing so well.'

'You still are. This is a blip. That's all. It's a wrinkle, and we've ironed it out. It's nothing to be frightened about.'

'Thank you,' I manage to choke out.

'Two o'clock next Thursday?'

'Absolutely.'

Chapter Fifteen

It's a pleasant afternoon. The sun is shining on the back garden and the wind has dropped, adding a few degrees to the single-digit temperature. I've boarded up the small windowpane in the shed and, as Nanook has made himself comfortable in a sunspot on the patio with his Kong toy, I decide to join him. I pour a large glass of Bushmills, grab a paperback, wipe the cast-iron chair, and sit down.

I enjoy days like this. It's still the middle of winter, but the sky is a gorgeous blue and I'm wrapped up against the elements, enjoying the fresh air in the privacy of my garden with a good book. I can see my breath as I exhale, and I wouldn't be surprised if my lips have turned blue. If anyone saw me, they'd think I was completely cuckoo, but I really don't care. I like this garden, it's serene. I like this weather too. I love being cold.

Something wakes me. I didn't even notice I'd fallen asleep. I certainly didn't feel tired. I must have nodded off mid-sentence. The book is on the damp ground and there's a crick in my neck from my head being slumped forward. Something has shocked me awake. The atmosphere has changed. The garden is no longer serene. It's suspicious. I don't like the way the evergreens at the bottom of the garden are swaying. The wind isn't strong enough to cause such movement. I think someone's hiding behind them. I look down at Nanook, who is asleep at my feet. His nose twitches as a new smell catches his attention on the breeze. Dogs are more hyper-alert than we are. If there was someone behind the trees, he would have sensed it; he would have woken up and barked.

I look up. The sky has dulled and the clouds are thin. It's going to be a cold night. I shiver at the thought. It's time to go back inside. It's time to lock myself away in my prison again.

I stand in the kitchen and look around. Something is wrong, I know it, but I can't work out what. Nothing is out of place, but it feels as if someone has been in here and left their presence behind. I limp through the kitchen, out into the hallway, my slippered feet hardly making a sound against the hard floor. There's nobody in the hall, but I have the heavy feeling that I'm being watched again. Why is that? Why now?

I don't think my home helps me. The grey walls are heavy and lifeless. There's nothing uplifting and vibrant about my décor at all. It reflects my mood, but it shouldn't, because my mood is pitch dark. There is no colour in my life. I live in greyscale. Maybe I should redecorate. And by I, I mean Luke, of course. I'm sure he'd love to paint my living room a brilliant red and the bathroom a glorious yellow.

I go into the living room to look out of the window and immediately I see it. There it is: there's the presence. There's a man at the top of the telegraph pole just to the left of my house. A small van with the logo of a phone company makes him seem official, but I don't like it. He's too close to the house. And so high up, he'll be able to look through the windows from there. He'll be able to see into every room in the house.

I fish for the house keys in my pocket. My fingers are shaking. I pull open the front door and limp out into the cool evening air. I'm halfway up the drive before I realise I've left the house. I stop and look back. I've left the front door wide open. It seems so far away. I can't go back. My whole body is shaking but I have to go on. I have to confront this intruder.

'What are you doing?' I call out to the man as I approach the gate. I try to sound assertive, but my voice is wobbling. I must look like a nervous wreck to him.

The telegraph pole is across the road from the driveway entrance.

'Sorry?' the man shouts.

'What are you doing?' I repeat. I try to sound more forceful by lowering my tone, but I don't think it's worked.

'What does it look like I'm doing?' he asks. His voice is soft and there's no accent to it. He's not local.

'I've no idea. That's why I asked.'

'There was a storm last night, mate. Lines are down all over the county.'

'Really?'

'Yes.'

'Oh. Do you have permission to be up there?'

'Of course I do.'

I look up at him, study him. He looks to be in his twenties, with a fresh, smooth face and red cheeks bitten by the cold. He has wavy blond hair poking out of the bottom of his hard hat and a tattoo creeping up his neck from his uniformed polo shirt.

'You all right?' the man asks.

'What? Yes. I'm fine. Why is everyone always asking me that?' I snap. 'How long is it going to take?'

'Not long. I'm just checking the connectors are still working.'

'And are they?'

'They seem to be.'

'So you'll be coming down soon?'

'Yes.'

'Good,' I say to myself. I turn and head back for the house. I can feel the man's eyes burning into me. There's something wrong, but I can't quite put my finger on it.

Back in the house, Nanook is waiting for me in the hallway. I close and lock the front door and limp up the stairs to the attic. I try to go as quickly as I can, but it's not easy with a crutch and a shooting pain running down your right side. I feel sick and try to remember when I last swallowed a couple of ibuprofen. I'm surprised I don't rattle with the number of tablets I take.

I perch on the stool and try to get comfortable. That's a joke. I'm never comfortable. I can smell myself. Sweat. I need a shower.

I bring the telescope into focus and aim it at the young man at the top of the telegraph pole.

He doesn't seem to notice that he's being studied, and continues to work. I can't tell if he's talking to himself or someone else through a wireless device. His lips are moving slightly, but I'm not good at lip-reading so I've no idea what he's saying. Maybe he's simply singing to himself. I've no knowledge of telecommunications, but surely if the phone company was going to send someone out, they'd let the local residents know about it?

How would they let you know when the phone lines are down? Dick!

I sit back on my stool and chew my bottom lip.

'Am I reading too much into this?' I ask Nanook, who's in his bed. 'I mean, it's just a bloke who's come to do some repairs after the storm. That's a normal thing, right?'

It's cold in the attic and, despite wearing layers, I'm feeling the chill. I've no intention of moving until the engineer, if that's what he really is, has gone.

It's starting to get dark and the man has switched on a light on his hard hat. I look at my watch. He said he was almost finished when I asked him. That was more than an hour ago. How much longer is he planning on staying up that ladder?

Exactly thirty-three minutes later, the man slowly climbs down the telegraph pole, places the ladder on top of the van, removes his hard hat, and … wait, no, before he removes his hard hat and gets into the van, he looks back at my house. Why has he done that? He purposely turns, glares at the house for a few seconds, then turns back to get in the van, starts the engine and drives away.

'What was he looking at?' I ask, peering through the lens to see him drive up the winding lane through the barren trees.

I point the telescope back at the wooden pole. The man has added something. There's a grey plastic box attached to the top. It wasn't there before. He said he was checking connectors. He said they were fine. Why has he added something to the pole? He wasn't an electrical engineer at all. That box, whatever it is, is a tool to either spy on me or record me, to watch me, to monitor my movements. Maybe he's the man who is committing these killings and now he's spying on me. Is his plan to set me up for his murders? Bloody hell, have I just been speaking to a murderer?

Chapter Sixteen

'**Y**ou've reached Luke Jackson. I'm obviously busy. Wait for the beep, you know the rest.'

'Luke, it's me. Aidan. Erm, do you know anything about telegraph poles? Give me a ring when you're free, please.'

I feed Nanook a little later than usual and he wolfs down his meal with his usual relish, making me smile. I love seeing my dog enjoy his food. But I'm not in the mood for eating myself. It's been a bizarre day. The stranger on the telegraph pole, whoever he was, has increased my anxiety, and I really don't need to add any more fuel to that particular fire. My mind is conjuring all kinds of scenarios. That man was not a telephone engineer, I'm sure of it. He didn't look old enough. I'm convinced, now more than ever, that I'm being watched. The question is, why? What have I done to someone to make them target me in such a cruel way?

It's too early to go to bed but I'm exhausted and I need to rest. I need to shut off my whirling thoughts and quieten my mind.

'Come on, Nanook, let's go upstairs.'

He follows me out of the kitchen and, together, we walk slowly up the stairs, tiredness making our limbs heavy.

My bedroom door is ajar. Nanook goes in first, jumps on the bed and walks around in a circle a few times before he's comfortable and curls up. I stop in the doorway. The stairs seem to be getting harder for me to climb. I've been neglecting my exercises lately and I'm feeling stiff because of it. I've been thinking of buying a treadmill for a while now. I could put it in the dining room and go for walks on it. Half an hour twice a day should be enough to loosen my muscles.

I lean the crutch at the side of the bed and remove my oversized jacket. I go to hang it on the hook on the back of the door and physically recoil at what I see. I let out a loud yell and snap my eyes shut so I don't have to look at it.

It's a mirror. There's a mirror hanging on the back of my bedroom door.

Chapter Seventeen

I find the business card DS Katherine Marshall gave me and call her mobile number. It rings for a while before it goes to voicemail. I end the call and try again. I do this three more times before she eventually answers. When I tell her what's happened, she says she'll be right over.

When I first saw the mirror, I froze. I clamped my eyes shut and didn't dare open them for fear of seeing my reflection. I made my way out of the bedroom like a blind man, feeling my way onto the landing. Once there, I opened my eyes. Nanook was on the bed, looking up, wondering what was going on.

Carefully, I made my way back into the bedroom. I felt around the back of the door. As soon as my hand hit the cold, smooth glass I recoiled. It wasn't my imagination. It was real. There was a mirror on the back of my door where a mirror shouldn't have been, where a mirror has never been. Someone has been inside my house and put it there. It can only have been the fake telephone engineer.

I shout to Nanook to get off the bed and we go back downstairs.

While waiting for DS Marshall to arrive, I stoke up the fire in the living room.

It's half an hour before headlights break through the gap in the curtains. I peel them back and recognise the car, and the shadowy figure of DS Marshall standing at the gate. I go to the front door and open it.

'DS Marshall, is that you?' I shout out into the dark night.

The range from the light above the front door doesn't quite reach the gate, and she's standing in darkness.

'Yes, it is, Aidan. Can you open the gate?'

'Are you on your own?'

'Yes.'

'OK. Hold on.' I retreat back into the house and unlock the gate with the touchscreen display on the alarm system by the front door.

As soon as the gate starts to open, DS Marshall pushes it back and comes down the drive. Once in the house, I wait until the gate is shut, lock it, and close the door behind her.

'What's happened?' she asks.

She looks tired. Her hair is a wild mess, and she has dark circles beneath her eyes.

'I'm sorry. I didn't know who else to call.'

'That's quite all right. Let's go and sit down and you can tell me everything.'

I hobble into the living room and sit down next to Nanook, leaving the other sofa free for her, but she stands in front of the fire to warm herself up.

'I fell asleep outside this afternoon. When I woke up there was a man outside fixing the telegraph pole, or at least that's what he said. Anyway, I decided to get an early night. I went upstairs to bed and there was a … there is a mirror behind my door,' I say, stumbling over the words.

'OK. Is that so unusual?'

'I don't have mirrors in my house. I never have mirrors in my house.'

I'm sitting on the edge of the sofa, knees together, arms clamped firmly around myself, rocking back and forth. I look up at DS Marshall, her brow furrowed as she observes me.

'So who put it there?' she asks.

'I don't know.'

'Has anyone been in your house today?'

'No.'

'Are you sure?'

'Well, maybe it was the man from the telecommunications company. You see, he could have snuck in while I was asleep outside.'

'OK.' DS Marshall perches on the edge of the coffee table in front of me. She's sitting too close. I don't like it. 'Before we discuss that, tell me, what is it with you and mirrors?'

I look up at her with wet eyes. 'It's … you'll think it's irrational.'

'I won't think anything. I'm not a psychiatrist. I just want to know.'

I take a deep breath. 'I…' I can feel the urge to cry building up inside me. I try to swallow, but it hurts. 'I … I just really don't like looking at myself.'

'Is that all?' There's almost a laugh in her voice. 'I don't like looking at myself, either. I've never liked my nose.'

'I don't look at my appearance. I physically hate what I see when I look in the mirror.' As I speak, I can detect the hatred I have for myself in my voice.

She seems to be studying me. I can feel her eyes burning into me. 'Aidan, what do you actually see? From where I'm sitting, all I see is a normal bloke.'

'I know. Luke is always telling me that.'

'So, what's the problem?'

I don't answer. I can't answer.

She nods and moves over to the sofa. It's a while before she speaks, and her eyes never leave me. 'Well, I'm glad you've got someone you can talk to.' She sighs. 'So, whoever put the mirror in your bedroom is someone who knows about your aversion to mirrors?'

'Obviously.'

'Who knows?'

'Nobody. Just Luke. Well, my agent does, too. And I have a therapist I talk to. She knows.'

'Anyone else?'

I shake my head.

'May I go upstairs and have a look?'

'Of course.'

I point up the stairs where my bedroom is and follow her up slowly, gripping the banister firmly with one hand and pulling myself up. Nanook races past me.

'This is a lovely house,' she says when she reaches the landing, looking around.

'Thank you. I like it.'

'It's very … clean and spacious. No pictures on the walls though.'

'No. I don't like clutter. Everything needs to be put away.'

'Fair enough.' She raises her eyebrows and goes into my bedroom.

I sit on the chair on the landing by the window. I'm shattered. I could fall asleep right here. I also feel sick. When was the last time I ate something? I didn't have any tea and I think I skipped lunch, too. I don't think I've eaten since breakfast.

'Do you recognise this mirror?' DS Marshall asks from behind the door.

'To be honest, I didn't look at it. As soon as I saw it, I closed my eyes and ran straight out of the bedroom.'

'It's a decent size. A dark wooden frame. It looks quite old.'

'No. I don't know where it's come from. I didn't bring a mirror with me when I moved in, and I've been here five years.'

'Your friend Luke,' Katherine says, coming back onto the landing. 'Does he have a mirror in his room?'

'No.' I smile. 'He jokes that one day he's going to cut his throat while shaving.'

DS Marshall leans against the landing wall. 'What's the relationship between you two?'

'We're friends. We've been mates since university.'

She smiles. 'If you're a couple, you can tell me.'

I laugh. 'We're most certainly not a couple.'

'I see. And you two get on well, no cross words?'

'No.'

'So, he wouldn't have done this with the mirror?'

'No,' I reply firmly. 'Besides, Luke's in Newcastle.'

'Is there—'

'Wait!' I interrupt. 'What about the man?'

'What man?'

'Outside. On the telegraph pole. He said he was doing some repairs to the phone lines after the storm. I don't know how long he was there for, because I was in the back garden when he arrived. He could have come into the house.'

'Why?'

'To … I don't know. But he's put something on the telegraph pole.'

'What?'

'A box. It's a grey box. I asked him what he was doing, and he said he was checking it was working. I asked if it was, and he said everything looked all right. But he was up there for a lot longer than he should have been and he put a box there. If everything was fine, he wouldn't have needed to do that. I think…' I quickly stop talking.

'What do you think?'

'Nothing,' I say, looking down.

'Aidan, do you think he's put something on the telegraph pole to spy on you?' she asks, her voice quieter.

I look up at her and nod.

'Why? Who would want to spy on you?'

It's a while before I answer, and, when I do, my voice has lost any shred of confidence it may have had. 'The killer.'

'What killer?'

'The person who killed Melanie Burton and the Hargreaves couple.'

DS Marshall looks away. A silence falls and envelops us both. I keep my eyes on the detective, waiting, hoping for her to say something reassuring.

'It's not likely, is it?'

I don't reply.

'Is it, Aidan?'

'I don't know.' I chew the inside of my mouth. I can taste blood. 'But there's no denying the fact that someone broke into my home and put a mirror on the back of my bedroom door.'

'Is there any sign of a break-in?' she asks. She sounds flustered.

'No. And the alarm…'

'The alarm?'

'It's still activated. I checked.'

'So, if someone had broken in…'

'A silent alarm would have been triggered. A security company in Derby would know about it and I'd have an alert sent to my tablet.'

'And have you?'

'No.' I look down.

'So, nobody broke in.'

'That only means someone I know came into the house and put it there.'

'Or…'

'Or?' I look back at her, confused.

'Aidan, I've seen the medication on your bedside cabinet. You take quite a lot of tablets. Have you missed a dose or taken more than you should? Have you been drinking?'

'What? You think *I* did it?' I exclaim.

'I'm just exploring all angles. Is it possible you could have done it?'

'Where would I have got the mirror from? I haven't left this house since I moved in five years ago. I closed that door when the removal men left and haven't been out since. Check my Amazon history. There'll be no mirrors on there. Someone, somehow, broke into my home and put a mirror behind my bedroom door to taunt me.'

Katherine folds her arms. 'OK. What do you want me to do?'

'Investigate. Find out who did it. Fingerprint the house. No, fingerprint the mirror,' I say, quickly, the words tripping over each other. 'You can take the mirror and give it to forensics. You said it's a wooden frame. They can get prints from it or maybe skin samples or something.'

'Aidan, I can't do that. My boss would not sanction such a request based on the hys—' She stops herself.

'Hysterical musings of a delusional writer? Is that what you were going to say?'

'No. I really wasn't.'

I pause and look at her. I take a deep breath to calm myself. It doesn't work.

'Right. Well, thank you for coming over, but I'd like you to leave now, please.'

'Aidan, I really…'

'Please, just go. You've said there's nothing you can do, so there's no reason for you to stay.'

'OK. I'm sorry. I didn't…'

I turn away. I don't want to hear her apologies.

'If anything else happens. Or … give me a call.'

She heads for the stairs. I follow slowly behind. I'll need to unlock the gate for her. We're silent as we descend.

I open the front door. On the doorstep, she turns back to say something, but I've already started to close the door. I secure the top and bottom with the bolts, fasten the chain in the middle and lock the door with the Yale and cylinder locks. I grab the door jammer from the corner of the hallway and wedge it in place. On tiptoes, I look through the spyhole to watch DS Marshall walk to the gate, head down, hands in her pockets.

Chapter Eighteen

There is no possibility of going to sleep in my bed with a mirror in the room. It has to be got rid of. How and where I've no idea, but I do not want that thing in my house. I stand outside my bedroom, struggling to think of what to do next. I chew on my bottom lip until I can taste blood, mixed with a good measure of Bushmills.

I have to go back into that room. Simply closing it off and waiting for Luke to come home is not an option. It's my room. I have important things in there. My clothes are in there. My medication is in there. But the thought of turning around and seeing myself looking back in the mirror fills me with horror.

I lean my crutch against the wall and take off my hooded jacket. Holding it firmly in both hands, I limp towards the door. If I can somehow place the jacket over the mirror and cover up the glass, I'll be able to go into the room, lift the mirror from the hook and take it down. I can't smash it, obviously, as superstition dictates I'd receive seven years' bad luck, and I really don't need an invitation for any more bad luck to befall me. There is only one place I can put the mirror where I'll never set eyes on it again: the basement.

I manage to fit the jacket over the mirror. It falls to the floor twice and I struggle with my muscular pain to bend down and pick it up again. I'm in agony and I yell out a couple of times when the pain is too much. Nanook looks on, head tilting from side to side. Sweat is running down my face and my long-sleeved T-shirt is wet. It's exhausting and frustrating work, and tears are forming as I strain to do something that should be so simple.

'I can't do it,' I whimper, banging my head hard against the door.

I take several deep breaths, psych myself up for one final push. Feeling blind, I reach around the door and hook the shoulder of the jacket over the far corner of the mirror. I let go. The jacket doesn't fall to the floor. I smile.

'I've done it, Nanook. I've done it.'

I lean against the wall at the side of the bedroom door and slide down to the floor. The dog comes over, tail wagging, and sits beside me. I put my arms around him and give him a hug.

It's early morning. The sky is empty of clouds and the moon is full and bright, casting a spotlight on Gallows View House. The roads are empty and the wildlife silent. The wind is still. Not a sound can be heard. A fox strolls down the road outside the house, daring to come out under the cover of darkness. Ignorant of the security features, it crawls under the gate and onto the gravel driveway. Its small paws crunch on the tiny stones as it makes its way carefully around the side of the house towards the back garden in search of bins, in search of food. A loud crash from inside the house causes the fox to bolt back to where it came from.

At the top of the landing, I look down the stairs to where the mirror has landed. It slipped out of my sweaty hands, through the fabric of the jacket, and bounced down the carpeted stairs. It landed on the wooden floor of the hallway with a smash. As I gaze down, I see my broken image in the jagged glass looking back up at me.

With my jaw set tight, my teeth clenched together, my entire body shaking in horror, I allow the pent-up anger to rise inside me before I open my mouth and let out a violent scream. The scream is so loud that it makes Nanook run into the bedroom and hide.

In a normal neighbourhood, lights would have turned on and people would have come out of their homes in their dressing gowns wondering which house was the scene of a murder. But this is Gallowsfield. Nobody comes running when you scream here.

'Seven years' bad luck,' I utter to myself.

Shards of glass litter the stairs. I can see them twinkling in the moonlight coming through the gap in the landing window curtains. The large pieces will need to be carefully picked up, the small ones hoovered so they don't stick in Nanook's paws.

I can't draw my eyes away from the broken frame at the bottom and my jagged reflection looking back at me. I hate what I see – cold, unfriendly eyes, a crooked smile. The face of a person who has nothing to offer the world but pain. As I look harder, I don't recognise the face staring back. I'm a complete stranger to myself.

Who are you? What do you want?

I run down the stairs, grab the jacket and throw it over what's left of the mirror. I bend down and begin picking up the large pieces of broken glass, trying not to look at them. I collect a black refuse sack from the utility room and a dustpan and brush and carefully put the shards inside. When all I can see left on the carpet are tiny twinkling pinpricks, I go for the hoover and spend more than half an hour vacuuming every single stair until I am confident it's safe.

I place the wooden frame and my jacket, now covered in glass, into the black bag, tie it up and carry it into the utility room. There is a door at the end of the narrow room that opens to a stone staircase leading to the dungeon of the house, the basement.

As soon as I open the door, I can feel the cold from below climb up and wrap its icy fingers around me. Without a jacket, I shiver. The bare concrete floor and exposed breeze-block walls cause my footsteps to echo and I can taste the dust as I slowly descend. Despite the exposed light bulb shining brightly against the dull backdrop, there are still areas of the basement where the light doesn't reach, and long shadows are cast into the corners of the angular room where anyone or anything could be hiding.

There's an old table running along the back wall with several cardboard boxes beneath it. I seem to remember Luke storing some of his belongings down here, and there are even some of my own keepsakes, things I don't want to look at but am not ready to destroy. Items from my mum's house, and my grandmother's.

I place the black bag on the table and pull open the flaps of the first box I come to, disturbing the dust and sending it into the air. I cough. I look at the reams of paper, my first attempts at writing novels. I'd forgotten all about these. I'd asked Luke to put them down here not long after we'd moved in. I wanted my move to Derbyshire to be a fresh start, put the nightmare of the knife attack behind me and start anew. Yet I didn't want to get rid of them completely. I thought I might use them for future ideas; you never know.

I rummage through another box, pushing past folders and picking up old clothes that really should have been donated to charity years ago but are now only fit for the bin. I pull out a jacket by the shoulders and lift it up. I don't recognise it as one I've worn in the past. Maybe it belongs to Luke. I fold it up to place it back in the box when I feel something hard in the front pocket. I put my hand inside, wrap my fingers carefully around the strange object and pull it out.

Despite the light being dim in this part of the cellar, there's no mistaking what it is: a flick knife. I hold it in the palm of my hand and stare blankly at it. I've no idea what to make of it. Who does it belong to? How did it get here?

The small button on the black handle is rusty. I press it and the blade shoots out in a violent movement. I gasp. The way it slices through the air brings back a painful memory. I hold the blade up to the light. There's dried blood on the knife. It's my blood. It has to be. Because this is the knife that stabbed me all those years ago.

Chapter Nineteen

'I'm sorry I scared you,' I say as I enter the utility room from the basement, a manuscript clasped to my chest.

Nanook is sitting in the doorway to the kitchen, waiting patiently.

'I didn't mean to shout. I'd never do anything to upset you. I'm so sorry. Would you like a Bonio?'

Nanook's ears prick at the sound of the only word in that sentence he knows. I smile.

I watch while Nanook chews on the biscuit. When he's finished, he licks his lips, then licks my cheek as if thanking me for the snack.

'I don't know what I'd do if you weren't here, Nanook,' I say. I'm sitting on the tiled floor in the kitchen, warm from the heat of the Aga. 'I'm so scared right now. I don't know what's happening.'

There is no chance of me going to bed. Even if I did, I wouldn't sleep. My mind is far too active to rest. I stagger into the living room with heavy legs and pour a large measure of Bushmills. I take a long drink and feel the golden liquid warm me up. The fire has long since gone out and the room is cold and dark. I place more wood onto the grate and light it. It doesn't take long for the room to warm and Nanook lies down in front of the hearth. By the light of the flickering flames, I make myself comfortable on the sofa, glass in one hand and a manuscript on my lap.

ONLY THE GOOD

Chapter One

I didn't mean to kill him. I didn't wake up this morning with murder on my mind, and when I left the house this evening, I didn't fill my bag with knives and weapons of destruction. It was just a normal, ordinary day. I had my usual breakfast, I caught the same bus I always do, smiled at the same woman I've been smiling at for the past six months, and spent the next eight hours staring at a computer screen messing around with people's taxes.

At lunchtime, I sat with Stuart in the canteen and made an excuse to pop to the shop when he got out more baby photos. Then, at five o'clock, I turned off my computer and headed for home.

What happened between getting off the bus and walking to my house is a blur. I'm sure it will come back to me at some point but, right now, there's a massive black hole where my life used to be, replaced by this madness that seems to have come from nowhere.

I'm holding a knife in my hand. The blade is dripping with blood. I know I have blood on me as I can feel it, smell it, taste it. My hand is shaking. I've killed someone. I've destroyed someone's life and the lives of those he knows.

I look down at the victim. He's looking straight back at me with a cold, dead gaze. It takes me a while to get my emotions under control. Every time I try to open my mouth to speak, nothing comes out, until this time, it does. I say I'm sorry. I know it's too late for that, and the words are meaningless, but I am, I truly am. I continue saying sorry to my brother as the dancing blue lights of a police car pull up in front of me.

I smile to myself. I remember writing this now. I've always been fascinated by what goes on behind the scenes of a murder. Not the police investigation, that's quite dull, but the mindset of a killer. What really goes on in their heads before they plunge in the knife, fire the gun, or strangle the life out of someone. Part of me wishes I'd studied criminal psychology at university. That would have stood me in good stead to become a crime writer. It's not too late, of course. I could do an Open University degree.

I remember showing this manuscript to my agent, Lucy, not long after she signed off on my second book. I was on cloud nine with another rave email about how talented I was, so I thought she'd like to read my very first novel. I knew the writing could do with a little tightening up here and there, but the story was there to evolve into something great. I knew it was.

Her reply wasn't flattering. She found the murder scenes gratuitous and the relationship between the main character and his family very stilted. She suggested I put it back in the bottom drawer and stick to my publishing schedule.

I wasn't hurt, but I got a glimpse into what Lucy was like as a person, as an agent, when she sets her mind to something. It's good that she's ruthless in business, but I felt she didn't need to be quite so harsh. Lucy's been so good to me, but I'm pleased she rarely leaves the confines of the M25 and I'm a hundred and fifty miles away.

A whimper from a sleeping Nanook makes me look down. The flickering flames catch my eyes and I look deep into the fireplace. The orange flames reach up like arthritic fingers grabbing onto oxygen to keep them alive. I stare, unblinking, until my eyes sting.

A noise from outside startles me. There's someone there. I hear a car engine right outside. My breath catches in my throat as I rush over to the living room window and slowly peel back the curtain to glimpse outside into the darkness. I've been too relaxed. I haven't been looking out for dangers. Who is it? Who's coming to harass me now? A set of headlights blind me. I let out a long sigh and allow the tension to fall away from my shoulders. I recognise the van straight away. Luke is home.

Chapter Twenty

The house comes alive the moment Luke steps over the threshold. I think we're both shocked to see each other.

'What are you doing up at this time?' he asks.

'I couldn't sleep,' I lie. 'What are you doing back so soon?'

'There was a problem with the apartments. Health and safety BS. I won't bore you with it but the job has been put on hold for a few days, so I thought I'd come home.'

'You're here for a few days?' I ask. I can actually feel my face light up.

He nods and heads for the kitchen. 'Got any leftovers? I'm starving.'

I'm hungry myself. There aren't any leftovers as I haven't cooked in days. 'I think there's some bacon in the fridge. Fancy a bacon butty?'

'I'd love one.'

There's plenty of bacon for two large butties and some left over to cut up and put in Nanook's bowl for him to join us. We sit at the island and devour our early-morning breakfast as if it's the finest meal in the world. After not having eaten properly for days, to me, that's exactly what it feels like. We wash it down with a mug of tea each and Luke fills me in on the drama with the carpets and how he's hired two young lads in their twenties to start the decorating in the student apartment block when he gets the OK to make a start.

I finish my sandwich first. I can't eat it fast enough. I don't see the point in making a full meal when there's just me here. All those pots and pans and plates to clear up and ingredients to buy and chop. Why bother? Usually, I have a boiled egg or a couple of crumpets. If I want a decent meal, I'll throw a chicken breast and a few veggies into the steamer, but it's not often I do that. My signature dish seems to be a crisp sandwich these days.

I watch Luke as he finishes his breakfast. I enjoy his company more than he can ever know. We've got a connection that goes deeper than him simply coming back to the pub on the night I was stabbed. I can't explain it. He's…

'What?' he asks.

'Sorry?'

'You're staring at me.'

'Am I?'

'Yes.'

'Sorry. It's just strange you being home again.'

'There's no place like it, so they say.' He smiles. 'Hang on a minute, why were you asking about telegraph poles?'

'What?'

'You left me a voicemail about telegraph poles.'

'Right. Yes. It doesn't matter now.'

'You sure?'

'Yes. We had a storm and the power went out. I just wanted to clarify something. It's fine.' I wave it off. I'm still unsure about the man up the telegraph pole but I don't want to think about that now. Hopefully, DS Marshall will look into him and be able to set my mind at rest.

'OK,' he says, licking his fingers. 'Well, I think I'm going to catch a bit of sleep. What are your plans for the day?'

'I've got a book to write.'

Luke climbs down from his stool and gets on the floor with Nanook. They're rough-housing and it's fun to watch. Nanook is a large, heavy dog with so much energy, but I can't do that with him. My injury won't allow it.

'I'll take him into the woods later, if you like.'

'I think he'd love it.'

Luke gets up and heads for the hallway. Nanook follows, leaving me on my own.

'Luke,' I call out. 'Have you got a mirror in your room?'

'A mirror?' He turns back with a frown. 'No.'

'Are you sure? If you've got one hidden away, you can say. I don't mind.'

'No. I know what you're like with mirrors. I wouldn't do that to you.'

'OK. Good.'

'Are you sure everything's all right?' His frown deepens. It makes him look childlike, vulnerable.

I smile. 'Everything's fine.'

LIAR. LIAR. BLOODY LIAR.

Chapter Twenty-One

It's strange hearing footsteps in the house while I'm at my desk. I can hear Luke above me, pacing around, singing to himself, chatting to Nanook. It makes me smile. It's almost as if normality has been restored and life is continuing as it should. I've put Melanie Burton and the Hargreaves couple to the back of my mind. Yes, what happened to them is tragic, and I hope their killers are swiftly caught, but Charlotte's right: it had nothing to do with me.

But then, there's the knife I found in the basement. I can't ignore that. In the aftermath of my attack, I was rushed to hospital and placed into an induced coma while the internal bleeding was dealt with. I hadn't given the knife any thought. I assumed the young lad who stabbed me had pulled it out and taken it with him when he fled. Obviously not. But then, if he'd left it in me, the doctors at the hospital would have safely removed it and given it to the police as evidence. It should be locked up in their storage area for when a cold case is reviewed at a later date. That's what I am, I'm a cold case. Shelved. Unsolved. Once a case is solved, all evidence is destroyed. So how did the flick knife that stabbed me end up in my basement?

'Aidan.'

I jump at my name being called. I turn around in my chair and see Luke in the doorway. He looks much fresher after a shower, shave, and a nap.

'I'm taking Nanook for a walk in the woods. Are you sure you don't want to come with us?'

'No, thanks.'

'See you later.'

I listen to them both leave. They'll have fun together. Much more fun without me tagging along.

It's been a couple of days since I've checked the emails from my author website. DS Marshall said she was going to send someone around to read them all. Although I'm not comfortable with a stranger reading them, I know they'll be trained to decipher any hidden meanings. I take them at face value. It might give me some answers.

Dear Mr Cullen,

Our book club recently read My Wife and unanimously loved it. Would you be interested in attending a virtual meeting and taking part in a Q&A session? They're held on the first Thursday of every month at 7 p.m.

Yours,
Talia McDonald
Chair of the Dulwich Women's Book Club

That's a simple message to reply to, but I'll stretch out the word 'no' to make it sound less abrupt.

Chapter One

Dear Aidan,

I recently discovered your books and while I thoroughly enjoyed Out of Darkness and The Loudest Scream, I thought The Science of Silence was a gross attack on the Church of England. I'm aware that it was a work of fiction, but there are some people who will read it and believe priests are capable of committing such despicable crimes. It's hard enough in this day and age to get people to trust in the Church, but when there is fiction like this out in the world, it is damaging and irresponsible.

Obviously, I would never call for a boycott on such a book. However, I think you have a duty as a man of influence to inform your readers that this is purely an exaggerated world you have created in these pages.

Regards,
Rev Stephen Morgan

I'm not sure how to respond to that. The fact that my books are found in the fiction section of bookshops should be sufficient. And since when was I a man of influence? I write books for entertainment, I'm not a cabinet minister. Delete.

My mobile bursts into life, making me jump. I look at the screen to see DS Marshall calling. I hesitate, wondering whether I should answer, given how things were left between us. Part of me feels embarrassed. Part of me feels outraged. However, if there is someone stalking me, I'm going to need her on side. I swipe to answer.

'Good morning, Aidan. I thought I'd ring to see how you are.'

She sounds bright and cheerful. I can't decide if it's forced or not.

'I'm fine. Thank you. I'm...' I stutter. 'I'm sorry about ... I'm sorry. I shouldn't have reacted the way I did. I was shocked by the mirror, and I took it out on you. It was wrong of me.'

'It's perfectly understandable.' She pauses to clear her throat.

'I thought you'd like to know I've been on to BT, and they said the engineer was booked to work on the telegraph pole outside your house and the grey box that was fitted is a new housing to protect wires from the elements. There is further work to do in the coming days.'

'Oh, that's good to know.' Hearing this news, I let the anxiety seep out of me. I can literally feel my entire body relax. 'Thanks for looking into it.'

'You're welcome. Is the mirror still there?' she asks.

'No. I managed to take it down. It's in the basement.'

In a million billion pieces.

'Good. Are you all right?' She seems sincere, here, and it makes me smile.

'I'm fine. Luke's home for an impromptu visit, which is nice, so I'm fine. I'm really … fine.'

'That's good. Would it be possible for me to have a word with Luke?'

'Why?' My smile has dropped.

'Just … I'd just like to ask him a few questions, that's all.'

'But Luke's been working away. He doesn't really know what's been going on … and he's not actually here at the moment. He's out with Nanook.'

'Oh. Could you have him call me when he comes back?'

I can feel my frown deepen. My hand goes to my hair. 'Why do you want to speak to Luke?'

'I'm conducting a murder investigation. I need to speak to everyone in the vicinity of the incident.'

'But Luke wasn't at home when Melanie Burton was killed. He was working in Newcastle. I told you that.'

'I know.'

I wait, wondering if she's going to continue. She doesn't.

'So you still want to talk to him?'

'Yes.'

'OK. When he gets back, I'll get him to give you a call.'

'Thank you, Aidan. Listen, if anything else happens, please, feel free to call me any time.'

'I will,' I reply hesitantly.

I don't know if DS Marshall said goodbye or not. I suddenly realise I'm listening to silence so the call must have ended. Why would the police, busy and understaffed as they constantly claim to be, want to speak to someone about a murder when they were more than a hundred and fifty miles away at the time?

She doesn't want to talk about Melanie, she wants to talk about me.

I squeeze my eyes closed. Sometimes, to completely close yourself off from the world, you have to shut down your senses. I can't see anything. I'm in the middle of nowhere, there's no sound from a television or radio, so I can't hear anything. I'm in my study with the door closed, no food, no coffee, no smells. My mouth is clamped shut, so I can't taste anything, and my hands are balled into tight fists so I can't feel anything. I'm completely devoid of emotion and feeling. I feel at ease with myself. Finally.

Chapter Twenty-Two

Luke was out for more than two hours with Nanook. I didn't write a single word in all that time. I've no idea what I've been doing. I hear them come back and go down to greet them.

While Luke's cleaning up Nanook, I grill a couple of pork sausages and make us both a sandwich for lunch. I don't want to tell him to call DS Marshall. I'm worried about what she's going to say to him. I don't want him knowing about how I reacted to the mirror. He'll think I'm crazy, or crazier than he already does.

'You're quiet,' he says.

'Am I?'

'Yes. Something on your mind?'

'No. Just … no.'

'You sure?' He's frowning at me. 'You know, you seem to be a bit different lately.'

'What's that supposed to mean?'

I stare at him and his eyes drop down to his sandwich. I decide to come clean.

'Listen, you know the detective I was telling you about, DS Marshall? She called while you were out and she said she'd like to speak to you.' I say it quickly so it's done.

'Me? Why?'

'I don't know. You live here so she probably wants to see if you knew any of the murder victims.'

'But I was in Newcastle.'

'That's what I said.'

'Fine. I've nothing to hide. Have you got her number?'

I hand him my phone. 'It's in there.'

He finishes his mug of tea and heads out of the room with the phone to his ear. 'What's she called again?' he asks, looking back over his shoulder.

'DS Marshall.'

He goes into the living room and closes the door behind him. I'm not sure why he does that. It's not long before I can hear a muffled conversation but not the actual words.

I really don't want to eavesdrop, that's not me at all, but I'd like to know the content of the conversation for myself, rather than titbits Luke tells me when he's finished.

I go out into the hallway and head for my living room, exaggerating my limp so it will make me walk slower and I can pick up more of the chat. Luke isn't the quietest person in the world and his thick Liverpudlian accent can often be heard from one end of the house to the other. Obviously, I won't be able to know what DS Marshall is saying, but hopefully I'll be able to piece the conversation together from Luke's side.

'… he's told me bits about what's been happening and how he thinks they're similar to what he's written but … no, not in the slightest … I do worry about him. I've tried to get him to leave the house for years, but he won't. It causes him great anxiety when he even thinks about it, so I think it's better all round if he stays indoors. He's able to function, do his work, pay his taxes, and he's not a drain on society, so let him be a recluse if he's happy, that's what I say.'

I'm outside the living room door. It's a double door with glass panels. I don't want to get too close in case Luke sees me. I smile when I overhear what he's saying. He's sticking up for me.

'What mirror?' Luke asks.

Shit.

'Someone came into the house? Who? … He was asking me if I had a mirror, but he hasn't told me any of this.'

Shit. Shit. Shit.

'Well, what do *you* think? Should Aidan be worried? … I see … Look, I'm working away in Newcastle at the moment. I'm very busy and I'm going to be away for quite some time. What are you telling me? … Oh … No, I understand … So what should we do? … Look, can I be honest with you?'

Luke lowers his voice and I struggle to listen. I edge closer to the living room door. I pick up the odd word – 'scared', 'worried', 'panic' – but I can't string together a coherent sentence.

Then Luke raises his voice. 'If there is a serial killer out there, and he's copying Aidan's work, then he's obviously got some kind of fixation on Aidan and it's the duty of the bizzies to protect him.'

My mouth falls open in shock. It's one thing to think these things myself, but to hear a police officer confirm them makes them very real. Suddenly, I'm scared. I was right. I *am* right. There is a killer out there committing crimes based on what I've written.

I look down at Nanook, who has made himself comfortable in the hallway. He's shattered after his run out in the woods. Would he be able to protect me if someone broke in? Would Nanook be hurt in an attack? I couldn't cope with losing him.

'Shit,' I say to myself, emotion rising up in my throat.

I walk as quickly as I can through the kitchen, throwing open the conservatory doors and stepping out into the cold winter air. I take a huge lungful to try and steady my nerves.

Why is this happening to me? All I want is to live a quiet life with no intrusion. I've chosen a house in the middle of nowhere with no neighbours. Nobody knows where I am. I do nothing to invite attention, yet one person out there is trying to destroy me. Who? Why?

'Well, she seemed nice.'

I jump. I didn't realise Luke was behind me. He hands back my phone and I put it in my pocket.

'What did she want?' I ask, not making eye contact so Luke can't see my red eyes filled with tears.

'She asked me where I was at the time of the murders and where you were. And she asked me how concerned you were about them. Why didn't you tell me someone had broken in and put a mirror in your bedroom?'

I sit on the wooden bench by the conservatory. 'I didn't want to worry you.'

'How did they get in?'

'I don't know. I thought…'

'What?'

'I thought at first the bloke who came to repair the phone lines might have somehow got in, but … I don't know.'

Luke sits down next to me and sighs. 'I can't turn this work down.'

'I know you can't, and I wouldn't ask you to.'

'Look, why don't you come up to Newcastle with me? The apartments are huge, big enough for the two of us, and Nanook. There are some great beaches along the coastline. It could be just what you need right now.'

I close my eyes. I try to imagine what it would be like to walk on a beach again. Barefoot. Sand between my toes. The sea breeze on my face. The ocean lapping at my feet. My dog running freely beside me. It sounds like bliss. It's an impossible dream. I shake my head.

'You can't stay here on your own, and I've got to head back tomorrow,' Luke says.

'I can. Look, I've got Nanook. I've got excellent security. I'll buy more locks.'

'I'll try and come back at the weekend.'

'No,' I say, and stand up. 'Luke, you need to go. I'm ruining my own life by not leaving the house. I won't drag you down, too.'

'That's not how I see it.'

'I know it isn't, but it's how I see it. Have fun. Do all the things I can't do, then tell me all about them when you get back.' I smile, but it doesn't reach my eyes. I must be the only person in the world whose smile makes him look sadder.

Chapter Twenty-Three

I'm engrossed in my work. The coffee beside me has gone cold and my biscuits are untouched. I woke up this morning feeling empty. I'm still coming down from Luke's visit. He has such a bright presence that, when he's gone, it's like I'm grieving. He was here for three days and two nights, but it feels like so much longer. On the last night, he cooked his signature dish – well, his only dish really – a screaming hot chilli. We sat in front of the TV in the living room and watched the original *Star Wars* trilogy, had a few drinks and chatted and laughed. It was a good night. The first night I've relaxed and enjoyed myself in a long time.

The next morning, he was gone before it was even light. Nanook and I waved him off from the front doorstep and watched until the lights of his van, high up in the valley, disappeared.

I appreciate everything Luke does for me. Since he left, I've been at my desk every waking moment. I need to fill the time with something until I get used to being alone again. Work is progressing well, and I'm pleased with the words I've written. This is shaping up to be a darker thriller than I expected.

The buzz from the intercom brings me out of my imagination

with a start. I was deep in the writing zone, and that harsh noise has pulled me out of it. I open up the camera feed and see DS Katherine Marshall standing at the gate, arms folded, hair being blown in all directions. Her face is blank. I can't read it, but I doubt she's here to bring good news. I turn on the microphone.

'Yes?'

'Mr Cullen, it's DS Marshall. Can I come in for a word, please?'

'Are you on your own?'

'Yes.'

'Is this official business?' I ask.

She pauses. I can see she's struggling to find the right words. 'It's … I … I want to run something by you.'

I don't like the sound of that.

I release the lock and watch as she pushes the gate open and walks with long, determined strides down the gravel driveway.

'We've got a visitor, Nanook.'

DS Marshall wipes her feet on the door mat. She's about to take off her jacket but feels the coolness of the house on her bare arms so keeps it on. I want to apologise for the house being cold, but I stop myself. I like it cold. I only light the fire in the evenings. We go into the kitchen, and I set about making her a coffee.

'I'm trying to cut down on my coffee intake,' I say. 'But it's not possible, I'm afraid. I'm a writer, I live on the stuff.' I give a weak smile. 'I did think about having decaffeinated coffee, but it's like having sugar-free sugar. What's the point? I also tried just sticking to tea. I mean, I know there's caffeine in that, even if not as much as coffee, I'm guessing, but I missed it too much. There's something about drinking coffee that helps me concentrate on my writing.'

'Mr Cullen…' DS Marshall's face is grim as she interrupts my ramblings. By the look on her face, I can tell what's coming.

'You've come to tell me there's been another murder, haven't you?' I ask and turn my back to her to focus on making the coffee.

'I'm afraid so.'

I bow my head. The kettle boils and I begin pouring the hot water into the mugs. 'I'm guessing it's similar to one of my books, or you wouldn't be here.'

'It is.'

I sigh. 'Which one?'

'*The Science of Silence*.'

I turn to her. 'Chapter One?'

She nods.

THE SCIENCE OF SILENCE

It's always the quiet ones

AIDAN CULLEN

Chapter One

It was an unusual summer. It rained for most of June and several festivals were washed out. After the damp problem had been sorted, I finally got around to decorating the back bedroom. I went on holiday in the first week of July to Cornwall and got terrible sunstroke. I read Hilary Mantel's excellent *Wolf Hall* trilogy and thoroughly enjoyed every one. Oh, and I committed my first murder.

To look at me you wouldn't think I was capable of killing someone. I'm often described as mild-mannered, quiet, but, as the saying goes, 'it's always the quiet ones'. It's people like me who pass under the radar undetected and are therefore able to get away with all manner of things, including murder.

I didn't set out, originally, to be a killer. I don't think I have any overly psychopathic tendencies. I didn't wet the bed as a child. I didn't torture animals or pull the wings off flies, and I've never had an interest in setting fires and watching things burn for pleasure. However, there was something about listening to Craig Torday that made me realise what a complete and utter fool he'd been, and how killing someone could be a work of art, if done correctly.

You'll know Craig Torday, naturally, so I won't go into all the gory details of how he ended up in Wakefield Prison by the age of twenty-nine and how the only way he'll leave that place is in a pine box. Stupid man. Low intelligence and little imagination. I knew from the first moment I set eyes on him that I wouldn't enjoy talking to him. It was hardly a meeting of equals. However, I was able to learn something from our times together, and that was how not to get caught.

I remember lying awake in bed at night after that first

chat with Craig. Something was running around my mind and I couldn't figure out what it was that was stopping me from falling asleep. I had a busy day the next day and needed to remain focused, but sleep eluded me, and it was just as the church clock in the village struck three that I realised what it was – Craig Torday could very easily have avoided capture if only he had a few extra brain cells.

I got up, went downstairs to the kitchen, made myself a mug of tea and sat at the table going through Craig's crimes. With the help of Wikipedia and several newspaper websites, I put together a timeline of his killings and everything he had done wrong. Trust me, it was a very long list. I then went about writing how he could have avoided even appearing on the police's radar, if he'd taken a different route home, for example, or perhaps chosen a different victim, or hadn't stopped off at that McDonald's drive-through. Like I said, he had little intelligence. It was so easy to turn his crimes into a baffling case that would have tortured the minds of investigators for decades to come.

Looking down at my A4 lined notepad in a dimly lit room, I saw that I had the ingredients for the perfect murder. And I, having a good reputation as a trusted member of society, could be the perfect murderer. As I sat back in my chair, I contemplated if I had it in me to kill, to take another life. Then, the perfect victim popped into my mind.

I've known Valerie St George for more than thirty years. She's in her late eighties and is housebound. Not much of a victim, I grant you, but I'm new at this killing malarkey and I want to start at the shallow end, so to speak.

Chapter One

Valerie has lived a good life. She taught in the local infant school for fifty years and was married to Raymond for over sixty years. I was actually at their sixtieth wedding anniversary celebrations before he died of a brain tumour three years later. They had four sons, all of whom have gone on to great things and are a credit to their parents. Two are now living abroad, one is in London and one is a member of the Welsh Assembly. For the past three years, Valerie's health has deteriorated and she doesn't leave the house at all now. She relies on the kindness of neighbours to fetch any shopping she may need, and I visit often to keep her updated on what is happening in the outside world. Despite her health issues, her mind is as sharp as a tack, and she enjoys our chats over a pot of tea and a Mr Kipling treat. I enjoy them, too. I'll miss them.

———

I gain entry to Valerie's house using the key inside the safe at the side of the house. Access to the safe is gained by using a four-digit PIN. The only people who know it are me, her sons, Daisy Appleyard, who runs the village store, and Clive Fairbank, the milkman. We'll all be questioned by the police. Clive has a criminal record, nothing major, something that happened almost twenty years ago, but he'll be looked at more closely, and Daisy has two children who have been caught shoplifting and joyriding, so suspicion may fall onto them for a while. It might do them good to be hauled in by police for questioning. Her eldest is on a slippery slope. All of us, however, will soon be eliminated from the enquiries. Why would we possibly want to harm dear, sweet Valerie St George?

'Valerie, it's only me,' I say, as usual, as I enter her

cottage. She worries about being burgled, so I always identify myself so she doesn't panic.

Her living room is small and cluttered with a lifetime of memories. It's also stiflingly hot. She's sitting by the fire with a blanket over her lap and it's twenty-three degrees outside. I'm surprised she hasn't already died from heat exhaustion. I can feel the sweat prickling at my armpits already. That might be nerves, I'm not sure.

'How are you feeling today?'

'My feet are in bloody agony, if you'll pardon my language.'

'You swear as much as you want, you've every right to.' I smile. She does look to be in great pain. I wonder if I could give her an overdose using all the paracetamol, ibuprofen and codeine she has in the house. 'Shall I pop the kettle on?'

'Lovely,' she says with a smile.

'Have you taken anything this morning? Do you want me to get you some medication?'

'I've taken the lot,' she shouts after me while I'm in the kitchen setting up a tray. 'I'm surprised I don't rattle with all the tablets I'm taking. Pills for pain. Pills for my stomach. Pills for my blood. Then there's that new white one I'm on. Have you seen the size of it? I never know which end to put it in. Oh, there's a piece of cod in the fridge; will you throw it out for me? I should have had it for my tea last night, but I couldn't face it.'

She continues to ramble on while I'm waiting for the kettle to boil. She mentions her son, Thomas, who called her yesterday afternoon to tell her he's going to take early retirement at the end of the year and is planning to move to Florida.

'Early retirement,' she tuts and rolls her eyes as I enter

the sitting room. 'I worked for twenty years after my retirement age.'

'I know you did. Nothing could stop you.' I'm looking past her, out of the window to see if there's anyone passing in the street. There isn't.

'I'm not one for sitting. That's what did it for my Margaret. You remember Margaret, don't you? She retired at sixty-five and was dead before her seventieth. All through inactivity.'

I've no idea who Margaret was but I don't tell her that.

'Could you pull that curtain to a bit? The sun glares something terrible on the TV. It's hardly worth having it on.'

Perfect. She's practically giving me camouflage to kill her undetected.

I tread carefully through the many armchairs and coffee tables she's got cluttering up the floor space and pull the right-hand curtain to.

'That's wonderful,' she says, eyes fixed on the blank screen. 'There's a tennis tournament in Miami later that I want to watch and snooker from somewhere in China after that. That'll take me up until bedtime.'

I scarcely hear a word she's saying. All I've had going through my mind since the early hours of this morning is murder, and now, here I am. I'm about to do it and she doesn't have a clue at all. She's still talking when I wrap my arms around her. One hand on her shoulder, one on her head. She doesn't have time to react. I pull down hard in opposite directions. A quick snap and she's gone.

I stay behind her in the armchair and look down at her from above. Is she dead? Is she really actually dead? Have I just killed someone? Is that all it took? I don't feel any different. Should I?

'Valerie?' I ask quietly. She doesn't react.

I move around to the front of the armchair, squat to my knees and look at her. She was beautiful in her youth, I've seen the photos, but age has been terribly cruel to her. Her skin is like parchment paper and severe blue veins run across the surface. Her eyes are sunken and rheumy and her hair thin and wispy. She's better off dead.

I need to act quickly. Obviously, if she's found in her armchair with a broken neck, all the signs will point to murder, and that cannot happen. I pick her up – she's incredibly light – and carry her up the stairs. Once at the top, I simply drop her and watch as she bounces off each step before landing with a light thud at the bottom.

Everyone in the village knows how unsteady she is on her feet, and, despite one of her sons having a stairlift installed, she still struggles to walk from the living room to the stairlift and from the stairlift to her bedroom. It wouldn't take much for her to lose her balance and plunge down the stairs to her death, which is what must have happened in this case. Such a tragedy.

There is an absurd hilariousness to this incident. In order for it to look like an accident, I need to put the chair lift to the top of the stairs. To do that, I have to sit in it and press down a button on the arm rest. There I am, travelling at a snail's pace up the stairs as if I've got all the time in the world while, at the bottom, Valerie St George is rapidly going cold. It would be funny if it wasn't so serious.

Back downstairs, I rearrange the lounge to make it look like she was simply sitting watching TV when she decided to pop upstairs for some reason before falling, and then I call the police.

'Emergency, which service do you require?' asks the voice at the end of the line.

'Ambulance, please.' I know it's too late for an ambulance, but as my medical training only goes so far as loosening someone's collar or putting them in the recovery position, I need a paramedic to formally pronounce death. And I need to look hopeful. 'I'm at the house of an elderly neighbour, well, a friend really, and I've found her at the bottom of the stairs. I think she might have fallen. I'm not sure if she's dead or not.'

'OK. I'll arrange for an ambulance, but I can talk you through a few steps to clear her airways and check her breathing. What's your name, sir?'

'Stephen Bryce. Reverend Stephen Bryce.'

Chapter Twenty-Four

DS Marshall and I are sitting in the conservatory with the door wide open so Nanook can come in when he's finished chasing birds. Our mugs of coffee are on the table and are rapidly going cold. There's a stiff icy breeze blowing in. DS Marshall, still with her coat on, holds herself rigid, but I embrace the cold.

'Are you allowed to tell me anything about the victim?'

'Is there any chance we can close the door? I'm freezing.'

'Oh. Sure.' I limp to the door, call for Nanook to come in, which he does, then close it, securing it with the Patlock covering the handles.

'You secure the house every time you lock the door?' she asks.

'Yes.'

'Even though you might be opening it again if your dog wants to go back out in an hour or so?'

'Yes.'

'Why are you so paranoid about someone wanting to break in?'

I baulk at the word 'paranoid'. Only I am allowed to call myself paranoid.

'This is my home,' I say, a croak in my voice. 'This is the only place in the world I feel safe. If someone tried to get in … if someone … that would be it.' I sit back down, place my hands tightly between my knees and bow my head.

'The other night with the mirror. You thought someone got into your house then?'

'They must have done.' I look up.

'So presumably you don't feel safe now?'

'I've ordered more locks and I've got someone coming out to give me a quote on more CCTV.'

DS Marshall studies me for a while.

I open my mouth to speak, but nothing comes out.

Eventually, I say, 'You were going to tell me about this latest victim.'

DS Marshall takes a deep breath and nods. She fishes her dog-eared notebook out of her inside jacket pocket and flips it open.

'Jean Maltravers was eighty-four years old. She lived in the village of Sheldon, which is—'

'Less than five miles away,' I interrupt.

'That's right. She lived on her own, and had done for the past twenty years since her husband died. One daughter.'

'Did she have a stairlift?'

'Yes. She did.'

'And she was found at the bottom of the stairs?'

'Yes.'

'Was her neck broken?'

'Yes.'

'Could it have been an accident?'

'No.'

'How are you so sure? In my book Valerie St George's death was made to look like an accident and was ruled as such.'

'The stairlift was at the bottom of the stairs. Her injuries were consistent with her falling or being pushed down the stairs. For it to have been an accident, she would have needed to have taken the stairlift to the top of the stairs then fallen. According to her daughter, there was no way she could have walked up those stairs by herself.'

I frown as I think. 'I don't understand. If she was killed but left at the bottom of the stairs to make it look like an accident, why leave the stairlift at the bottom?'

DS Marshall shrugs. 'I can only assume the killer wanted us to know it was no accident despite it potentially looking like one.'

I nod. 'I suppose the killer wants you to know that he's copying my books, so he needed this one to be clearly a murder.'

DS Marshall nods.

'This is real, then, isn't it? I was right all along. This is someone copying my work.'

'It would appear so,' she says softly, almost reluctantly.

'Why is he doing this? Why my books?'

'I've no idea. I've arranged for someone to come out later this morning to look at your computer, if that's all right?'

'That's fine.'

'If someone is copying your books, it's possible it's a fan who's trying to impress you.'

'Why would that impress me?' I ask.

'I don't know what goes on in the minds of fans. I'm sure you know of John Hinckley Jr and his attempt to impress Jodie Foster by assassinating President Reagan. To us it sounds bonkers, but in his head it seemed perfectly natural.'

'You think I might have a stalker?'

'It's possible,' she says.

'Wouldn't I know about it?'

'Not necessarily. Given your circumstances, how you live, it's not easy for people to meet you. I'm guessing you don't attend book conventions and award ceremonies, so whoever is doing this can't come up to you and introduce themselves. The only way people can talk to you is through messaging your website, and I assume you receive a lot of emails from around the world?'

'I do.'

'So, for one to stand out, they need to do something different to get your attention.'

I stand up, grab my crutch and go over to the window, where I look out into the expanse of garden. 'But why is this happening here, on my doorstep? Nobody knows I live in Derbyshire. It's not mentioned on my website or in the bio section of my books.'

DS Marshall shrugs. 'All I can assume is that he or she has managed to track you down somehow. If someone is determined enough, they can achieve anything.'

I feel an icy grip on my spine, and it has nothing to do with the strengthening wind outside. I watch as the bare branches of the trees clack together, birds struggle to fly, and the deepening grey clouds gently roll in over the hills.

'I think it might snow later,' I say. 'Nanook loves the snow. If it's deep enough, he can spend hours out there. I have to keep calling him in so he can warm up,' I say with a half-laugh.

'Aidan...' Katherine says softly.

'Maybe even another storm on the way.'

'Aidan, we need to talk about who could be targeting you.'

I turn to her, my back to the window. I can feel the tears building up in my eyes. 'I have one person in my life. Luke. I purposely don't have anyone else so that I can't get hurt, and now...' I stop and swallow my tears.

'Shall I make us another drink?' DS Marshall suggests.

'I spoke to Luke. He seems nice. Very thick accent. I couldn't understand him at times,' DS Marshall says with a laugh as we take fresh coffee into the living room. I start a fire and it's not long until it's blazing, and the room is warming up.

'Yes. Even though he's not lived in Liverpool for six years and he travels all over the country for work, he can't seem to shake the accent.' I smile.

'Same as you, really. How long is it since you lived in Ireland?'

I take a sip of coffee and place the mug carefully on the coffee table. 'I left Dublin when I was eighteen to go to university in Liverpool, which is where I met Luke. I never went back after that, not until after my gran died.'

'What about your parents?'

I sigh. I don't want to tell her my story, but it's all in the media anyway. 'I never knew my father. He was there, occasionally, in the background, but I didn't know him. When I was five years old, we were on our way home from a school Christmas party when Mum lost control of the car and we went down an embankment. I was asleep in the back at the time. I don't remember much of what happened, but I remember being trapped in the back. I couldn't get my seatbelt off. Mum was … she kept asking me if I was all right, trying to talk me through what to do, but her voice … it kept fading. I didn't know it at the time, but she was dying right in front of me. I had to sit there for hours until the emergency services arrived. I listened to my own mother die.'

'I'm so sorry,' she says, and she seems to genuinely mean it.

'You don't get over something like that, do you?'

She shakes her head.

'My gran took me in and she brought me up. I was lucky to have her.'

'Didn't your dad try to make contact?'

It's a while before I answer. 'There are echoes of memories. There's a man who pops up every now and then who I think is my father. I remember he and my gran having very heated conversations in hushed tones so I wouldn't overhear.'

'Do you think your gran was trying to protect you from your father?'

I can feel the tears rising up inside me. I nod. 'I think my dad raped my mum and that's how I came to be born. My parents were married but I get the impression he was a violent man. I'm not making excuses for him, but I'm assuming he didn't see it as rape, whereas my mum did. I think him returning, sporadically, was him trying to make amends for what he did, to be a presence in my life that neither my mum nor my gran wanted.'

'Aidan, I'm so sorry. Do you know where your dad is now?'

'No. I thought he'd turn up at my gran's funeral, but he didn't.'

'While you've been living in England, have you had anyone trying to contact you?'

I snigger. 'You mean, has someone turned up on my doorstep proclaiming to be my long-lost dad?'

'Something like that,' she says with a hint of a smile.

'No. Surely you don't think the killer is my father trying to get my attention somehow?'

'No. I don't.' She takes a sip of her coffee. 'Is there anyone from your childhood in Ireland you're in touch with?'

'No. My gran died a year or so after I left to go to uni. She was my last relative.'

'What about from when you were living in Liverpool? Are you still in touch with your university friends?'

'No,' I answer quickly. 'There was a tight group of us when we were at uni, but we seemed to drift apart once we left. I found that out on the night I was stabbed.'

'How do you mean?'

'We'd drifted apart. Everyone had made a life for themselves, and I hadn't noticed. All I wanted was to be a writer, but it's not a job you can apply for. So, while I was getting my work rejected by publishing houses all over the country, I was working in libraries and bookshops and spending all of my spare time trying to come up with an original and exciting thriller. The next thing I knew, ten years had gone by in a flash. The world had moved on and I hadn't.'

'But then you were published?'

'Yes. I arranged a get-together with the old gang, but I realised the old gang wasn't there anymore.'

'After you were stabbed, didn't that bring the group back together?' DS Marshall asks.

'No. I sort of withdrew into myself. To be honest, I don't remember much of those early days after the stabbing. I'm not sure if anyone came to see me in hospital. You'd have to ask Luke.'

'So why has your friendship with Luke stayed so strong, when it didn't with your other friends?'

'I'd rather not answer that.' A tear rolls down my left cheek, and I let it.

'Why not?'

'Because if I think about why and how Luke and I are friends, I may discover that we're not really friends at all.'

Katherine frowns. 'I don't understand.'

'I do,' I reply with a sad smile.

It's lunchtime and the computer expert from the police still hasn't arrived. DS Marshall makes a call and is told he is running late. We're in the kitchen and I'm making us sandwiches after the noise of DS Marshall's stomach grumbling made even Nanook look up.

'So, you move from Liverpool to this gorgeous house in Derbyshire, and Luke comes with you. Isn't that a little strange?'

'Can we change the subject?' I ask.

'OK.' She puts her hands up in surrender. 'What would you like to talk about?'

'Well, you've spent all morning questioning me about my life, tell me something about you.'

She looks taken aback. 'There isn't much to tell.'

'No history of parents abandoning you or of being stabbed?' I ask as I place slices of ham on brown bread.

'No. Thankfully. Though I have a distant uncle who was a bigamist. I'm afraid that's as exciting as my family gets.'

'Any brothers and sisters?'

'I have an elder brother. He's an estate agent in Didcot.'

'Where's Didcot?'

'I've no idea,' she says, taking the proffered plate and sitting down at the island. 'We're not that close. I know he's married to an incredibly mousey woman. They have twin girls, and both drive identical Volvos.'

'What about you? Are you married to a mousey man?'

DS Marshall takes a large bite of the sandwich and chews slowly. She seems to be thinking of her reply. 'No. I'm permanently single.'

'By choice?'

'Actually, yes. My last three relationships were doomed from the start, and I ended them before they could become disasters.'

'I'm sorry,' I say, simply because it seems the right thing to say. I start eating my sandwich.

'I'm not. I'm better off on my own. I don't seem to function well in a relationship.'

'Don't you want to settle down and have children?'

'I'd like to get married at some point, but I'm not bothered about having children. And part of me thinks I only want to get married so I'm not lonely in old age. Hardly a sound reason, is it?' She smiles, but it's not a happy smile. I don't think she needs to wait until old age to be lonely. She's lonely now.

Snap.

I watch her while we both eat. She seems to be fine while she's asking the questions, but when the topic of the conversation is turned to her, and I'm in the interviewer's chair, she withdraws into herself, almost as if she's afraid of what she might reveal about herself. I can certainly understand that.

'What made you want to join the police force?' I ask.

'I'm not sure. I studied criminology at university and thoroughly enjoyed it. When I left, joining the police seemed like a worthwhile thing to do. Which it is, until you get into the politics of it all.'

'What do you mean?'

'Well, there's so much red tape, form-filling, budget cuts, what you can and can't say or do. You touch a suspect and they shout assault; you look too long at a woman in a hijab and you're branded a racist. The balance has shifted. Suddenly the police are the bad guys and everything we do is wrong. Almost all of my colleagues are unhappy in their work and that affects their home lives. We didn't join the force for this.'

'I'm sorry,' I say, and genuinely mean it. 'I had no idea.'

I'm pretty sure there's a plot in there somewhere for a future book.

'No. I'm sorry. I shouldn't be moaning to you like this. I could get into a lot of trouble.'

'I'm not going to say anything. Who would I say anything to?' I laugh, making light of the situation.

She smiles, and looks more relaxed than she has the whole time she's been in the house.

'Do you think you'll ever leave the police force?'

'Well, actually…'

Her mobile starts to ring, and we both jump at the sound. She fishes it out of her pocket and swipes to answer. She says a few words then ends the call.

'The technician is here. He's wondering how to open the gate.'

I stifle a smile. 'He has to pass a test before it opens.'

Chapter Twenty-Five

Having one stranger in the house is bad enough, but for there to be two, and both of them in my inner sanctum, is difficult for me to cope with. Nobody comes into my office, not even Luke.

DC Erik Lindhardt is a digital media investigator and is able to access all of the emails sent to my author website, even the deleted ones. He entered my house wearing a winter Barbour coat, woollen beanie hat, heavy leather boots and a battered satchel over one shoulder. He didn't wipe his feet and he didn't shake hands when he looked at me with a blank expression. I wonder what he's already been told about me. He tore off his hat to reveal a shock of white-blond hair and shook himself out of his coat, which he draped over my office chair. He sat down and made himself comfortable, not seeming to care that this was someone else's place of work.

I want to stay in the office and watch him work. The thought that this man might be putting something on my hard drive that could let the police know every website I visit, every person I email and every keystroke I make fills me with horror. But the room isn't large enough for three people and a German Shepherd, so me and Nanook decide to retreat to the living room.

'Please remember that I'm a crime writer when you look at my Google search history,' I say from the doorway. 'I have to research weapons, methods of murder, and forensic information for my work. I'm not a terrorist or a serial killer.' I try to sound light-hearted but there's a desperation in my voice.

DS Marshall laughs, while Erik simply shrugs.

'Is there a coffee going?' Erik asks over his shoulder. I detect a hint of a Nordic accent.

'Not at the moment, no,' I say, walking away with Nanook at my heel.

I sit in the living room and try to work out how old my computer is and what I've been googling over the past few months and years. There's nothing suspect that could get me arrested, especially when my job is taken into consideration, but work isn't the only thing I use the computer for. I do all my shopping online – food, clothes, books – and I've bought all my locks and security via the internet. I thought I'd be safe by ordering from different companies, but it's only taken one man at my computer to have access to everything. This Erik Lindhardt will know my bank account details, my passwords, every single lock and safety device. I don't like this. Not one bit.

And how do I know he's even a policeman? He didn't show me any identification. I've only got DS Marshall's word that he is who he claims to be. How do I know they're not in this together and they're not both in there right now, planting something on my computer, setting me up?

'Is everything all right?' DS Marshall asks from the doorway of the living room.

I jump. 'Sorry?'

'You look nervous.'

'Is he finished?'

'Erik? No.'

'Shouldn't you be watching him?'

'To be honest, I don't have much of a clue when it comes to computers. I know what I need to know, but that's about it.' She smiles. 'Is something wrong?'

'I … no.' I try to look more relaxed. 'I'm just not used to this invasion.'

'I know it's not easy, but if someone is stalking you, chances are they will have made contact, somehow, and we need to find out how.'

I take a deep breath. 'Tell me about this new victim,' I say, wanting to take my mind off whatever Erik Lindhardt is doing to my computer. 'What was she called again?'

'Jean Maltravers. There's nothing much to say, really. She lived alone, virtually housebound. She had a few close friends who did some shopping for her, and her daughter popped in every day. It was very much how you wrote in *The Science of Silence*.'

'Did her daughter find her?'

'Yes.'

'She must be heartbroken.'

'She is. Aidan, when you're researching your novels, who do you talk to?'

'Well, a lot of what I need is nearly always online. I chat to a pathologist via email who is very helpful when it comes to postmortem information. Why?'

'Do you tell anyone about your plots before you write them?'

'No. Well, I have to write a synopsis for my agent and publisher. When they give the green light, I start writing. But these books are in print. They've been on the shelves for years. Anyone could have read them.'

'I know. I'm just trying to understand the process better,' she says, smiling. 'Where do you get your ideas? *The Science of Silence*, for example, is about a vicar who is a prison visitor and believes he can commit the perfect murder because of the things he's listened to over the years. Where did that come from?'

'The idea for that one came from a film I was watching. Someone went into the confession box and poured his heart out to the priest about a crime he'd committed. It got the cogs in my mind turning and I came up with *The Science of Silence*.'

We both look up when Erik Lindhardt enters the room.

'I've found your nut job,' Lindhardt says with a grin.

I really don't like you.

Dear Aidan,

I've recently been made redundant. I knew it was coming as the business has been struggling for a while, but it was still a blow to lose the job I've had for fifteen years. Unfortunately, it's provoked my insomnia and I'm back to kicking the covers and being wide awake at three o'clock in the morning. Do you suffer with insomnia? I read somewhere that a lot of creative people have mental health issues. I've started reading Out of Darkness again. I love Beth as a character. I know she murders her husband, but she's wonderfully drawn. I'd like to have known her in real life. I really should try and get some sleep. I need to start job hunting in the morning.

Regards,
Rebecca

Aidan,

Will you be attending Bloody Scotland this year? I've been to a few festivals but not that one and wondered what it was like. I have a friend in Edinburgh who I could stay with and drive over to the event on both days. I've never seen your name on any programmes, which

*is a shame, I'd love to meet you in person, shake your hand, and have
you personally sign my Aidan Cullen collection for me. Hopefully
our paths will cross one day.*

Bye,
Rebecca, xx

Aidan,

*I've joined a book club. My therapist said that I need to put
everything that happened with Malcolm behind me and learn to trust
people again. I realised that it turns out I don't have any friends, so,
in order to make some, I looked up book clubs online and my local
library runs one. My first meeting was last night. There were about
ten of us there and they all seem like nice enough people – a mix of
ages, sex, and race, which is nice. I mentioned you and said how I
was a fan and how we'd chatted, and they all seemed really
impressed. I'm going to try and get them to get your latest book as
one of our reads, though Brian, he's the bloke in charge, isn't much of
a fan of contemporary fiction. That started a huge debate, and he was
severely outnumbered. I know this is naughty of me, but I did
mention that I might be able to sweet talk you into making a virtual
appearance via Zoom if we read one of your books. Would that be
possible? Please say yes. Pretty please.*

Love,
Rebecca, xx

'This Rebecca Charlesworth has sent over a thousand emails to
you in the past four years,' Erik says.

We're all back in my office. Erik is in my chair, scrolling
through the pages and pages of emails Rebecca has sent, while DS
Marshall and I stand nearby watching the screen.

'I hadn't realised it was that many,' I say. I turn to look out of the window. DS Marshall's car is parked in line with the gate, whereas Erik looks like he just pulled up in his dirty blue Mondeo.

'Who is she?' Katherine asks.

'I don't know. Just a reader.' I don't turn back from the window.

'Do you reply to her?'

'Occasionally.'

'You've replied to sixty-seven per cent of her emails,' Erik adds. 'Anyway, they're all pretty friendly, but there's a new one she sent today. And let's just say she's not happy.'

Aidan,

> *I don't know what I've done to upset you but there's obviously something the matter. Why don't you reply to my messages anymore? All I've ever done is admire your work and support you. And you reward me with silence? Is that really the way you treat your fans? You ignoring me has crushed me and I've never felt more hopeless and alone. I thought you were different. I thought you were like me. I guess I was wrong.*

Bye,
Rebecca

Erik reads it aloud and I'm genuinely shocked by the tone. Why has she gone defensive all of a sudden? There have been times, over the years, where I've thought she's shared far too much information about herself and she has asked me some very personal questions, all of which I've ignored. But to turn like this, almost accusing me of abandoning her, is bizarre. We're not friends. We've never met. I don't even know what she looks like.

'Can we trace her?' Katherine asks.

'Yes. I've got IP addresses on the emails. However, here's the even weirder part: she doesn't always message you from the same computer. So far, I've counted over one hundred different IP addresses.'

'What?' I say. 'Why? Why would she do that?'

'I can only assume it's to avoid detection,' DS Marshall says.

'But even I know that you can trace someone through an email, so surely just changing computer isn't going to work, especially if she's using the same email address?'

'She hasn't. Again, I've noted more than fifty different email addresses. All of them are variations on her name,' Erik says, sitting back with his arms folded.

I suddenly feel dizzy and sit down on the padded seat in the window. 'She really is a stalker, isn't she?' I ask.

'She looks like a weirdo, that's for sure,' Erik sniggers.

'How do you know?' I ask.

He leans into my computer and brings up a Facebook page. He increases the size of the profile photos and scrolls through them all. They all show the same thing – a middle-aged woman with deep, sad eyes, a drawn expression and dull, black hair. Occasionally, she's smiling, but it never reaches her eyes and makes her look almost frightened of something, as if she's been held at gunpoint and forced to smile. So, this is Rebecca Charlesworth. It's not how I imagined her. Her messages have often been fun, light, bouncy almost. I've pictured her as having a permanent smile on her face. There's actual misery in her eyes. I suddenly feel very sorry for her. Or should I be frightened of her?

'Will you be able to track her down?'

'Erik, get the locations of all the IP addresses and we'll go from there,' DS Marshall says, before turning to me. 'This woman obviously has some kind of fixation on you. She likes you. All the personal information she's shared with you in her emails will be correct, for the most part. We can look for someone who has recently been made redundant, moved house, or joined a book club. We will find her, Aidan, I promise you.'

'I've put all her messages on a flash drive,' Erik says, handing DS Marshall a small device. 'Can I use your toilet, mate?'

'What? Oh, sorry, yes, it's the room next to the kitchen,' I say, distracted. There have been times when I've seen a new email from Rebecca sitting in the inbox and I've sighed, wondering what she's going to be droning on about next. I've always thought of her as a fan; lonely, perhaps, but nothing sinister. But all these emails, from different addresses and computers, is unsettling. And this last message is really angry.

Erik leaves the room and I gaze out of the window. The sky is grey and heavy, and a few small flakes of snow are starting to fall.

'A big storm last week and now snow. Don't you think the weather in this country has gone bonkers over the past few years?'

'Aidan, I know this is frightening, but you have good security, and you've ordered more. You're doing everything right. I can also ask a patrol car to keep passing your house on a regular basis.'

'She's killed four people,' I say quietly.

'We don't know that. We're just covering bases. She could simply be a harmless fan.'

'Oh great, so I've got a stalker *and* a murderer following me? Two separate lunatics.'

'Just wait to see where our investigation takes us before we start jumping to conclusions,' she says, trying to placate me. 'Is there anyone you can call to stay with you? Can Luke come home?'

'No.' I fold my arms tightly across my chest. I suddenly want them both to leave. I want to be on my own.

'OK. Well, you have my mobile number. You can call me any time. Day or night. I'm not far away. I can be here in about ten minutes if I break the sound barrier.' She stifles a small laugh.

'Thank you.'

Erik enters the office and snatches his coat up from the back of the chair. 'Well, my work here is done so I'll be off. By the way, your order from SecurityUK has been dispatched. The email came through while I was in your account. That's some serious piece of kit you've ordered.'

'You read my email?' I ask.

'What do you think I've been doing here for the past couple of hours?' he scoffs. 'I'll see you back at the station, Katherine.' He stops in the doorway and turns back to me. 'How do I get out of this fortress? That gate's a fucker to open.'

'It's supposed to be,' I reply, malevolence evident in my tone as I show them both out.

Once I'm alone in Gallows View House, I set to work.

There are two rooms DC Erik Lindhardt has been in – my office and the downstairs toilet. The office will take a long time to search so I start with the bathroom.

It's only a small room, large enough for a toilet, sink and a cupboard for storing toilet rolls and cleaning products. If Erik has hidden a camera or microphone device, it shouldn't be too difficult to find.

I run my hands along the top of the door frame, search behind the toilet and in the cistern. I take everything out of the cupboard, check each and every product, shake the towel to see if anything is attached to it and look behind the blind. Nothing. It's clean. But how long was Erik actually away from the office? He said he was going to the toilet, but what if he went somewhere else? Did he go into the kitchen or the living room? Did he plant something in one of those rooms and simply rush into the bathroom to flush the toilet to give the illusion of using it?

I stand in the expansive hallway and look around. It could take days to search the entire ground floor. There are so many places a hidden camera or recording device could be planted, and I really don't know what I'm looking for.

'Shit!' I say as I lean against the wall and lower myself to the floor. I can feel emotion rising up inside me and the tears building up behind my eyes. I don't want to cry. I refuse to allow myself to cry.

Nanook pads up to me and lowers himself beside me, resting his head on my lap.

'I shouldn't have let him in. I shouldn't have allowed any of them in. What have they done, Nanook?'

The computer is my biggest worry. DS Marshall said that Erik was the force's go-to guy for anything related to cybercrime. If he's able to recover deleted emails and track a person who has seemingly covered their tracks, then he can easily leave something behind. Has he installed a recording device to keep an eye on me while I'm at my desk? The camera system for the front gate is on the computer; Erik could access it remotely and disable the alarm, unlock the gate. He could come and go as he pleases, or, if he's working with someone else, he could let them in whenever they want.

Tears pour down my face as I sit at my desk, glaring at the black mirror of the computer screen. My entire life is in this machine: my whole body of work, notes for my current work in progress and future books, my bank accounts, my royalty statements, my tax returns, the contracts with my publishers, private emails with my agent – and then there are my Skype calls with my therapist. Are they stored on a hard drive somewhere? Could a video call be stored somewhere deep in the ether? Would Erik and DS Marshall and the whole of Derbyshire Police have access to my private conversations with Charlotte?

'No. No. No. No. No.'

I lean over the desk, pull out every cable of the monitor and keyboard, unplug it at the mains and sit back in my chair. I've only had this computer for about two years, but it will have to go.

I order a new computer from my tablet. Erik didn't touch that. All of the files I need are on a backup drive, so I carefully box up the computer and keyboard and carry it down into the basement. When Luke returns, I'll ask him to go to town on it with a sledgehammer or something, destroy every circuit board and wire, obliterate it.

By the time I'm finished, I'm soaked with perspiration. It's dark outside. The sky is clear and the snow hasn't materialised. I feed Nanook, but don't bother with anything for myself; I'm not hungry. Once Nanook has been outside to pee, and I've secured the house, I limp upstairs to have a bath. I need to wash the day off me.

With the water as hot as I can stand it, I lower myself carefully into the deep bath.

Beads of sweat fall down my face, mixing with my tears. I stare at the far wall and study the plain white tiles, my eyes refusing to blink.

I think about sinking under the surface of the water and not coming back up. I could just disappear and not have to deal with any of this. I want the pain to stop, the thoughts to stop. I lower my shoulders and dip my face below the surface of the bath. Bubbles erupt from my nose and break on the surface. Everything is peaceful, everything is calm. This is the way it should be. I let the warmth envelop me. Then I remember Nanook. He needs me. I push my face up into the air and take a deep breath. If it wasn't for Nanook, it could all be over now.

Chapter Twenty-Six

It's another two days before the snow finally arrives. When I open my eyes, I notice the light from the gap in the curtains seems brighter than usual for a winter's morning. I hobble out of bed and over to the window, throw back the curtains and see the Christmas-card view in front of me. It makes me smile. Thick snow covering roads and fields, heavily laden branches and the roofs of barns and farmhouses hidden beneath a blanket of white. Leigh Road will be closed. It's always impassable in bad weather. I'll be cut off from the village of Gallowsfield and, judging by the depth of the snow, it could be several days before I see a moving car again. The thought makes my smile even deeper.

I turn and see Nanook by the bedroom door. His tail is wagging.

'You're going to love this.' I grin.

I leave the room without taking any of my tablets.

Nanook runs down the stairs faster than usual. I'm sure he can sense the change in my demeanour and can probably smell the snow. He barges his way through the kitchen and nudges at the conservatory doors as I remove the Patlock over the handles and turn the key in the lock before throwing them open. I shiver immediately at the cold, but Nanook delights in running out into the snow and jumping in the drifts.

I stand in the doorway, dressing gown pulled tightly around me, and grin as Nanook finds his inner puppy and ploughs through the snow. He rolls in it, eats it, kicks it, jumps into it and barks at the falling flakes.

After half an hour, I call Nanook in. The snow is falling heavier, and it's not good for him to be out in freezing temperatures for too long. He needs his breakfast, a warm in front of the Aga, then he can go back out. Reluctantly, and with the aid of a Bonio *and* a Smacko, Nanook comes into the house, the conservatory doors are closed and locked, and we both begin to thaw in the warmth of the kitchen.

The best thing about living in the middle of nowhere, at the end of a village with very few neighbours around, is that nobody can see what I get up to. So, on the rare occasion that I decide to act out of character for a reclusive author with severe anxiety and paranoia, I can do so in absolute privacy. After breakfast, I change into jeans, a T-shirt, a thick sweater and wellington boots. I put on a waterproof padded coat, woollen bobble hat, scarf and gloves, and join Nanook in the back garden to play in the snow.

I find a tennis ball, lob it down the garden and watch as Nanook hops through the drifts, picks it up and comes running back with it. I trick him a few times by throwing a snowball which, naturally, disappears as soon as it lands. Watching the confused look on his face as he stands in the middle of the garden, ears pricked, tongue lolling, makes me laugh out loud for the first time in as long as I can remember. I call Nanook back and make a fuss of him before we return to playing like two children having a snow day off school. That's exactly how it feels.

By lunchtime, I'm actually hungry. Usually, I will have a crisp sandwich while I work, but all the energy I've burnt off in the back garden has left me with an appetite. There are some sausages in the fridge and a couple of potatoes need using before they start sprouting, so I make myself bangers and mash. I throw an extra sausage under the grill for Nanook and give him a spoonful of the mash, too, along with a covering of thick gravy.

After lunch, it's not long before Nanook wants to go back outside and play in the snow, and, if I'm honest with myself, I want to, too. I know I'm going to be in great pain later, and I'll be suffering for the next couple of days, but right now, I don't care; I'm enjoying myself.

While I'm out in the garden playing with Nanook, I'm not thinking about Melanie Burton or the Hargreaveses or Jean Maltravers. I'm not worried about a killer stalking me or about being watched. I'm in the moment. This is what it must be like to be Luke.

A large glass of Bushmills in front of a roaring fire with a sleeping dog at my feet and a good book on my lap is the perfect way to end the perfect day. I'm not reading, I'm staring into the flames. I can feel the heat on my face and there's a smile on my lips. I haven't done anything remarkable today. I haven't conquered anything. I haven't spent any money, and I haven't written a single word. But I've had one of the best days of my life.

I pull the blanket off the back of the sofa and wrap it around me. I'm so comfortable, I don't bother going up to bed. I'll sleep here tonight.

The second before sleep claims me, I realise I haven't taken a single tablet today. I haven't needed one.

Take your tablets.

Chapter Twenty-Seven

It snows on and off for the next three days, but each day, the temperature gets a degree or two warmer and it's not long before the snow turns to rain. As I look through the telescope in the attic, I can see patches of green appear in the fields where the snow is melting. It makes me feel sad. The roads will start to open and the path to my door will clear for people who want to deliver bad news or torture me with their mind games.

'I'm sorry, Nanook. It looks like playtime in the snow is over with for now. Fingers crossed winter continues long into February and March and we get a few more snowfalls.'

There's a farm up the valley that I can see clearly from the attic. There's no direct foot route to get there, and by car I'd have to go right into the village of Gallowsfield and along Leigh Road to get to it, but it's interesting to watch my closest neighbour. I only ever see one figure, a tall, lean man who wears green wellington boots and a wax jacket all year round. There's no wife or children, no farmhands to help him. It's just him and his herd of black-and-white cows.

He's a blank canvas of a man and I often invent a backstory for him. He married young. He and his wife were going to have eight children and raise livestock, but a terrible tragedy befell them a couple of years into their marriage. His wife was struck with a rare and incurable illness and she was dead within six months. The man decided to realise his wife's dream of having a rural farm, but he couldn't face marrying someone else. He kept the memory of the only woman he truly loved alive through his work.

Perhaps he has a dark past. He was a killer, committed his first murder as a child and was imprisoned to serve a minimum of twenty-five years. When released, he was still a young man, not quite forty, but rather than have the press hound him, he retreated to live an isolated life on an isolated farm, not to be bothered by anyone.

It doesn't seem to matter what story I choose for the farmer; it's always a sad one. Maybe I should send Luke over to befriend him one day, get the real story.

A car coming down the road catches my eye. I point the telescope at it and recognise the Peugeot straight away. DS Katherine Marshall is paying a visit.

———————

'I hate the winter,' DS Marshall says as she stands in front of the Aga to warm herself up. She's dressed in multiple layers and still has a long woollen scarf wrapped around her neck and an oversized bobble hat pulled down firmly over her head. 'My boiler packed in. I had no heat at home for three days. Why do boilers always break in winter?'

I hate stupid questions like this. Of course, they break in winter because you don't turn them on in the summer months. I don't reply. I continue to make the coffee, my back turned towards her, so she can't see me roll my eyes.

'I can't wait for the summer. I'm determined to get a holiday abroad this year,' she says.

'Anywhere nice?'

'To be honest, I don't care where it is as long as the temperature is in the high twenties and there's a golden beach for me to sit on every day. A week of doing sod all is looking like heaven to me right now.'

'I prefer the winter,' I say, handing her a mug. 'I love having a fire blazing and long dark nights.'

DS Marshall wraps her hands around the mug and takes a few small sips. 'This is lovely, thanks. The coffee at the station has no taste to it. It doesn't matter how strong you make it, it's bland. This is very nutty.'

'Thanks. I order it in. If there's one thing a writer can't stand, it's cheap coffee.' I smile.

'I guess you were cut off during the snow?' she says, nodding to the view out of the conservatory, which shows the garden still covered in patches of white.

'We don't get many cars coming this way anyway, so it's difficult to tell,' I say.

'You've not experienced any … unwanted attention?' she asks, choosing her words carefully.

'No. All quiet.'

'That's good. I've been in touch with Rebecca Charlesworth.' She places her mug on the island and pulls a file out of her bag. 'She lives in Etwall, just outside Derby.'

'Oh. Not far away, then?'

'No. She's rather a sad woman, quite lonely. I felt sorry for her.' DS Marshall hitches up onto a stool. 'She's one of those people who take a step forward then a few months later take two backwards. She's had failed marriages and relationships, job losses, redundancies. Not much has gone right for her. I think she's a bit … erm …'

'What?'

'I think she may have behavioural problems.'

'What does that mean?' I frown. I remain by the kettle in the corner of the kitchen, leaning against the worktop, my arms folded.

'I don't know how to describe her.' DS Marshall becomes uncomfortable and doesn't seem keen on making eye contact. 'She wasn't exactly normal.'

'In what way?'

'Well, like I said, she was very sad when talking about herself, her life and her past, but when I mentioned you, her face sort of lit up. Your books have been a lifeline to her.'

'Oh.' I don't know how to respond.

'Her book collection was massive, and how it's all arranged must have taken her ages. It's like she lives in a branch of Waterstones. Your books, however, take pride of place in her living room. She's quite the fan.'

'But is she capable of committing murder?'

'It's hard to say, but I don't think she's our killer. I did mention that she should perhaps not email you as much as she has been doing, that her constant messages may be construed as veering towards the stalker.'

'How did she take that?'

'She was very contrite. Like I said, I felt sorry for her.'

'Why did she send the emails from so many different computers?'

'She currently works at the Royal Derby Hospital on the nightshift in security. She's in different departments all the time. It's rare for her to be at the same desk two shifts in a row.'

'And the different email addresses?'

'She's slightly … paranoid when it comes to internet security. She says she doesn't like online companies having access to her whole life, so she limits what she does to separate devices and accounts.'

I can understand that.

'Does she have an alibi for the time of the mirror being placed in my bedroom?' I ask.

DS Marshall maintains eye contact with me a little too long before sifting through her notebook. 'No. Not as such.'

'What does that mean?'

'We're looking into her timesheets at work, which so far all seem to add up. But when she's not working, she's at home either sleeping or reading.'

'She doesn't have friends or family?'

'No. I spoke to one of her neighbours and they thought she'd moved out as they hadn't seen her for months. A couple of others said she was a loner.'

'A loner with a fixation. That doesn't exactly make me feel any safer.'

'There's nothing we can do, I'm afraid. She hasn't committed any crimes.'

'I know.'

Just like the plot of My Wife.

'I honestly don't think she has anything to do with this. I think she's sad and lonely and she's simply latched onto you because she likes your work. If she reads another book that grabs her, she'll move on to that author.'

I give a weak smile. 'Did searching through my computer reveal any other results?'

'I'm afraid not.'

'So you're still no closer to discovering who the killer is?'

'No.' She bows her head.

'I have a new book out in a couple of weeks. That's another potential murder victim.'

'We are working around the clock on this. I promise you.'

'I don't want anyone else to die because of me,' I say, a catch in my throat.

DS Marshall clears her throat and leans forward. 'When these murders were committed, were you here on your own?'

I frown. 'Yes. Why?'

'Where was Luke?'

'In Newcastle.'

'You know that for a fact?'

'Well, not being able to see him, no, but … hang on, why are you asking about Luke again? You were questioning me about him last time you were here. You don't suspect Luke, do you?'

'You know him. I don't.'

'Exactly. I know him. Luke Jackson is my best friend. He's been with me through a great deal. He wouldn't hurt a fly. If you knew him, you wouldn't even suggest such a thing,' I say, my voice brimming with frustration.

DS Marshall holds her hands up in submission. 'I'm sorry. I have to ask difficult questions in my job. I didn't mean to upset you.'

'Luke wouldn't put me through this. He's not like that.'

'I'm sorry,' she repeats. 'Look, I should be getting back. Thanks for the coffee,' she says, and begins to pack her files back in her bag. 'If anything comes up, I'll be in touch, and, if anything else happens or you just want to chat, you know where I am.'

'Thank you.'

As I lead her to the front door, DS Marshall glances into the living room and notices the empty HP cardboard boxes at the door to my office.

'New computer?'

'Yes.'

'Erik didn't break the last one, did he?' she asks with a smile.

'No. Time for an upgrade, that's all.'

'Oh. There didn't seem to be much wrong with the last one.'

'There wasn't. You know what technology is like these days. You buy a state-of-the-art computer and within a week something new and shiny comes out to replace it.'

'Like phones.'

'Exactly.'

I unlock the door and pull it open. We both feel the cold blast and shiver.

'Thanks for the coffee,' she says.

'Any time.' I don't mean it.

I watch while she makes her way carefully up the gravel drive. I wait in the open doorway until she has driven away and I can no longer hear the engine.

I close the door, lock it, and secure it with the door jammer. Then I take my mobile out of my pocket and send a text to Luke.

Are you really in Newcastle?

Chapter Twenty-Eight

Luke doesn't reply straight away to my text. I sit on the sofa for over an hour with the phone in my hand, looking at the blank screen, waiting for it to light up, but it doesn't. The silence is deafening.

I try to go back to work, but I can't concentrate. I read through some emails. My agent has sent a few requests for interviews for publication day next week. The *Sunday Times* wants to write a feature about me to run alongside a review of the new book, which, according to Lucy, is practically a love letter. Radio 4 also want me to do an interview which could be recorded via Zoom then edited and broadcast as if live.

I don't want any of this. I'm pleased my books are getting publicised and gaining in popularity, but I'd rather the books speak for me than rely on me doing interviews. I know exactly how they'll go. They'll start by asking me about the book, where my ideas come from, and a few questions later, things will turn personal. 'So, Aidan, are you married?' I shudder and fire off a quick reply to Lucy saying I don't want to be interviewed at all and the review will be more than enough publicity. I've written a short story exclusively for a special Waterstones edition of the hardback and signed a thousand title pages, and there's even a special edition Goldsboro Books are selling that has sprayed edges. There are plenty of ways to publicise the book without me having to bare my soul to the nation's press.

A reply from Lucy comes back within ten minutes.

Aidan, I'm aware of and sympathetic to your unusual circumstances, but there is only so far the mystique of a reclusive author can take you. Eventually, your readers will tire of your lack of public persona and move on. These days readers want to interact with their favourite authors, and you're not even allowing them to do that via social media. While we expect The Confession of Billy McLean to enter the Sunday Times bestseller list, it won't be the coveted number one spot. We'll be lucky to hit top five. Your preorder figures are starting to wane. I'm coming up to your neck of the woods this week. My mother is marrying her boyfriend in a village outside Burton-on-Trent, so I won't be far from you. I'll pop over and we can have a heart-to-heart over a glass of your famous Bushmills and sort out a plan for how to increase your visibility. This needs to happen, Aidan, and I'll be with you every step of the way.

I read the email several times before it sinks in. There is so much wrong with what Lucy has said. First of all, I don't want her at my house. Secondly, I don't want to increase my visibility. Thirdly, I don't want to be on social media. I don't want any kind of interaction with anyone.

'WHY CAN'T PEOPLE JUST LEAVE ME THE FUCK ALONE?!' I scream.

Nanook jumps down from the sofa and runs out of the room. I've scared him. I've scared myself.

I slump back onto the sofa. I look at my phone. Still no reply from Luke. Where is he? I need his help.

Chapter Twenty-Nine

It was Melanie Burton's funeral yesterday.

I haven't looked at the news for a few days. The news is another voice in my head screaming for attention. I don't want to read about poverty and war. I feel for the victims, I really do, but I can't switch off when I hear bad things. I'm trying to protect myself.

The service was at the Holy Trinity Church in the village where she lived, Ashford-in-the-Water. Looking at the pictures, there was a small congregation inside and, despite the cold temperatures, a large crowd gathered outside. The stories don't mention anything about readings or what music was played, but everyone wore black and looked sombre, as they're supposed to do on these occasions.

One woman had to be held very tightly by a man as she left the church. I'm guessing this was Melanie's mother. She looked haunted. I know people say that parents shouldn't bury their children, but it's no picnic for children to bury their parents either, especially when you're only a child.

It's getting dark, and there has still been no word from Luke.

I feed Nanook, let him out into the back garden and watch from the safety of the house as he walks around, does his business, and comes back with his tongue lolling.

I close the conservatory door, lock it with the key and place the Patlock over the handles. I set the alarm and walk back through the house to the living room.

It's still early, not quite eight o'clock, but darkness has fallen around Gallows View House.

I'm not in the mood to watch a film so I curl up on the sofa next to the raging fire and read an old Barbara Vine paperback with a large glass of Bushmills single malt.

The house is deathly silent. I don't have a single clock throughout the whole building. I hate the sound of a ticking clock. The only noise comes from the cracking of the wood burning in the fireplace. I lose myself in the fiction, turning page after page without once looking up. The only time I stop reading is to refill my glass.

Nanook lies in front of the fire, his usual position in the evenings. When he becomes too warm, he gets up, jumps onto the sofa opposite me and closes his eyes. He's content.

If truly engrossed, I can read a book in a single sitting. There's something about immersing myself in another world that I find relaxing. A world away from my agent making demands, a local murderer on the loose and a stalker knocking on my front door. When I'm finished and look up at the real world, I'm almost always disappointed by my surroundings. I wish so hard that I could belong among the pages I've just read. I don't care if I'm reading a psychological thriller, a police procedural or a horror, fiction is far more enjoyable than reality.

My eyes grow heavy, and I've started to go cold. The fire is dying, and it's not worth adding more wood. I look at the time on my phone. It's almost one o'clock. I've been reading for more than five hours. It's time to go to bed.

'Nanook,' I say gently.

The dog opens his eyes.

'Time for bed.'

Nanook carefully climbs down from the sofa and stretches. He heads lazily for the door and makes his way up the stairs while I take one last look around the ground floor, double-checking the locks on the doors and windows and making sure the alarm is set. Once satisfied, I limp my way upstairs and into my bedroom, where Nanook has already made himself comfortable on the double bed.

I'd finished the Barbara Vine, but on my bedside table there is the new thriller by Benjamin Black that I'm halfway through. I read a couple of chapters before putting it down. My eyes sting with tiredness and my constant yawning is annoying me. I turn out the light and snuggle down beneath the duvet. It's three minutes past two.

———

Wake up.

I can feel movement on the bed.

'Stop fidgeting, Nanook,' I say, halfway between sleep and being awake. I turn over and pull the duvet over my head.

Nanook barks.

I wake up.

Nanook never barks in the middle of the night. Even during storms when gale-force winds are buffeting the house, Nanook sleeps right through.

I reach for the lamp, switch it on and sit up. Nanook is by the door.

'Do you need the toilet?'

I sweep the duvet back and look at the time on my mobile. I sigh. I haven't been asleep an hour yet.

I grab for my crutch and heave myself up. I feel stiff.

At the door, I pull it open and Nanook shoots out. I remain in the doorway, my arm stretched out for my jacket with the keys in the pocket. I freeze as soon as I hear the sound. The noise cuts right through me and I start to tremble.

An alarm is blaring.

I step out onto the landing, go to the top of the stairs and look down. That's when I smell it. Smoke is starting to drift along the hallway. For a moment, I wonder if I've left the fire in the living room burning and an ember has fallen, but the smoke isn't coming from the living room. I hear barking from downstairs.

'Nanook!'

I struggle to run downstairs, gripping the banister firmly with one hand and my crutch with the other. I almost fall and have to steady myself.

I cough as the intensity of the smoke mounts and hits the back of my throat. Nanook is at the front door, barking to get out.

Chapter Thirty

Help me!!

Chapter Thirty-One

I can hear the sound of flames cracking, eating into my home, destroying my sanctuary, but all I can see is smoke. I go into the kitchen, but there's nothing there. I turn back into the hallway and then I see it, beneath the door to the dining room, my library, a glowing strip of orange. My books are on fire.

I know I should call for the fire brigade, leave the house and wait outside in safety for the firefighters to arrive and save my home, but I have no idea how long it will take for them to come out. I've never had a reason to call them before. Will they have to come all the way from Derby? My house will have burned down by then.

I look to the door where Nanook is cowering in the corner. The smoke is getting thicker. My keys are in my jacket pocket and my jacket is still hanging on the hook behind my bedroom door.

'Shit.' I panic. 'Stay there, Nanook. I won't be long. I promise you.' My voice is filled with terror.

I grab the banister with my right hand and hoist myself up the stairs, two at a time – not easy when using a crutch. I practically throw myself up the final few steps. Sweat is pouring off me, the heat from the fire is already intense and the exhaustion from climbing the stairs in a hurry is taking all of my energy.

As I fumble in the jacket pockets for my keys, I spot my mobile on the bedside table. I grab it and begin scrolling through the contacts as I return to the top of the stairs. Looking back down, I can no longer see the hallway. It's lost in the thick smoke.

DS Marshall's voicemail kicks in after several rings: *'You've reached Katherine Marshall. I can't take your call at the moment...'* She's probably sleeping.

I disconnect the call and ring it again while I practically throw myself down the stairs. I need to get my dog to safety. At the front door, I knock the door jammer away with my crutch and fumble with shaking fingers as I open all the locks. The smoke is intense. I can feel it stinging my eyes and scratching the back of my throat each time I inhale. I'm coughing and spluttering as I struggle with the door.

'You've reached Katherine Marshall. I can't...'

'Wake up, for fuck's sake!' I scream as I disconnect and call again.

I pull the door open and feel the cold night air on my face. Nanook shoots out and heads for the locked gate. My dog is safe. That's the only thing that matters.

I breathe in the fresh air before turning around and heading back into the house.

'Hello?' DS Marshall answers, groggy from being woken.

'It's Aidan. My house is on fire. Someone's set my house on fire!' I scream.

'What?' She suddenly sounds very alert.

'My fucking house is on fire!' I shout.

'I'll call the fire brigade. Get out of there now.'

I hang up. Help is on the way, that's all I want to know.

I choke as I run deep into the house. The roar of the flames eating away at my books is deafening. I look around. The entire ground floor seems to be hidden in a thick cloud of black smoke.

Chapter One

This is my home. It has taken five years to feel safe here and minutes to destroy it.

Safety- and security-conscious as always, I have a fire extinguisher in the cupboard under the stairs. Ignoring Nanook's barks from outside, I pull open the door and grab the extinguisher, ripping off the plastic safety tag to make it work.

Standing in the hallway, struggling to read the instructions in the poor light, I shoulder open the door to the dining room and stand back in case I'm hit with a wall of flames.

Nanook's barking intensifies. I turn and see the German Shepherd by my side.

'Get out, Nanook. Run. Go.'

Ahead is a wall of orange flames, destroying everything in its path. I struggle to hold the heavy extinguisher in one hand and the nozzle in the other, my crutch abandoned, lost somewhere in the smoke. I aim at the flames and douse them with foam.

It seems to take an age for the fire to come under control. The smoke stings my eyes, it chokes me. I can feel the flames almost touching me, licking my skin. I'm hot and the sweat is pouring off me. I'm in danger. I should drop the extinguisher and leave the house, but I can't. I can't give up. I can't lose my home. I can't lose my books.

I fight against the blaze, and it's almost under control, almost out, when the foam runs dry.

'Fuck!' I scream.

I drop the extinguisher and limp heavily into the kitchen.

'I should have bought two. I should have bought two,' I chastise myself as I pull out a bucket from under the sink and fill it with cold water.

Dragging my leg behind me, limping through the pain, I run back into the dining room and throw the water over the final flames. It takes several trips, but eventually the fire is out. I stand back to observe my favourite room and watch the black fingers of smoke rising from every book.

Nanook's barking brings me out of my dark reverie.

'Come on. We have to go.'

Exhausted, I limp to the open doorway, fall out of the house and onto the gravel driveway.

I turn onto my back, Nanook by my side, and survey my house. It doesn't look too badly damaged. I've managed to put the fire out before it had a chance to spread through the rest of the place. I can't understand how the fire started in the dining room. There's nothing in there to start a fire accidentally. It's full of books, nothing else. The only way books can catch fire is if someone sets them alight.

I wrap my arms around Nanook, holding him close. I'm freezing cold and in so much amount of pain, it's excruciating.

'Someone tried to kill us tonight, Nanook. Someone wants me dead.'

Chapter Thirty-Two

DS Marshall arrives at Gallows View House first. She brings the car to a screeching halt at the gate and jumps out.

I'm crouched with Nanook by the front door, my coughs echoing into the night.

'Aidan, it's me, Katherine. Can you open the gate?'

'I can't. The fire must have knocked out the alarm system. It won't unlock. You'll have to force the latch open.'

DS Marshall looks around her for something to use. Unable to find anything, she gives the latch a swift kick. That's all it takes for the metal housing to be thrown off the heavy wooden gate, and it swings open. DS Marshall runs down the drive. In the distance, the sky is lit up with flashing blue lights from the approaching ambulance and fire engine.

'Are you all right?' she asks, squatting in front of me, concern etched on her face.

I cough before I'm able to speak. I could murder a Bushmills right now. 'Someone set my house on fire.'

'Are you sure?'

I nod. 'It was coming from the dining room. There's nothing in there to catch fire on its own.' I can taste ash and smoke. I feel sick.

'Shit,' she says, looking up at the front door as black smoke wafts out of it.

A fire engine drives through the gate and pulls up by the garage. Uniformed men and women jump out of the large vehicle and head for the house. DS Marshall helps me to my feet and leads me away from my house as an ambulance stops in the road by her car.

'I'm not going to hospital,' I say, panic loud in my voice. 'I'm not leaving.'

'It's OK,' she reassures me, squeezing me tight by the shoulders. 'Let's get you checked over first.'

'Nanook?'

'He's here. Don't worry.'

A green-suited paramedic leads me to the back of the ambulance. As I climb inside, I look back at my home and the chaotic scene of firefighters walking in and out without permission. I shudder. It's no longer my sanctuary.

'How is he?'

'He's fine. Minor smoke inhalation, that's all. He seems reluctant to go to the hospital for a check-up,' the paramedic says, as if I'm not here.

DS Marshall smiles. 'I think this is the furthest he's gone from his house in five years.'

'Oh. I see.' The paramedic cottons on. 'Well, we've given him oxygen, and he seems to have calmed down, but I can't tell if there's damage to the airways and lungs without taking him to hospital for further examination.'

I rip off the mask. 'I'm not going to hospital.' I cough. 'I'm fine.'

With a red blanket around my shoulders, I step out of the back of the ambulance and squat where Nanook is waiting for me. I wrap my arms around him and pull him close.

'You're going to need a bath. You smell of smoke.' I kiss him, and Nanook licks my cheek in return.

'Is there anywhere you can go?' DS Marshall asks me.

I stand up. 'What do you mean?'

'You can't go back in there.'

'Why not?'

'It's full of smoke.'

'I'll open all the windows.'

'It's also a crime scene.'

'Only the dining room. This is my home. I'm not leaving.'

'Come with me.'

She leads me to her car. She sits behind the wheel with me in the passenger seat and Nanook in the back. She switches on the heater and turns to me.

'Tell me exactly what happened.'

I take a deep breath and cough. 'I was late going to bed. I was in the living room, reading. It must have been about one o'clock when we finally went upstairs. I'd not been asleep an hour when Nanook barked, waking me up. I thought he needed to go for a pee or something. I opened the door and I heard ... I heard the smoke alarm.' I bow my head.

'Did you hear anything else? Someone running away, or a car or something?'

I think for a few seconds. 'No. I saw the smoke from the top of the stairs. It was ... it was awful,' I choke, and a tear falls from my left eye. 'I couldn't let my house burn down. I couldn't lose everything.'

'I was talking to one of the firefighters. The dining room is gutted, I'm afraid, but the rest of the house is just smoky. You might need to redecorate the hallway, but it's fine. You haven't lost everything.'

'I've lost my books.'

'You can buy those again, though.'

'True.' I give a painful smile. 'When can I go back in?' I ask, almost a whisper.

'Not tonight. I really don't think that's wise.'

'I can't go anywhere else.'

DS Marshall looks at me. I expect her to say something, but she doesn't. Her eyes are darting left and right: she's thinking.

'You can come and stay with me for tonight,' she says reluctantly.

I want to thank her for her kindness, but I know she's only offering by rote. She doesn't really want me in her house. And I don't want to go, either.

My smile is weak. 'That's not possible. Do you have any idea how exhausting it is for me just being in this car with you?'

DS Marshall looks at me. Her face softens as she begins to understand the mental pain I'm suffering.

The fire brigade has gone, and DS Marshall waves away the ambulance. She pushes the gate closed at the top of the drive and walks back towards me and Nanook waiting impatiently outside the house. I'm shivering in the cold despite still having the red blanket wrapped around my shoulders. It's a good blanket, thick. I wonder if I can keep it.

An emergency electrician is en route to restore the power that had been knocked out in the fire, and a joiner is coming to board up the external door on the sun terrace leading into the dining room. When it's light, a fire investigator will visit with a specialised fire dog to search the wreckage. According to one of the firefighters, a glass panel in the door had been smashed and the curtain behind it had been set alight. He wouldn't be surprised if an accelerant was used. It was definitely arson, a deliberate attempt to kill me and my dog.

Chapter One

The three of us step into the house, treading carefully on the soaking-wet floor. The air is heavy with smoke and the rancid tang of ash. As much as I want to look at the destruction in the dining room, Katherine advises against it. She asks to review the security footage to see if there's any sign of the intruder, but without the power, we can't. We go into the living room and close the door behind us. The windows are wide open, and the cold night air plunges the temperature inside to below freezing. I'm tempted to light the fire, but the last thing I want to see is more flames. I pour myself a large glass of Bushmills and offer DS Marshall the same.

'It's been a long time since I've had whiskey,' she says as she recoils after sniffing the golden liquid. 'I'm usually a bottle of Chardonnay at the end of a long shift kind of woman,' she says, smiling.

'It's all I drink,' I say. 'Well, apart from coffee.'

'Wow. It's strong.' She baulks after the first taste.

'It's twenty-one years old.'

'I can feel it warming me up.'

We sit on opposite sofas.

'I should phone Luke,' I say.

'He's back in Newcastle?'

'Yes. I'll need to order a new fire extinguisher, as well. I'll get two this time. Maybe one for upstairs, too. What do you think I should do about the door in the dining room? Should I replace it with a strong fire door, or have it bricked up? I suppose if I brick it up, I'm blocking off an escape route if I need one.'

'Aidan, calm down. You don't need to think about any of this right now.'

'I do, though. The house is exposed,' I say, looking around me. 'You said a fire investigator is coming out in the morning? I'll ask him how I go about fireproofing my home.' My hand is still shaking as I bring the glass up to my mouth and have another long drink.

Silence hangs in the air. DS Marshall leans forward, an intensity on her face I've not seen before. 'Aidan, who's doing this to you?'

I sigh. 'That was going to be my question to you.'

'On paper, you don't have any enemies. There was one suspicious fan, but we can't connect her to the murders and, although we don't know her whereabouts for the fire yet, I doubt this was her doing. You know very few people. Who would try to burn your house down with you inside it?'

I look up at her. 'I don't know,' I croak. 'There is only one person who I'm close to. Luke. After him, there's my agent, Lucy Graham, and my...'

'Go on,' she prompted.

'My therapist, Charlotte.'

'Oh yes, you mentioned you see a therapist. What's her full name?'

I tell her and watch DS Marshall write her name down.

'How do you see her? Does she come to you?'

'No. We have weekly meetings via Skype.'

'Oh. And, I'm guessing, she knows everything about you?'

'She does. I've also extensively researched her and she's a genuine therapist.'

'Anyone else?'

'I have a freelance researcher who digs up things for me I can't find on the internet. She visits places and takes photographs for me,' I say.

'Has she ever been to the house?'

'No. Never. We chat via Zoom and communicate by email.'

'Do you know where she lives?'

'Nottingham. I think. I've got her details in my phone.'

'Anyone else?'

'My publisher. My editor. My publicist. I really can't see any of them wanting to kill me.'

'What about other authors? Do you have any writer friends? Is there any jealousy when you've won an award?'

I smile. 'No. I don't actually know any other writers. I receive emails and we all wish each other the best of luck when we have a new book out, but that's as far as my relationship goes with them.'

DS Marshall is about to take another drink of her whiskey when she catches the smell, wrinkles her nose, and decides against it. She places the glass down on the coffee table. 'The thing is, with this kind of crime – someone killing people based on your books, setting fire to your house – it's usually someone you know. It's incredibly rare for a complete stranger to seemingly be so obsessed with you and not make themselves known.'

'If it's not Rebecca Charlesworth, then who else could it be?'

'I don't know. But I will find out.'

I study DS Marshall's face, trying to read her perplexed expression. 'You think it's Luke, don't you?'

'We'll need to speak to him, obviously, but I really don't know what to think.' She stifles a yawn.

A bright light from outside illuminates the living room. We both stand up and look out of the window. It's either the joiner or the electrician. It seems strange to see a vehicle come straight into the driveway without pressing the intercom at the gate. That's something else that needs adding to the list of things to take care of. I hadn't realised how easy it would be for the gate to be opened by an intruder. DS Marshall had given it a swift kick, and it buckled and swung open. I need a complete rethink of my exterior security.

I watch from a distance as the joiner cuts a piece of boarding and screws it into the door frame of the dining room. DS Marshall makes him a coffee and chats to him. It seems so simple for her to be friendly and animated with a complete stranger. Had I been alone, I'd have let the joiner get on with the job without a single word passing between us.

As he's packing away, the electrician arrives and sets to work capping off the supply to the dining room, then reinstating the rest of the house and the alarm system. It doesn't take long before he tells DS Marshall that the video surveillance is now back up and running and he'll return to reconnect the dining room once it's safe to do so.

Again, DS Marshall takes control in organising them, leaving me in the living room with Nanook, dark thoughts running around my mind. The person taunting me is known to me. How is that possible? I intentionally have few people in my life precisely so they can't turn against me.

'The fire's wiped out the CCTV; there's no record of anything saved. What are you thinking?' she asks from the doorway.

I jump. I hadn't realised she was there. 'I'm just thinking that, if they really want to kill me, why not just come and stick a knife in me like they did all those years ago? They can even use the same knife if they want to,' I say, taking the pen knife from my jacket pocket and slamming it down on the coffee table.

DS Marshall stares at it, wide-eyed. 'What's that?'

'That's the knife that was used to stab me six years ago.'

'What are you doing with it?'

'I don't know. I found it.'

'Where?'

'In the basement. I was looking through some boxes when I put the broken mirror down there.'

'How do you know it's the same knife?'

'Have you ever been stabbed?' I ask.

'No.'

'Good. I hope you never are, but trust me on this. When you have a knife sticking out of your stomach and you're looking down and seeing the blood pouring out, there's very little else to focus on. I know every single thing about this knife. I know there's a tiny piece of silver missing from the handle measuring three millimetres. I know the mechanism isn't as smooth as it should be, probably because of the dried blood in there.'

'Aidan, you shouldn't have that knife in your possession. It's evidence for your attack.'

I reach for the knife and pick it up before she can.

DS Marshall looks at me, speechless. I take another sip of my drink and gaze off into the distance through the open window. 'If the killer wants to finish the job, he can use what he started it with.'

Chapter Thirty-Three

Luke's back. He was on his way home when I called him in the early hours to tell him about the fire. He went straight into protective mode the moment he stepped through the front door. Once the electrics have been sorted and the place has dried out, he'll redecorate my hallway for me and take charge of gutting the dining room and disposing of my ruined books.

I can't look in that room just yet. There were times, when things got too much for me, that I'd go in there and simply stand in front of the floor-to-ceiling shelves and marvel at my vast collection. I can't do that anymore. All my books have been destroyed. Every. Single. One.

I'm drained. I'm mentally and physically drained. I want to go to sleep and never wake up again. Luke would take care of Nanook. I've no doubt about that. It wouldn't matter in the slightest if I simply ceased to exist.

It's early morning before Luke practically forces me to go to bed. I doubt I'll sleep as the smell of burning is everywhere. It's making me cough and is stinging my eyes. Still, I don't want to have to watch Luke shovelling out soaking remnants of my books, so I allow myself to be taken to bed.

There is one saving grace of the fire, and that is I can't have my agent, Lucy Graham, come to the house for a friendly visit. I send her a quick email and make it out to be worse than it is. Hopefully, she'll cancel her visit, but she's a formidable woman. She may take it upon herself to come over to see if she can help. Hopefully Luke will still be here, and he can make an excuse on my behalf.

I fall asleep almost as soon as my head hits the pillow. When I wake, it's still dark. I look at my phone and see that I've been asleep for the whole day. It's now late evening. I still feel unrested, though, and consider turning over, pulling the duvet over my head and going back to sleep. But I can't do that. I can hear noises from downstairs. Luke's laughing and Nanook is growling. They're playing and it makes me smile. I'm missing out on all the fun. I'm bloody hungry, too.

I limp downstairs. The door to the dining room is closed; the burning smell is still lingering. In the kitchen, Luke is making enough scrambled eggs to feed an army.

'How are you feeling?' he asks.

'Fine. I think,' I say. The thing is, I feel numb to everything. 'Has Nanook eaten?'

'He has. I've also had him out in the woods for a long walk and a run. I've had a skip delivered, and emptied the dining room, and stripped all the cushion covers from the sofas. They're currently going through their second cycle in the washer. The smell really lingers, doesn't it?'

'Wrong time of year to have the windows permanently open, I suppose.'

'You could move out for a while.'

'I think we both know the chances of that happening are slim,' I say with a slight smile.

Luke smiles back.

'Hungry?' he asks.

'Starving.'

Luke makes me three slices of toast and spoons a generous

helping of scrambled eggs and fried mushrooms on top. He sets it down in front of me at the island and hands me a huge mug of tea. It's a simple meal, but it's delicious and I devour it.

'I had a phone call earlier, while you were sleeping,' Luke says as he watches me eat. 'A DI Victor Finch.'

'Oh yeah? That's DS Marshall's boss. We've gone up a level. What did he want?'

'He wanted the full story on what happened. I didn't like him. He called you infirm.'

'Cheeky sod.'

'He asked where I was at the time of the fire,' Luke says, taking a large swig of water.

'So, they still think you're behind all this?'

'It would appear so.'

I look around me. The kitchen, once a clean and bright room, suddenly feels damp and dirty. 'Do you think this room will need redecorating?'

'Probably.'

I sigh. I hate the upheaval of redecoration. 'What about my office?'

'That's fine.'

'Are all my books ruined?'

'I'm afraid so.'

I want to cry. 'Some of them are first editions.'

I can't replace my books. I don't think I want to, either. I had hundreds. And now I have none. I don't have it in me to start again. I'll be the only writer who doesn't own a single book.

'Finch asked if I knew who would be doing this to you,' Luke says.

'What did you say to that?'

'I told him that I can count on one hand the number of people you've spoken to in the past five years and still have fingers left over.'

'I bet he didn't like that.'

'No. This is obviously a case where he's going to have to engage his brain, and I think his might be missing in action.'

'He's not one for thinking outside the box?' I ask.

'I think he prefers the cases where he walks into a room and finds a man holding a bloody knife over a corpse.'

'Ah.'

'He even asked if this could all be directed at me.'

'What did he mean?'

'That maybe whoever set fire to the house was trying to target me.'

'Do you have enemies?' I ask him.

'Not that I'm aware of. You know me, I get on with everyone,' he says with a huge grin.

That's true. Luke has always had a habit of being able to chat, laugh and joke with anyone, even complete strangers. People are just drawn to him.

I go back to eating my eggs, but they don't taste the same. There's a bitterness to them now. The police are questioning everything, which is what they're supposed to do, obviously, but it feels like they're trying to destroy what little life I have.

I put my knife and fork down.

'Are you all right?' Luke asks.

'Yes. Not as hungry as I thought.'

'You've got to eat. Keep your strength up.'

I climb down from the stool, grab my crutch and slowly make my way out of the room.

'I've done a shop,' Luke says, following me. 'I was going to do my famous chilli. I thought we could sit in front of the TV and have a *Star Wars* night.'

My mind keeps going back to what DS Marshall said about someone close to me doing all this. I remember telling her that I only have one person truly close to me and that's Luke. Do they suspect him? Do I? No, I don't. He's my best friend.

Isn't he?

Besides, he's been in Newcastle.

Hasn't he?

'I'm not hungry.'

'Fair enough. Just the films, then.'

'I think I might go back to bed.' I'm in the hallway now and I stop to rest at the bottom of the stairs. A shooting pain has run up my right side. I hold onto the banister for stability.

'Aidan, I know this has been a really hard time, but you're OK, aren't you, mate?'

'I'm fine.'

'No, you're not.' He comes towards me. 'You've got that intense look on your face. What's wrong?'

I pause and frown while I think of what to say. 'Why didn't you answer my text?'

'What? When?'

'The other night when I asked if you were really in Newcastle. You didn't reply.'

'Didn't I? Oh, no, I didn't. I was out with a few of the lads having a curry. I was going to reply when I got back to the flat, but I just went straight to sleep. I'm sorry.' He shrugs defensively.

'You've never not replied to one of my messages before.'

He pauses and then replies, his tone blunt. 'I'm sorry. But I have got a life, you know.'

That comment stings. We both know what it implies: he has a life, and I don't. He looks down at his feet. We stand in silence before he breaks it.

'Why did you want to know if I was in Newcastle?'

'I just wanted to know where you were, that's all.'

'Why?'

'DS Marshall asked.'

'She asked you where I was? Why?'

'She said … she wanted to know where you were at the times of all the murders, and I couldn't tell her.'

'I was in Newcastle.'

'But we only have your word for that,' I say quickly.

'What does that mean?'

I can't answer him. I want to, but I can't.

'What does that mean, Aidan?' Luke asks, an edge to his voice. 'Do I need an alibi all of a sudden?'

'We all need an alibi.'

'Do you have one?'

'No.'

'There you are then. We're all suspects.'

'I'm not.'

'No. You wouldn't be, would you? I don't believe this. After everything I've done for you, this is how you thank me. I was in Newcastle, Aidan. I was nowhere near here at the time of the murders. And what would my motive be, anyway?'

I shake my head. 'I don't know.'

'You know what? I've had enough of this. You need to change, Aidan. You need to do something about the way you live. All I've ever done is look out for you and be your mate, and now you're accusing me of… You're twisted, mate. I'm heading back to Newcastle.'

'I thought we were going to have a meal together.'

'You're not hungry, remember? Also, do you really want to sit down and have something to eat with a man who's killed four people and set fire to your house?'

'Luke, I wasn't accusing you.'

'No? It certainly sounded like it.'

He turns, grabs his coat from the cupboard in the hall and storms out of the house, slamming the door behind him. I'm frozen to the spot, gripping the banister for dear life. I want to go after him, but I can't. I want to shout to him, scream at him that I'm sorry, that I need him, but I don't.

His words hurt, and they hurt because they are true. I know they are. I'm twisted. I've thought it myself for a long time, but to know that someone else has thought it, too, that someone I thought was my friend has looked at me and had the same concerns, is hard to take. I'm stuck in a prison of fear and paranoia and now I've pushed away the one remaining person in my life who cares about me. He's never done anything but be a good friend – my best friend – and now he's gone, and I'm alone. Maybe that's how it's supposed to be. Maybe I deserve to be alone.

Chapter Thirty-Four

I go upstairs. It takes me a while. I'm in so much pain. When was the last time I took any tablets? I can't remember, and I really don't care anymore.

I sit on the seat by the window on the landing and look out. It's dark. The beautiful, yet cold, Derbyshire landscape is lit up by a brilliant moon high up in the sky. I could sit here all night and lose myself in the sprawling view. Nanook comes and sits beside me.

'Do you think he'll come back?'

Nanook looks up at me, his head tilted to one side.

'I wouldn't blame him if he didn't. How could I have accused him like that? I've known him for such a long time, then sodding DS Katherine Marshall comes along and stirs everything up with her textbook suspicions. She's wrong.'

I look back out of the window.

'I've ruined everything, haven't I? What am I going to do to—'

I stop. Something's caught my eye. There was a flicker of movement by the trees just outside the drive, where the gates used to be. What was that? A squirrel? No, it was too big for that.

'You see,' I say to Nanook. 'This is what the police have done to me. I know I'm not the most stable of people, but now I'm jumping at the slightest shadow. I live in the countryside, for crying out loud: of course there's going to be things running across the road.'

Nanook steps towards me and places his head on my lap. I stroke his soft fur and his big eyes look up at me. I'll be sad if Luke doesn't return but, as long as I have Nanook by my side, I know I'll be fine.

'I know we've had our tea, and you've had your dental chew, but how about we have a cheeky snack and…'

There it is again. Something outside caught my eye. I saw something move behind the tree just to the left of the opening to the driveway. I've seen foxes and squirrels and even a rat scurrying along before, but this was different. This was … bigger.

'Come on,' I say to Nanook.

I get up off the chair and we climb to the attic. The shooting pain down my right leg is torture tonight. I really need to make sure I take my medication on a regular basis.

I hop up onto the stool and point the telescope at the front of the garden. I bring the lens into focus, and I see a cat slink along the road. It disappears behind the stone pillar but doesn't come out the other side. Why not? What's behind there to grab its attention? Then it reappears, tail high, turns around and rubs against something. Then, I see it. I see a cloud of breath against the night sky. There is someone hiding behind the stone pillar at the top of my driveway.

I plunge my hands in my pockets but they're empty. What have I done with the flick knife? Where did I put it once DS Marshall had left?

Shit.

I look back through the telescope and see the cat has moved on. It's far up the road now and there's no cloud of breath coming from behind the pillar. I've let my guard down and they've taken the opportunity to come closer to the house.

There are no gates. My security is erratic. I'm exposed and vulnerable and a prime target.

I freeze. I've heard something. At night in the countryside, everything is silent and the slightest sound is magnified. I can hear the quiet noise of gravel crunching. Someone is walking down my driveway. They're taking tentative steps. They don't want me to know they're there. They're sneaking up on me. Ready to shock me. To attack me.

I need to call 999, or DS Marshall at least. I don't even know where I put my mobile.

I jump off the stool. The pain is excruciating. I hobble down the stairs as quickly as I can with Nanook nudging me to get past. He stops on the first landing and looks at me – tongue lolling, tail wagging. He thinks we're playing a game. If only.

I go into my bedroom and pull open the drawers of my bedside table. I'm looking for my phone. I'm looking for anything I can use as a weapon. But there's nothing there.

'Shit, shit, shit,' I say quietly. Even I can detect the fear in my voice. Whoever is out there has succeeded. I'm scared.

I go out onto the landing and stand by the window. I look, carefully, out into the night to see where they are, how close they are to the house, and wonder if I have enough time to run into the kitchen and grab the biggest knife in the cutlery drawer.

'They're coming for me, Nanook. They're coming.'

I go downstairs, struggling to hold onto the banister with my palm covered in sweat. I go into the dark kitchen and don't turn on the lights. There's enough light coming through the conservatory from the full moon. I open the cutlery drawer and straight away I see something I can use that will cause more damage than a mere knife. I grab the meat cleaver by the stainless-steel handle, feel the cold against my clammy skin and lift it out of the drawer. It's heavy, and I know it's insanely sharp as it cuts through bone like a hot knife through butter. If anyone tries to hurt Nanook or me, I'll cut them up.

I go back into the hallway and sit on the bottom step of the stairs. Nanook follows and sits next to me. In the silence, we wait. All I can hear is the humming of the fridge and the pounding of my heart in my chest. Whoever is out there may end up killing me, but I'll not give in without a fight.

I don't know how long I can wait before the pain of being in one position for so long is too much. Did I imagine the noises outside? I haven't heard anything more for a while now. I have to stand up. I walk into the kitchen. I need a drink. I need medication. As I'm throwing back two ibuprofen, I see something in the back garden. There's a shadow outside the conservatory door. In the darkness, all I can make out is a silhouette, but it's obviously a person. It's definitely not Luke. I'd recognise his shape anywhere. This is someone I haven't seen before. This is a complete stranger.

I pick up the cleaver from where I set it down on the counter next to the sink. I wish I'd continued searching for my phone. It's too late now.

'I don't know who you are, but I've called the police and they're seconds away from turning up here with sirens blaring and lights flashing,' I shout. 'If you don't want to be arrested, I suggest you leave right now.' I try to sound forceful, but I can see the cleaver shaking in my hands. I'm guessing my voice is quivering, too.

The shadow moves. They're making hand gestures but, through the double-glazing, I can't hear what they're saying, which means they probably haven't heard me.

Slowly, I step closer. I have to lower the cleaver so I can hold my crutch and steady myself towards the window.

'I've called the police,' I shout again. 'They're on their way. You're trespassing and you're in a great deal of trouble already, so don't go making things worse.'

Nanook barks. He's finally noticed the shadow outside and

he's bounded into the conservatory. He jumps up onto the sofa, front paws on the windowsill and his bark resounds around the empty room. He has a fierce, frightening bark.

Good boy. Scare them away.

The shadow doesn't move.

I lean into the conservatory doorway, fumble on the wall for the switch for the outside lights and turn it on. The garden is lit up and the person holds up an arm to shield their eyes from the brightness. They're wearing a long dark purple duffel coat with the hood up. They have a backpack on their shoulders. When the hand lowers, I see that it's a woman and I immediately think of my agent, Lucy. She's in the area. But it's not her. I have regular video calls with her. I have no idea who this woman is, though she does look vaguely familiar.

'The police will be here any minute,' I shout again. I doubt she can hear me over Nanook's barking. It's an empty threat, anyway.

The woman steps closer and is knocking on the glass now, making Nanook even more frantic. She's mouthing something but I can't hear her. There's no way I'm letting her in.

Then it dawns on me where I've seen her before. DC Erik Lindhardt showed me her face on my computer. It's Rebecca Charlesworth. I'm sure it is.

What is she doing here? How the hell did she find out where I live? She really is a stalker. Adrenaline courses through me. She's here to set fire to my home again. Or am I the final murder victim on her list? She's fed up with the copycat murders and she's here for the ultimate prize: to kill the creator. Either way, I know I'm not safe.

Nanook jumps up at the window. She seems frightened by him. Good.

'You need to leave!' I call out. Then I remember where my phone is. I turn back to the kitchen and find it on the counter next to the kettle. I scroll through the contacts and select DS Marshall's number. I go back into the conservatory so Rebecca can see me on the phone.

'DS Marshall, it's me, Aidan…'

She says something, but I can't hear what over Nanook's barking.

'Can you hear me? You need to send someone to my house right now. It's Rebecca. She's turned up. She's in my back garden!'

The barking suddenly stops.

'Aidan, are you still there?'

Slowly, I turn around. Rebecca has gone. The lights are still on in the garden, but there is nobody there. Nanook still has his front paws on the windowsill, his eyes searching.

'Aidan. Aidan?' DS Marshall calls out.

'It was Rebecca. She was here, but now she's…' The front doorbell rings. 'Jesus Christ! Please, you need to come now.'

'OK. Aidan, stay where you are. Make sure the doors are locked. I'm coming over right now.'

The call ends.

The doorbell rings again and Nanook runs out into the hallway, barking at the intruder.

I manage to pull him back. I push him into the living room and close the door on him. He's still barking, but it's muffled.

I'm in the hallway. All that separates me and this psycho stalker is a front door that's been weakened by the fire. I've still got the cleaver in my hand. I don't want to use it, but I will if I have to.

The letterbox lifts.

'Aidan. It's me. It's Rebecca Charlesworth. I read about your house being set on fire in the news. I—'

'Listen,' I interrupt. 'I've called the police and they're minutes away. You're in enough trouble as it is, so just FUCK OFF, YOU CREEPY BITCH.'

I grab the handle of the living room door, open it and rush inside, closing it behind me. Nanook is barking. The doorbell is ringing. If DS Marshall doesn't get here soon, there's going to be blood spilled.

I don't know how long the ringing went on for, but once it stopped, Nanook stopped barking. I poured myself a large measure of Bushmills and sat on the sofa waiting for DS Marshall to arrive.

My phone rings. It's her calling. She's outside the front door and wants me to let her in.

'Are you on your own?' I ask.

'Yes.'

'Where's Rebecca?'

'Aidan, there is nobody else out here. Can you please open the door? It's bloody cold and I'm only wearing a thin jacket.'

I go into the hallway. I start to unlock the door, but I've seen my fair share of horror films and know that Rebecca could have overpowered DS Marshall and be forcing her to lie in order for me to open the door. I look through the spyhole. There's only DS Marshall there on the doorstep. But Rebecca could be hiding just out of sight.

Shit.

I open the door and stand back. Whoever is going to come rushing into the house is going to have to face a snarling German Shepherd.

Nanook's tail wags when he sees DS Marshall and I close the door quickly and lock it as soon as she comes in.

'Are you all right?' she asks, looking me up and down. I'm guessing I look a mess. I'm sweating and I'm not ashamed to say that I'm scared.

'No. I'm not. Rebecca was here. She was right here, ringing on the doorbell. And she was in my back garden.'

'What did she say?'

'I don't know. I couldn't hear her. She … she said something about reading about my house fire on the news. I didn't know it had made the news.'

'Of course it had. Listen, Aidan, how sure are you it was Rebecca? Is your security back up and running?'

'I … I assume so, yes.'

I walk towards my office, and DS Marshall and Nanook follow.

I sit down at my desk and wince at the pain. I log on to my security system and angle my body so DS Marshall can't see me type in my passcode. I select the footage from the camera at the front of the house and scroll back the time until a figure appears on screen. I pause it as Rebecca comes to the front door from the back of the house. She pulls down her hood and her face is revealed.

'There. That's her, isn't it?'

She nods. 'Yes.'

'How does she know where I live?'

'I'm not sure.'

'Can you arrest her?'

'For what?'

'For trespassing.'

'She hasn't trespassed, Aidan. Your gates are wide open. She's walked up to the front door; you've told her to go away and she's complied. She hasn't broken any laws.'

'She's stalking me. You said so yourself.'

'I never said she was a stalker, Aidan. She's a fan. She's a superfan but she hasn't done anything illegal.'

'She set fire to my house!' I shout.

'We don't know that.'

'Then ask her. Pull her in for questioning. Search her home for accelerants. Test her clothing. Get that bag off her and test that. I bet she has a canister of petrol in there or something.'

'Aidan, please, calm down,' DS Marshall says in soothing

tones. It works. I take a deep breath. 'I will go and visit Rebecca in the morning and ask her why she came to see you. I'll tell her that, if she contacts you again, then I'll take steps to issue her with a restraining order. That's all I can do.'

'You need to ask her about her alibis for the murders, too.'

'I have no proof that she's the killer.'

'Because you haven't looked.' I can feel myself getting riled up again.

Do I need to do her job for her? No wonder people get pissed off with the police so much these days.

'Aidan, leave it with me. I know what I'm doing.'

I don't feel as placated as she wants me to be, but I know ranting and raving isn't going to get me anywhere.

I take a deep breath and try to calm myself. It doesn't work. I need another drink.

'I'll get on to a patrol unit and ask them to make regular drive-bys of your house to keep an eye on things. Now, I suggest you go to bed, and I'll be in touch in the morning when I have more information.'

I don't look at her. I can't. I don't know whether I want to cry or scream or ask for a hug.

'Are you going to be all right? Do you want me to call Luke for you?'

'I'll be fine with Nanook. I think he actually helped in scaring Rebecca off.'

'Good.'

DS Marshall asks me to email the footage from the security camera to her, which I do, then I show her out. I lock the door behind her and secure it with the jammer, but I don't feel as safe as I used to.

I decide to go to bed. There's nothing I can do. My gates are broken, my security is compromised, and my home is no longer a safe haven. On top of that, Rebecca fucking Charlesworth is out there and who knows what she'll do next? I've heard about psycho fans turning against the people they claim to love. What has she got planned now I've threatened her with the police?

Nanook jumps on the bed and makes himself comfortable. I snuggle up to him, close my eyes and pray we'll both wake up in the morning.

Chapter Thirty-Five

'What's happened to you?' Charlotte asks, leaning into the screen.

'Someone set fire to my home,' I say.

'What? When? Why? Who?' She's genuinely concerned, which makes me smile slightly.

'A few nights ago. I don't know who or why.'

'Was anybody hurt?'

'I managed to get out. Nanook barked and woke me up.'

'Thank goodness for Nanook. Are you sure you're all right?'

'I'm fine.'

'You said someone *set* fire to your house, which means it was a deliberate act.'

'Yes.'

'Do the police know who?'

'No. Not yet. The investigation is ongoing.'

'No clues?'

'A window was broken in the dining room door leading out onto the sun terrace and petrol poured through onto the curtain. And then, the next day, a woman – well, one of my fans – showed up at the house, trespassing.'

'Oh my goodness,' she says, a hand slapped to her chest. 'You could have been killed.' I nod. 'And what was that woman thinking, showing up to your house like that?'

'I don't know. I feel like she's responsible for the fire, and maybe even the murders. The police are dealing with it, with her, but, I don't know. I just … I don't know what's going on.'

'Are you sleeping? Eating? Any panic attacks?'

I hold myself rigid. I'm sitting on the office chair, my hands clasped tightly in my lap. My head is lowered, and I look briefly up at the computer screen to make eye contact with Charlotte. I keep biting my lower lip and the feel of my heavy frown seems to be a permanent feature now. I really want to cry, but I don't think I have any tears left.

'I'm sleeping less. I keep waking up, thinking I've heard something. I know I haven't, but … I think I'll be like this until I can get the door and gate repaired.'

'Has Luke come down from Newcastle?'

'He was here for a few days but he's gone back up.'

'So, you're on your own?'

'Yes. I don't mind.'

'You really shouldn't be on your own, Aidan.'

I try to speak but choke. I swallow my emotions, which is painful. 'We had an argument.'

'You and Luke did? What was it about?'

'He has his own life. He's got this new contract in Newcastle. He obviously loves the city. He may stay there.'

'But he's still your friend. You don't stop being friends with someone because you have a new job.'

'I don't think he *is* my friend,' I say, after a moment of silence.

'Why?'

'If I say something to you, you can't tell anyone, can you?'

Charlotte licks her lips. 'Aidan, everything you say to me is in the strictest confidence. The only time I will tell someone else what you say is if I believe you may harm yourself or harm others,' she states slowly and professionally.

I nod. 'I think the police think Luke may be behind the murders. And, if he is, he's also the person who set my house on fire.'

'What evidence do they have?'

'They don't, that I'm aware of. DS Marshall asked about Luke's whereabouts for the times of the murders. He says he was in Newcastle, but I only have his word for that. I don't know any of his mates up there so can't ask.'

'Are the police looking into Luke's whereabouts?'

'I assume so.'

'What do you think?' she asks.

'Honestly? I have no idea. Before he left, me and Luke sort of … well, we had words.'

'About?'

'I voiced similar concerns to DS Marshall's and asked him to account for his whereabouts. He went on the defensive. Understandable, really.'

'And he just left?'

'Yes.'

'But he knows what's going on with the fire, the murders, and now this obsessive fan. It's not wise, surely, to leave you on your own? Safety in numbers and all that.'

I'm trying my hardest not to cry. 'I think I'm probably better off on my own, until all of this is over.'

'I'm worried about you, Aidan. You look petrified.'

'I am.'

'Is there anything I can do?'

Help me.

I shake my head.

I'm sitting alone in the conservatory, watching Nanook having his final run-around of the day outside.

I rarely spend time in the conservatory. Had it not already been here when I bought the house, I wouldn't have had one installed, but it is tastefully decorated and designed to fit in with the period of the house. There's a calming serenity about it. In the spring, I occasionally sit in here with a book and a coffee when I've finished working, but it's always stifling during the summer. I don't like all the glass. It makes me feel open and exposed, and, despite the fact the house is very private, I can't help but feel someone might be watching. After all, I spend many an hour looking through my telescope in the attic; someone could be doing the same and watching me.

I don't feel safe in the house. I might feel better once a new gate is installed, a replacement fire door fitted in the dining room and the acrid smell of smoke is replaced with fresh paint, but will it change the way I feel about living here afterwards? Maybe, once Rebecca Charlesworth is caught and jailed. I had hoped Gallows View House would be my forever home, but now I'm wondering if I might have to move. I'd sought isolation, and certainly had it here, but maybe I do need people close by – the odd neighbour dotted here and there – to wave to or say hello to when I pop into the village for milk and eggs. I could do that, I know I could, if I put my mind to it. I don't necessarily need people living with me or a close circle of friends, just an occasional acquaintance to be on first-name terms with.

I feel a cold, wet sensation on my hand. Nanook has come into the conservatory. How had I not noticed? I'd let my guard down while my mind wandered. Anyone could have walked through the open door and I wouldn't have noticed.

'What's happening to me, Nanook?' I ask. 'If someone wants me dead, why don't they just come and do it, and put me out of my misery?'

Chapter Thirty-Six

I've just settled down in the living room with a book and a glass of Bushmills when my mobile starts vibrating on the coffee table. I look at the screen, hoping it might be Luke calling, and feel slightly dejected when I see it's DS Katherine Marshall. Reluctantly, I swipe to answer.

'I was just ringing to see how you are.'

'Have you arrested Rebecca?' I ask, ignoring her question.

I hear DS Marshall take a breath. 'OK, firstly, Rebecca is truly sorry about coming to your home. She's a very lonely person. She has a few trust issues and she's latched on to you and your books. She wanted to come over to apologise to you in person. I told her that wasn't the right thing to do. She won't do it again.'

'That's it?'

'Like I said, Aidan, Rebecca hasn't broken any laws.'

'So, you're just taking her word for it that she won't come to my home again?'

'If she does come again, we can take further steps.'

'If she comes again, she may kill me.'

'I don't believe she will.'

'So, because you don't believe she will, that makes it OK?' I sigh. 'Did you ask her for alibis for the murders?'

'Yes, I did, and they check out. She was working. She is not the killer, Aidan.'

I don't feel any better about this. I would prefer for Rebecca to be behind bars. That may sound harsh, but it's my own safety I'm concerned about here.

'DI Finch spoke to Luke. He said Luke seemed to be very worried for your safety.'

I don't know how to reply to that.

'I wanted to let you know,' DS Marshall continues, 'that we've questioned your closest neighbours. Nobody heard or saw anything on the night of the fire. We sent the door off for testing and it's come back clean – no fingerprints, nothing. And there are no identifiable footprints around the door either.'

'So, you've no clues, then?'

'I'm afraid not.'

'What does that mean? Where do you go from here?'

She pauses. 'There isn't much we can do without evidence or witnesses. The only thing I can suggest is to tighten up your security, which you are doing. Change your locks, contact us if you see anything suspicious, and don't be alone.'

'Don't be alone?' I almost laugh. 'I'm always on my own.'

'I know Luke is working away at the moment, but he'll keep coming back, and he'll return eventually.'

'I wouldn't bank on that.'

'What do you mean?'

'You made me doubt him. I questioned him,' I say. I'm suddenly angry with her. I grip the phone tighter.

'What?'

'You put it into my head that he might not have been in Newcastle like he said he was, and I asked him.'

'Ah.'

'Is that all you can say? It's ruined. Our friendship is ruined.

The trust has gone. I've known him for more than half of my life. He was like a brother to me, and it's gone. It's all gone.' I'm crying and I can't stop it from sounding in my voice.

There's a long pause before DS Marshall speaks. 'I'm sorry,' she says. It sounds pathetic. 'Would you like me to speak to him?'

'And say what?'

'That is was me who made you doubt him.'

'You'll make it worse.'

'Aidan, I really am sorry. It wasn't my intention…'

'I think, unless you have some new information, you shouldn't call anymore.'

She starts to say something, but I don't hear it because I end the call.

It's difficult for me to settle after the harsh conversation with the detective sergeant. I finish my drink in one gulp and pour another. I stand in the centre of the living room, in front of the huge fireplace, the flames roaring, the low ceiling weighing down on me. I feel claustrophobic, trapped in my own home, for the first time since moving in. I need to get out. I need air.

I open the door in the conservatory leading out to the back garden and step out into the cold, black night. Nanook shoots past me and charges up the grass to the trees. I stand on the patio, my hoodie fully zipped up to my neck to stave off the chill, a full glass of Bushmills in hand. I can't remember how many I've had this evening.

I look up at the dark sky and close my eyes. I inhale deeply, feeling the cold sting my nostrils. It's a pleasure to breathe in the fresh air after being surrounded by the lingering smoke fumes. I exhale and my breath forms a huge cloud in front of me which drifts out across the garden and disappears. I wish I could do the same.

I look down and see that Nanook has found a tennis ball and brought it to me. He stands back, looking from me to the ball and back again. It's dark and far too late to be playing ball, but screw it. I smile. I bend down, pick up the ball and lob it as hard as I can to the far end of the garden. Nanook charges off, his paws pounding on the cold, firm ground. He brings it back and drops it at my feet.

'You could do this all night, couldn't you?' I say as I throw it again.

I don't care that it's late. I don't care that my teasing Nanook by pretending to throw the ball results in the German Shepherd barking loudly and excitedly and the sound echoes around the village. I have no direct neighbours to complain. And if they did, who cares? Where were they on the night my home almost burned to the ground?

I throw the ball again and this time follow my companion, my last surviving friend, up the garden. Nanook isn't too happy the game is ending, but falls into step with me, the ball in his mouth. I limp into the thicket of trees, their naked yet thick branches blocking out the light from the moon, plunging me further into darkness. I carry on walking until I reach the wall, my boundary, and turn, looking back at the house. I can just about make out the light in the conservatory from here. Apart from that, it looks to be in complete darkness: abandoned, almost.

I lower myself down the wall and sit on the cold, wet ground. Nanook joins me.

'If it wasn't for you,' I begin, putting my arm around the dog's neck and cuddling him, 'I'd stay here all night. I'm sure it's cold enough for hypothermia to set in. I wonder how long I'd be here before someone found me. There's no chance of Luke coming back any time soon. Maybe DS Marshall or that DI Finch might turn up wanting more answers to their pointless questions. They'll knock and knock and, when there's no answer, they'll go away, but they'll be back. Eventually, they'll realise something's amiss, and they'll search the grounds and they'll come across me back here like Jack Nicholson at the end of *The Shining*. I wonder if it's a painful death. Do you actually feel your blood going cold, your heart rate slowing and your organs freezing? I may have to look into that. It could be good for another book.'

I look down at Nanook. His tongue is out, and he's panting. The ball is between his front paws.

'I'm only here for you, Nanook. When you go, I'll go. We'll go together.'

Chapter Thirty-Seven

Dear Aidan,

I've wanted to write this email for days, but I didn't know how to start it. Every time I did, I deleted it and started again, but was never happy with it. I don't really know if I should be writing to you at all.

I had a visit from the police, a DS Marshall. I'm guessing you already know about that. She told me that you've been receiving some unwanted attention. That's how she put it. She asked a lot of questions and seemed to want to know my whereabouts for certain dates but wouldn't tell me why.

I'm not a stalker. She never mentioned the S-word, but that's what she was hinting at. I could tell. I'm a fan. That's all. I've been through some dark times and your fiction has helped me. I enjoy your books. You really are a brilliant writer. You create amazing, real characters and always wrongfoot me when I think I know where the story is heading. I didn't mean you any harm with my emails. I just wanted someone to talk to.

I shouldn't have turned up at your house like that. I truly am sorry. I don't know why I did, a momentary lapse into madness, let's say. I often look out for you online and your agent has updated her

website recently. It mentioned that you live in the village of
Gallowsfield in Derbyshire. It's not far from me, only an hour's drive.
It didn't take much asking in the village to find out where a reclusive
author is living. I wanted to apologise to you in person. I wanted to
show you how much you've meant to me over the years. I've had a
few problems. My ex-husband, well, I won't go into details, but he
was a horrible man, and your books were a salvation for me. People
think books are just there to be enjoyed, but they're not, they're more
than that. They can be life savers. Yours saved my life.

I'll not email you again, and I certainly won't turn up at your
house again. You have a beautiful home, by the way. I'm sorry if I've
upset or frightened you in any way. I'll still read your books and I'll
always be a big fan.

Take care,
Rebecca Charlesworth

I wonder now if I'll hear from Rebecca again. She seems contrite and almost embarrassed to have caused me distress. After reading this, I feel more convinced that Rebecca isn't a threat. She has alibis for the murders and her apology seems sincere. And now that I think about it, I'd never been worried by her emails. Yes, they were frequent, especially around the time I had a new book out, but I never assumed I'd open my front door one morning to find her camping on my doorstep. It was DS Marshall and that supercilious computer so-called expert who said she represented a threat. Again, the seed of doubt was planted and through their intrusive investigation they have made a harmless fan feel pathetic, small, unworthy, bordering on the deranged. Yes, she shouldn't have turned up at my house. That was wrong and she knows that. Hindsight is a wonderful thing. But she's been through a great deal and my books offered her comfort. I can certainly sympathise with that. After my mum died, it was only by reading *Charlie and the Chocolate Factory* on a loop that I stayed sane.

I want to email her back, tell her I forgive her, say she can still email me if she wishes, just maybe once a month perhaps. But, at the back of my mind, I can hear DS Katherine Marshall telling me what a stupid idea that would be.

The police don't care about the effect they have on people's lives when they're investigating a crime. They storm in and take over and, once it's finished, they leave and to hell with the debris they've left in their wake.

Should I email Rebecca back? Should I keep the line of communication open? It sounds like she needs a friend. But then, friends can do more harm than good, as I know only too well.

I can't believe Lucy has practically posted my address on her website. Gallowsfield is only a small village. I doubt there are more than thirty buildings here. I may not leave the house much, but people around here obviously know there's a reclusive writer living on their doorstep and exactly which house I'm in. I'm bloody furious with Lucy. What was she thinking? I'll send her an email later and ask her to amend the details. I'm too angry right now to engage in a dialogue with her.

I answer a few messages before making a fresh coffee, giving Nanook a Bonio and getting out the notebook I'm working from for my next thriller. There's another nine months before the deadline, but I'm already more than halfway through the first draft. I could write more than I do. I never go out and my days are relatively empty, but I don't want the pressure of producing more books and making the writing process harder than it already is.

Ernest Hemingway once said that writing was easy. All you do is sit at your typewriter and bleed. I think that sums up writing perfectly. Every time I'm at the beginning of a new book, I start a fresh notebook, open up a new document on my computer and tear open a vein. It's a back-breaking, anxiety-inducing, soul-sapping job, but I love every minute of it. I'm obviously a fan of self-flagellation.

―――――――

I'm an hour into my work when my mobile rings. I look at the screen and see that Lucy's calling. She's obviously read my email. I swipe to answer and she's full of apologies. She's already called the office and asked them to remove the details of where I live. Too late for that: the damage has already been done.

'I just wanted to see how you're doing after the fire,' she asks.

'Fine. The house is going to need redecorating, but structurally, everything's fine.'

'Have the police made any headway in finding out who did it yet?'

'No. Not yet. Investigations are still ongoing – the usual line they peddle out when they haven't a clue.'

'I'm still in your neck of the woods, Aidan. I can pop across and see you, help out, if you like?'

'No. I'm fine. Honestly. Thank you, though,' I answer quickly.

'It really is beautiful up here, isn't it? I think this is the furthest north I've ever been. Such wide-open spaces, and quiet, too. You don't get this in London.'

I'm not sure what to say to that so I remain quiet.

'We don't need to talk about business. We can have a chat about anything you want.'

'Lucy, it's fine. Besides, the house is in a mess. The fire knocked out the heating. It's freezing here,' I lie, but I'll tell her anything to stop her from coming.

'OK. Well, I'm here for a few more days so, if there's anything you need, or if you just want to talk, let me know.'

'I will.'

I won't.

'I'll leave you to it, then. Take care, Aidan.'

'Bye.'

I hear a car engine start just before she ends the call. Out of the corner of my eye, I see a white car pass my house. Coincidence? Or was Lucy Graham making the call from outside my home?

The sooner I get some new gates for the end of the driveway, the better.

Chapter Thirty-Eight

When you do the same thing every single day, the days tend to merge into one another. Weekends and bank holidays don't exist.

I wake up, eat, work, read, feed Nanook, go to bed, and start again the following morning. This is my routine seven days a week, three hundred and sixty-five days a year.

But today is an unusually busy day. A fire door is fitted in the dining room by a man in his fifties and two men from a company in Sheffield come to measure up my new gates, talk me through the designs and give me a ten-week waiting time. There are no phone calls or texts from Luke. I'm not disappointed. Communication is a two-way street, and I haven't made an effort to contact him. I truly am on my own now.

With the oak gate no longer working remotely, the postman is able to walk up to my front door without being buzzed in. The only time I know he's been is if Nanook barks or the doorbell is rung.

I'm busy writing an interview chapter. A suspect had been identified and the detective is giving him a grilling, despite the suspect being confined to a hospital bed.

The doorbell rings. Nanook barks and I jump. I'm much more nervous of someone coming to the house since the fire, since Rebecca's appearance.

I look out of the window and see the bright red Royal Mail van at the top of the drive and the postman heading for it. He's obviously dropped off something that doesn't need a signature. I wait until the van drives away before opening the front door.

There are two packages of a similar size by the doormat. I pick them up and take them inside, locking the door securely behind me.

In the kitchen, I open the first one carefully and pull out a bottle of expensive Bushmills whiskey. A note is attached, from my agent's office, wishing me a very happy publication day.

I frown as I try to remember the date. I didn't even realise it was Thursday. Of course, today is publication day. It's completely slipped my mind. The second box contains a bottle of champagne from my publishers. I don't mind a glass of champagne, but it brings back painful memories of the defunct launch night of my debut novel all those years ago, when I realised how friendless and alone in the world I was – and still am. Champagne is a drink for company. I doubt I'll ever open this bottle, but I smile at the gesture.

Back in the study, I log on to Amazon. *The Confession of Billy McLean* is riding up the crime fiction charts. There are already seven reviews, all of them five stars, and, if memory serves me correctly, there is to be a love letter of a review in this weekend's edition of the *Sunday Times*. It would appear I have another success on my hands.

I sit back in my chair and fold my arms across my chest.

My success is bittersweet as I have nobody to celebrate and share all of this with. I often read of other authors' publication day celebrations with partners and family members, whereas I continue working. There's nothing else for me to do.

It's times like this when the loneliness sets in, and the dark thoughts return. Everything I work hard and strive for ends in a huge anticlimax. I shake my head. I know I'm being needlessly melodramatic. Writing, for me, is not about the adulation, the bottles of champagne and expensive whiskey. It's not about going for celebratory meals to give myself a pat on the back. I truly love what I do. It's what I've dreamed of doing since I was a child. I always wanted to write and now I'm living my dream. And I love my characters, too, all of them, even the bad ones who commit such heinous crimes. I have to love them in order to write them. I love getting inside their heads, working out their backstories, discovering why they become killers and, indeed, why the victims become victims. It's fascinating. People often say I should write a series, but I wouldn't write one from the point of view of a detective. That would be dull. I'd love to write one in the first-person narrative from the killer's point of view, like the Tom Ripley series by Patricia Highsmith. I'd love to dream up a killer who goes from book to book, gaining sympathy from the reader even though he's committing the worst crime of all. Something to think about.

'You've reached Luke Jackson. I'm obviously busy. Wait for the beep, you know the rest.'

'Luke, hello, it's me, Aidan. Erm … how are you? Busy, I'm guessing. I'm not sure if you remember, but today is publication day. Book seven, if you can believe it. Anyway, I thought I'd check in, see how you are, and I wondered if … well, if you fancy having a chat and drink later to celebrate, give me a ring.'

It took me three hours and a couple of glasses of Bushmills for me to find the courage to phone Luke, and that was the state of the message I was able to leave. And I'm an award-winning writer, apparently. I look down at the blank screen and wish I hadn't even bothered. I doubt Luke will ring back. I've opened myself up to being hurt, waiting for a phone call that I know won't come.

———————

I open my eyes. I must have nodded off, or passed out, more likely. I have an empty glass in my hand and my hoodie is wet from where the alcohol spilled out all over me while I was asleep. I'm more disappointed by the waste of alcohol than I am about the hoodie. My phone, beside me on the sofa, is blank. No messages or missed calls from Luke.

It hurts. Yes, I've brought it on myself by questioning Luke's loyalties and motives, but I don't deserve this.

My phone rings. A smile spreads across my face, but when I reach for my phone, I see that it's DS Katherine Marshall calling. My smile drops. My head aches slightly from the amount of whiskey I've been drinking, and I'm in no mood to speak to her, but after our last conversation, maybe she's calling with news. I take a deep breath and swipe to answer.

'Aidan, are you well?' she asks, sounding genuinely interested in the answer.

'I'm fine, thank you.' My standard reply. 'You?'

'I'm OK. I wanted to ask for your help. A body has been found in Monyash. I'm at the scene now. I've not read all your books but, if I describe the setting, will you be able to tell me if it's from one of your novels?'

I swallow hard. *Not another one. I don't want to hear this.*

'OK.' I brace myself and pull Nanook closer. I feel cold, as if the blood in my veins is beginning to freeze.

'I'm at the Lathkill Dale Campsite. A man in his mid-twenties with his throat cut. He's naked and there's blood everywhere. There are signs of a disturbance, but we don't know if there's anything missing.'

I tune her out. The background seems to fade, and I can't focus. This isn't happening. What the fuck is going on?

'Aidan, are you there?'

'Did you say you were at a campsite?'

'Yes.'

'Is the body in a caravan?'

'Yes.'

'Oh my God!' I run a shaking hand over my hair.

'What is it?'

'Are there many other caravans close by?'

'A few. It's out of season.'

'You need to check the others. There might be a body in another one.'

'What?' she asks, her voice rising an octave.

'In my book, a body is found in a caravan. When police knock on the doors of others to see if they've seen anything, they find another victim killed in exactly the same way.'

'Jesus! Right, I'll get on it.'

'Wait. Is this a recent crime?'

'Hang on.'

I wait. I can feel tears building up inside me while I hear a muffled conversation in the background.

'Aidan, I've been speaking with the pathologist, and she reckons he's been dead for at least thirty-six hours.'

'Rigor mortis has been and gone,' I say.

'Yes. Is that significant?'

'No. It's just that the book this crime refers to is my most recent one, *The Confession of Billy McLean*, and it only went on sale this morning.'

'This young man was killed before your book was released.'

'Oh my God,' I exclaim.

'Look, calm down. We don't know if this is like your book yet. There may not be a second body. I'll get uniform to search. I have a few things to attend to here and then I'd like to come over to yours to ask you more about this, is that OK?'

'Yes. Thanks.'

'Aidan, make sure all your doors are locked.'

I hang up the call. I can't believe this has happened. And who has read the story before it's released? My publishers, Lucy, early reviewers. And, of course, Luke could have read it at any point while he's been in the house. That last thought makes me shiver. The last time I'd tried to reach Luke and my calls went unanswered, my house was almost burned to the ground. He's not answering now. Where is he?

THE No1 SUNDAY TIMES BESTSELLER

AIDAN CULLEN

Can you trust an innocent man?

THE CONFESSION OF BILLY McLEAN

'An accomplished
and original thriller'
THE SUN

'Cullen is a master
thriller writer'
THE SUNDAY TIMES

Chapter One

It's strange how life can change so dramatically so quickly. He had never meant to kill anyone. That wasn't his intention when he left his flat less than an hour ago. It was supposed to be a normal, regular appointment. Within minutes it descended into a nightmare. A real-life hell.

And now, here he was, at almost one o'clock in the morning, standing in the middle of a caravan park, the cold winter wind whipping around him, drying the blood spatter on his exposed skin.

He brought his hands up to his face. They were shaking. Not just a shiver from the cold, but an actual uncontrollable shake, like his nan's used to have towards the end of her life when she had severe Parkinson's disease. His bottom lip quivered at the memory and tears formed in his eyes. The wind wouldn't allow them to drop and blew them out of his eyes.

If his nan could see him now, she would be so disappointed. One of the last things she said to him was that he had a brain somewhere in his head and, if he didn't start using it, he'd be in prison before he was twenty-five. It looked like her prophetic warning was about to come true.

Unless.

His nan was right. He did have a brain in his head. He did very well in his GCSE exams, and he would have achieved decent A-Level results had he not fallen in with the wrong crowd. He was easily led, that was his problem. No. Now wasn't the time for excuses. He needed to act. He needed to use whatever brain power he had to find a solution. He could get away with this if he put his mind to it.

The easiest way was to set fire to the caravan and

destroy all evidence of him being there, but that was flawed. One, he didn't have anything to set it on fire with. Two, people in the neighbouring caravans were bound to wake up at the sound and smell of the fire and call 999 before it had time to get hold. Three, the police would know exactly who was in the caravan and reach a very simple solution.

He needed to be creative. He needed to throw the police off the scent. This could not look like a targeted attack, which was how they'd view it. This needed to look completely random.

He looked around him in the darkness, shaking wildly as adrenaline and horror began to take hold. This was madness, but it had to be done. He was going to have to kill someone else.

There were eight caravans dotted around the site, all of them in darkness. He had no idea if they were all occupied or how many people were in each one. A young family here for a long weekend, an elderly couple having a few days away, mates on a weekend piss-up. It was going to be pure bad luck for whomever he chose. Whoever it was would lose their life, but there was no other solution.

He stepped out of the shadow of the caravan in which Marcus Braithwaite was rapidly going cold.

The one next to Marcus's was a large family caravan. He immediately ruled out that one. There could be children sleeping in there. There was no way he could kill a child. The thought alone made his blood run cold.

The one next to that looked clean and brand new. He imagined a young couple sleeping inside. With not enough money to holiday abroad, they had bought a caravan to go touring around the country in. It wouldn't matter where they went as long as they were together.

He moved on to the next one. He ran in short bursts, head down low so as not to be seen.

'For fuck's sake, just pick one,' he chastised himself.

He knew he was making excuses, and soon he would run out of options. It didn't matter who was in there – an elderly man, a young woman, a child, a baby or someone in a wheelchair. All he had to do was break in and kill whoever was inside in the same way he'd killed Marcus, and then fuck off home. Within half an hour he'd be back in the safety of his own flat, standing under the weak dribble his landlord laughingly called a power shower. Then bed. Then sleep. Then oblivion, hopefully.

He braced himself. He took several deep breaths to try to settle his nerves. It didn't work. He was heading towards a single-berth caravan at the far end of the park, his steely eyes firmly fixed on the door. He gripped the knife in his left hand; his right was a tight fist. He could hear the blood thundering through his veins. He licked his lips several times and tasted the metallic tang of Marcus's blood. He swallowed hard.

'I've got no choice. I've got no choice,' he repeated over and over to himself like a mantra as he reached the off-white caravan with a thick blue stripe around the middle.

He looked around him. There was no one there. He took one final deep breath, placed his cold, bloodied hand on the handle and yanked it open. It took three attempts, but eventually the lock snapped. He was in.

Chapter Thirty-Nine

I'm in front of the computer looking at the camera feed from above the gate. All I see is blackness.

As soon as I ended the call with DS Marshall, I limped around the house, making sure all the doors were locked and the windows secure. The sensors were on, and alarms set. If anyone tried to gain entry, I'd soon know about it. Although, if they did, what could I possibly do about it? I live too far away from anyone for my alarms to be heard. I doubt even the farmer in the next field would hear. Maybe his cows would. Maybe they'd become distressed, start mooing and wake him up. But by then it would be too late. Whoever had broken in could have killed me and Nanook.

I limp into the kitchen. My back is hurting me tonight. It might be from the unnatural position I was in when I nodded off on the sofa, or it could be the nervous tension I'm feeling. I can't remember the last time I did my exercises, and I've been drinking more than usual lately. Could the alcohol have lessened the impact of my medication?

I put my hand in my pocket and my fingers touch the flick

knife. I'd forgotten it was there. I take it out, rest it in my palm and look at it. This was the knife that stabbed me. It's old. It's scratched. It's chipped. It's rusted. There's dried blood in the mechanism. I press the button and the blade comes out in a stunted motion. It still looks sharp. It can still cause some damage. I look down at Nanook, always by my side.

'I'll protect you. I know I'm not Luke, but I'll protect you until my dying breath. I promise you.'

Nanook tilts his head to one side as if he understands every word I've just said. Maybe he recognised the word 'Luke' and thought the confident, good-looking one was returning to take him for a run in the woods. I grab the red box of Bonios, pull one out and offer it to Nanook. His eyes light up as he opens his mouth and gently takes the biscuit from my palm.

Back in front of the computer, my attention remains fixed on the screen. I have a glass of Bushmills on the desk, next to the flick knife. Did DS Marshall say she was coming over or did I imagine it? I remember her telling me to make sure I lock the doors, but that doesn't mean she's coming. She's only in Monyash. She should have been here by now. Unless. Has the killer got to her? Has she been run off the road? Is she lying in a ditch struggling to reach for her phone as she gasps her dying breath?

The security screen lights up with approaching headlights. I wait until I can see what car it is, who's driving and how many people are in it. The last thing I need right now is a house full of people. It's a dark red Peugeot. I don't recognise the number plate and the last time DS Marshall visited she'd been driving a blue Peugeot. I pick up the knife and wrap my fingers tightly around the cold handle.

The doorbell rings. Nanook barks.

It's strange to no longer hear the intercom buzz.

I go to the front door and peer through the spyhole. I feel myself relax when I see that it's DS Marshall and she's alone.

I remove the door jammer, unlock the four locks I now have on the door, and remove the security chain.

'Hello, Aidan,' she says, solemnly.

I give a weak smile and stand back to let her in.

She unbuttons her coat and removes her beanie hat while I close the door and secure the locks behind her.

'Sorry it took me longer to come over than I … what's that?' she asks, noticing the knife in my hand.

'Oh. Sorry. I thought I … I don't remember picking it up. I had it next to me. For protection.'

'You really shouldn't arm yourself with a knife, Aidan,' she says, gently taking it from me. She heads for the kitchen.

'I had to use something in case someone broke in.'

She places the knife on the counter. 'A couple of years ago, a woman in Chesterfield stabbed her husband in the stomach. He died and she was charged with murder. Her defence was that he'd been abusing her for years and she'd finally snapped. However, the prosecution argued that, because the attack happened in the bedroom, she'd have had to have gone from the kitchen up two flights of stairs to the attic with a knife before stabbing him. A premeditated act and not one of an abused woman snapping.'

'What happened to her?'

'Eventually she was found not guilty of murder but guilty of manslaughter on the grounds of diminished responsibility. She was given a suspended sentence, but it was a lengthy trial which, I think, affected her more than the abuse did. What I'm saying, Aidan, is don't walk around your house with a knife in your hand. If you stab someone in your bedroom and say it was self-defence, the prosecution is going to go into every detail about why you had a knife in your bedroom in the first place. I've seen the way victims are treated in the courtroom. It's not pretty.'

I watch her as she goes to the other side of the kitchen.

'Can I help myself to a coffee? I've not stopped all day.'

'Sure.'

She fills the kettle up and switches it on.

I clear my throat. 'There was a second body, wasn't there?'

With her back to me, she nods.

'Oh my God!' I buckle and grab onto the worktop to keep myself upright. 'Why is this happening? Why on my doorstep?'

'That's not my main concern at the moment,' she says. 'Your book was only released yesterday. I need to know the name of everyone who knew the plot before the book was published.'

The kettle boils.

'Would you like me to make you one?' she asks.

'Please. There's a bottle of whiskey in the cupboard above the kettle. Pour a measure into my coffee, please.'

'Is that wise?' she asks, an eyebrow arched.

'After the day I've had, I've never needed it more.'

The living room is lit only by a standard lamp in the corner and the flames from the fire. DS Marshall and I sit on opposite sofas. Nanook is next to me. He can sense I'm tense, but his head resting on my lap is relaxing me.

I take a long sip of my coffee. The hit of strong caffeine and even stronger Irish whiskey is like a shot of adrenaline straight to the heart. I look up at DS Marshall; her face is blank.

'Tell me about your latest book,' she says.

I have another sip of my drink and take a deep breath. '*The Confession of Billy McLean* is a novel about misdirection,' I begin. My voice is quiet, barely above a whisper, but it sounds tired and hoarse. 'From the point of view of the detectives, the identity of the first victim will lead them directly to the killer, but when they take in the scene at the caravan site as a whole, find the second victim, the bloody fingerprints on other caravans, they believe it was a random spree event. One man murdering and robbing in a blitz attack.'

'But the first victim is key?'

'In my book, yes. The first victim is a drug dealer. He's killed by a customer in a deal gone wrong. The murderer covers his tracks by killing again, as he knows the police will knock on his door. Were there attempted break-ins on other caravans?'

'Yes.'

'Jesus! It's exactly like the book, then.'

'And, as I said on the phone, the pathologist who attended the scene believed the victims to have been killed at least twenty-four to thirty-six hours before your book was released.' She leans forward, her face searching. 'Aidan, who knew the plot of your book?'

'I've been thinking about this. My agent, my editor, my publisher. Copy-editors, proofreaders, beta-readers, sensitivity readers, bloggers, reviewers, anyone with a subscription to NetGalley, newspaper and magazine reviewers. Then there's my editors in other countries, their assistants, translators. And then there's the people I've sent free copies out to. I received my complimentary copies more than a month ago. It's a big list.'

'OK. I'm going to need contact details for your agent and publishers. Hopefully they'll be able to draw up a list of people who read it once you submitted it to them.'

'No problem.'

'What about Luke? Does he know the plot?'

I look up at Katherine slowly. 'No. I don't discuss my plots while I'm writing. It's a weird superstition I have.' I half smile.

'Did you give him a complimentary copy?'

I shift in my seat. 'Yes. He always gets a signed copy of my books. But I don't think he's read it.'

'Why not?'

'I've never seen him read a book in his life.'

DS Marshall places her mug on the coffee table and rests her elbows on her knees. 'Why are you two friends?'

'I'm sorry?'

'The way I see it, you have absolutely nothing in common, yet you've been friends for so long.'

'I think if we did have a lot in common, we wouldn't get on as well as we do. Two matching personalities don't make for a good relationship. I think our strength is that we don't share similar traits.'

She sighs and leans back on the sofa. 'Who else did you give copies to?'

'A couple of authors I know. And I did a competition on my website. I gave away five signed copies.'

'I'll need their names and addresses, too.'

I nod.

'Aidan,' DS Marshall says, leaning forward again, 'do you feel like you're in any danger?'

'Of course, I do. Wouldn't you?' I almost snap.

She blows out her cheeks. 'I need to get to the bottom of why someone would be targeting you, Aidan. It's either someone from your past, when you were living in Ireland or Liverpool, or someone from your present, either a work-related acquaintance, someone who works for your publisher or a jealous author, or, and I'm sorry to say this, even Luke.'

I stand up, put my arm in the crutch and limp over to the table that holds variously sized bottles of Bushmills. I pour a healthy measure into a glass and take a swig. I go over to the window, push back the curtain and look out into the black night.

'I haven't lived in Ireland for over twenty years. I don't have any family left alive.'

'Friends?'

'No,' I answer without turning to look at her. 'Although...' I begin, but stop myself.

'Go on.'

'My agent. Lucy Graham. She's a very good agent, don't get me wrong, but she likes her authors to be more publicity-focused. She wants them all over social media and attending events.

At first, I think she liked the idea of having a reclusive author to try to sell. She really built up the whole mystique about who I was, but, well, I think she's getting bored of it now.'

'Why do you say that?'

'She's been trying to get me to do interviews and telling me I need to change, to put myself out there more. I don't think she realises how difficult it is for me. I'm sure she thinks I'm playing a game rather than this being my actual way of life.'

'So why do you suspect her?'

'I don't. I just … she's in the area.'

'In Derbyshire?'

'I think she said Burton-on-Trent. She's up here for a family wedding and said she could pop over for a visit. I used the fire as an excuse to put her off visiting me.'

'Let me have her details. I'll give her a call.'

'Don't … I mean, I need Lucy. Like I said, she's a very good agent.'

DS Marshall smiles. 'I'll be very succinct.'

I try to smile, but I'm feeling anything other than optimistic.

'What about when you were living in Liverpool? You mentioned that on the night of the launch of your first book you realised you had nothing in common with your friends, that you'd all drifted apart. Could any of them resent your success?'

'Why would they?' I frown. 'They're all successful in their own fields.'

'You know that for a fact?'

I pause. 'I … well, I don't know, but Floella Montrose is doing well. She's on TV in an advert for Médecins Sans Frontières. You know, doctors without borders. The first time I saw the advert, I looked her up online; she's been all over the world. It doesn't look like she's married to Grey anymore.'

'Did you contact her?'

'No.'

'Why not?'

'I didn't have a reason to.'

'But you're friends.'

'Not anymore.'

'Surely it would have been nice for you to catch up? If I'd seen an old friend on TV, I'd message and say hello,' she says with a slight smile.

'My books are advertised in newspapers, magazines, airports and train stations. *The Science of Silence* was a Richard and Judy Book Club pick, and *My Wife* was talked about on *Loose Women*. My name has been plastered everywhere. She, and all the others, will have seen it many times. The lines of communication run both ways. Any one of them could have fired off a quick email saying they'd seen my books in an airport kiosk and were pleased I was doing well, but they didn't. They've moved on.'

'You sound upset about that.'

I limp back to the sofa and sit down. 'No. I think, on some level, it would be nice to have someone from my past contact me and say well done, but it just goes to show how little you mean to some people. Like I said, we've all moved on.'

'Then that only leaves the people who are in your life now,' DS Marshall states.

I shake my head. 'We're just going around in circles. I don't know anyone who would murder all these people, set fire to my home, and taunt me in this way. The only person who knows where I live is Luke. Yes, my agent and publisher have my address, but they don't know the house. They don't know Derbyshire. Everyone in this business is in London. They probably only ever venture beyond the M25 to go to the airport for a holiday abroad.'

'Which brings us to Luke.'

I wince.

'I know this isn't easy for you, but I have to ask these questions. Aidan, have you made a will?' she asks. I nod. 'Who benefits if you die?'

'Luke gets the house and everything in it. He also gets a fifty per cent share of my bank accounts. The other fifty per cent is divided between my agent and various charities. It's quite a simple will, really.'

'What about your literary estate? Who'll get future royalties and decision-making responsibilities if someone wants to make a film out of your books?'

'Royalties go to Luke. My agent will handle my literary estate.'

'So, Luke would stand to inherit a great deal if you died?'

'Yes. But you're forgetting that he seems to be the only suspect in this. Why would he be doing something where the finger of suspicion points directly at him? He can't inherit if he's in prison.'

'Unless he's planning to set someone up to take the fall for him.'

I let out a burst of laughter. 'That's ridiculous. You're making it sound like the plot of one of my novels. If Luke wanted to kill me, he could have pushed me down the stairs, made it look like I tripped over my crutch or something. He could have given me an overdose of my painkillers and made it look like suicide. There is no need for this elaborate charade.'

'Well, I will be contacting him to find out more about his whereabouts in Newcastle. I've got his number.'

I don't know what to say to that. After a long silence, she stands up from the sofa. 'I should be going. Will you put that list together for me and email it over as soon as you can?'

'Of course.'

'If there's any development with the case, I'll let you know straight away.'

'Thank you.'

'In the meantime, keep your security level up to maximum. And if you have any worries or concerns, phone me straight away.'

'I will.'

I follow her to the door, remove the jammer and unlock it.

'DS Marshall, Katherine, thank you for coming out here this evening. I appreciate it.'

She looks into my eyes, smiles, and rubs my arm. It's the first physical contact I've had with anyone for years. I'm not sure if I like it or not. 'I will get to the bottom of this, Aidan. I promise you.'

Chapter Forty

It's late by the time DS Marshall leaves, but I'm too wired to go to sleep.

I run myself a bath. I rarely take a bath, despite my physiotherapist telling me a soak in hot water is good for my back. But tonight, I feel a bath is needed to silence the miasma of dark thoughts screaming for attention. While the bath is filling, I return to the living room, where I pick up a near-full bottle of Bushmills and a clean glass, and limp back upstairs.

Nanook isn't allowed in the bathroom while I'm using it. Given the chance, the dog would happily curl up beside me on the mat, but there's something uncomfortable about a dog staring up at you when you're naked and drying yourself. So, after I enter the bathroom, I close the door behind me and lock it with the small bolt.

While the cast-iron bath is filling, I sit on the side, sipping my drink. I can feel the warmth from the steam enveloping me. I'm beginning to feel relaxed already. I should have a bath more often.

The room is large, and the walls tiled halfway up from the bottom. The bare walls above are painted a deep grey. It looks cold and empty, and every sound echoes. As the water pours from the taps, the gushing resounds, making it as loud as a waterfall.

I close my heavy eyes. I concentrate on the noise of the water and try to imagine myself floating in a wild river, being carried along with the current to deeper waters, the open ocean and into oblivion. I like that imagery. What would end my life, I wonder, if I walked into the sea? Drowning? Exposure? Hypothermia? I open my eyes and stand up from the edge of the bath. I sway slightly in a boozy haze.

The bath is more than three-quarters full. I turn off the taps, undress and step carefully into the bath. The water is hot, and I can feel the heat rising up my body, sweat prickling at my forehead. I lower myself into the water, very slowly, wincing at the heat. I could add more cold water, but I welcome this pain to draw my attention from the dark thoughts in my mind. Although, for once, my disturbed beginnings in Ireland are no longer my principal torment. All I can think about is Luke. Is my best friend trying to make me think I'm going mad? If so, why? Does he want this house? My money? I'm not super rich, but I'm comfortable. If he wants it, he can have it. I just want to know why he's doing this. Why now? What's happened to him? What's changed that's causing him to hurt me so much?

I lean back. Everything is submerged apart from my head. I reach out for my glass and take a long drink of whiskey. I've lost count of the amount I've drunk today. More than usual. I don't care. With everything going on at the moment, I need the alcohol to dull the stress and anxiety I'm feeling. A cuddle and a chat with Nanook are no longer enough.

The silence is loud in my ears. There's the odd drip from the tap, but all I can hear is my heart thumping loudly in my chest, the blood racing through my veins, the screams in my head. Who is screaming? I can never work out who it is, vying for attention. I wish they'd shut up, though.

Nanook sneezes outside the bathroom door. I open my eyes.

'Are you all right out there, Nanook?' I call. I hear the dog move about, settling down with a heavy slump against the door.

Sweat is dripping down my face. It mixes with the tears. I open my mouth to let out a sob and it opens the floodgates. I'm crying hard and I can't stop. I'm struggling to catch my breath as the dark emotions are released.

I lean over the edge of the bath and pick up my whiskey. With a shaking hand, I try to drink, but I spill most of it in the bath.

'I'm sorry, Nanook,' I cry. 'I'm so sorry.'

I drop the glass. It shatters on the tiled floor. I lean back, wipe my eyes and look up at the ceiling.

The room dances in my vision, a mixture of the steam from the hot water and the whiskey. My whole body is beginning to relax, and my head rolls forward, lolling on my chest. My eyes grow heavy, and sleep starts to claim me.

You should get out of the bath.

Why?

You could drown.

So?

You don't care that you'll drown?

Not anymore.

What about Nanook?

Luke will take care of him.

Wake up.

No. Go away.

Wake up!

Go. Away.

Aidan, wake up, right now.

Aidan?

Aidan??

Chapter Forty-One

I'm in my bedroom, lying on the bed, a towel around my waist. I feel cold. I'm always cold. I open my eyes and look at the white ceiling. I feel movement next to me on the bed, turn, and see Nanook staring at me. I reach out for him, stroke his warm head and close my eyes again.

There's a noise from somewhere in the room. A cough. My eyes snap open. My head hurts. I try to sit up, but my body is weak. I'm drunk.

Luke is standing in the doorway wearing dirty blue jeans and a blue sweater. His face is like thunder. His arms are folded tightly across his chest.

'Luke,' I slur.

'What the fuck is wrong with you?!' he shouts.

I wince. 'What are you talking about?'

'I come home. I find Nanook on the landing, barking at the bathroom door, water pouring out from underneath and you unconscious with your head under the water and an empty bottle of whiskey on the floor.'

'Ah.'

'"Ah." Is that all you can say?'

'I must have nodded off,' I say, struggling to sit up.

'You could have died.'

'Would it really have mattered if I had?'

'What if I hadn't come back? What would have happened to Nanook? He could have starved to death. I thought you loved him?'

'I do,' I say, reaching out to my dog again.

'You obviously don't, or you wouldn't have been so bloody stupid as to get pissed and try to drown yourself.'

'I wasn't trying to drown myself.'

'Really? What were you doing, then? Because from where I'm standing it looks like a suicide attempt.'

'I was just … taking a bath. I didn't realise how much I'd had to drink.'

'I've looked in the recycling bin. You've been drinking a lot lately. More than usual.'

'It helps me sleep. Look, Luke, can you stop shouting? I've got a headache.'

'I'm not surprised. I'm going downstairs to make you a strong coffee. Follow me down. We need to talk.'

Luke turns and heads for the stairs, his large feet banging hard on the floor.

I turn to Nanook. 'I think I'm in trouble.'

I enter the kitchen with Nanook in tow. I've swapped the towel for a dressing gown. I pull out a stool at the island and heave myself up onto it, placing the crutch carefully beside me. My head is pounding. There's a dullness inside me, as if I've had a heavy sleep. Things are missing, but at least the screaming has stopped.

'Are you going to tell me what's going on?' Luke asks. He's standing with his back to the sink, arms folded, face red with rage.

'There's been another murder. Two, actually. DS …

whatshername, Katherine, she came round and gave me all the details.' Luke's face softens as I tell him what's been happening. 'Have you read my latest book?'

He quickly looks away. 'Erm … no. Not yet.'

I smile. 'You haven't read a single one of my books, have you? Be honest.'

'No. I'm sorry. I'm not a reader. You know I'm not.'

'It's OK. I don't mind. The latest murders were like the ones that happen in my new book. But it only came out yesterday … or the day before. What day is it? Anyway, according to DS Marshall, the murders happened before the book was published, so whoever is doing this knew about the book before. If you get what I mean. I'm really tired,' I add. I slump forward, my head resting on my arms.

'Aidan, here, drink this.'

The smell of the strong coffee makes me sit up.

'So, what are the police doing about it?' he says.

I shrug as I lift the mug up to my lips and take a sip. I recoil at the taste. 'Bloody hell, that is strong. The police still think it's someone I know,' I say, looking at him over the top of the mug.

'Are we really doing this again? Have the police actually said they think it's me?'

'Not in so many words, but it's kind of obvious if you think about it.'

'What do you mean?' He stares at me in disbelief.

'I've tried to call you a few times and you've been suspiciously out of contact,' I slur. 'And you just seem to show up like you've popped in from next door, like tonight. I fall asleep in the bath and there you are to save me. It's like you knew that I was going to need your help. Are you really laying carpets and decorating student flats in Newcastle?'

'Of course I am.'

'So why are you here now?'

'Because I got your message. You mentioned that it's

publication day. I'd forgotten. I thought I'd come down and we'd celebrate or something.'

'Why not call?'

'I thought it would be a surprise.'

'None of it … I don't understand,' I say. 'It's like you're there when I need you. It's as if you're watching and stepping in at the right moment.'

'That's what friends are for. Aidan, I did not kill those people.'

I look up at him, meet his eye directly. 'The police think you did. DS Marshall is going to speak to you.'

'And what do you think?'

I don't reply.

Luke moves slowly around to my side of the island. He leans over me, our noses almost touch.

'You're out of your fucking head, mate,' he says, his voice low and filled with venom. 'You're batshit crazy, and I'm not going to stick around to be accused of this anymore. If you want to stay locked up in this house forever, go for it. Drown yourself for all I care! I've honestly had enough.'

I look into the eyes of my only friend in the world. There's a darkness there I've never seen before. And there's a feeling I've never felt around him before – fear.

Chapter Forty-Two

I'm slumped in my office chair staring at a blank computer screen. I'd had to adjust the brightness as it was hurting my eyes. My hands are folded together on my lap. I've been sitting like this for over an hour and haven't made any attempt to start work. I just don't have it in me today. Luke has gone, and I'm pretty sure he's not coming back this time. And, for the first time in years, there's a fire inside me, a desire to get my life back. I want this madness to stop. I want to reclaim my freedom and let the killer know that I will not be pushed into a corner.

'I think the only way the killings will stop is if I stop writing, or I die,' I say, turning to Nanook, as if hoping he will give an opinion. 'Mind you, even if I stop writing, they may still continue, as the killer hasn't been through all my books yet.'

I turn to look out of the window. The sky is a light blue with thin fingers of cloud dotted about. It looks Baltic but it's dry and bright. A beautiful winter's day. After the incident in the bath, I feel like something has shifted. If Luke hadn't come back then, I wouldn't be here. But there was something about that fight that left me feeling scared. In a way, I'm glad he's gone. I've never felt that about him before. Thinking about it, Luke has always been the one to keep me here. Whenever anything's needed doing or whenever there's been a need to go outside, Luke has been the one to stand up and do it, leaving me in the house. He said he was looking out for me, that he knew I was afraid after the stabbing, but he's enabled me to become a recluse. Has he been holding me prisoner in my own home all this time without me even noticing? Wow, that is an incredibly dark thought.

I look down at Nanook. I feel a warmth growing inside me.

'I can't take this anymore. I fancy doing something different,' I say with a hint of a smile. 'Shall we go out for a walk?'

Nanook recognises the word 'walk'. He jumps up, ears pricked, tongue lolling and tail wagging. He's definitely up for this.

By the time I've changed into jeans and a sweater, put on a heavy winter coat and a pair of tatty walking boots, doubts have set in about whether I'm doing the right thing or not. It's been more than five years since I went further than the garden gate. I'm not sure if I can physically do this. However, I've promised Nanook and he's pacing the hallway. His face has the look of an excitable puppy. I can't let him down.

From the cupboard next to the door, I take out his lead and clip it on his collar, and then I unlock the door.

'Now, before we go out,' I say to Nanook, 'I need you to be by my side, OK? Don't go charging off and pulling me in every direction. We're just going for a leisurely stroll.'

I open the door and breathe in the cold air. I suddenly feel scared; I'm stepping into the unknown. Ever since the fire, I've felt the urge to go outside. It might be because I can't get the underlying smell of smoke out of my nose. Who knows, the killer might have done me a favour and unlocked whatever it is that's keeping me in the house.

Chapter One

I close the door behind me, lock it with all the keys and place them in my coat pocket, then zip it up to make sure they're secure. I take tentative steps towards the gate. Slowly but surely, I walk forward, concentrating on regulating my breathing and ignoring the sweat forming on my brow. I know I can do it, just one step at a time. Once over the invisible line where my property ends and the road begins, I stop and look back at the house.

'I'm doing this, Nanook. I'm really doing this.' I can hear the excitement in my voice.

We set off up the small incline. It's a narrow road with barren bushes on either side. A slight breeze makes the thin branches rub together. I can hear birds in the trees and somewhere overhead a plane is flying to an unknown destination.

Surprisingly, I'm enjoying myself. I look down at Nanook, who looks back up at me. He seems just as happy to be out on this walk.

After five minutes, we reach a crossroads. Turning left would lead to the farm next to my house and Leigh Road; straight ahead would take us into the village of Gallowsfield itself; and turning right would mean a very long countryside road leading to Sheldon. I'm not ready for Gallowsfield yet. There aren't many shops there: a newsagent and post office, a Co-op and a vet. Although there might be a coffee shop. I could buy a latte and a slice of cake and sit outside, soak up village life, show people that I'm not a recluse, that I am capable of being a normal person.

'Which way?' I ask Nanook. My voice sounds strong and confident.

Nanook turns left and I follow. I'm pleased. I'm not brave enough for the village. Not yet.

The road is long and narrow, and the incline is steeper the further we go. No cars pass us and neither do any people. It's like we have the whole countryside to ourselves. When we come to another junction, we don't even stop. Nanook continues walking and it's not long before we're on the Leigh Road and we reach the sad shrine to Melanie Burton. A few bunches of flowers are laid at the side of the road, but they've long since died, the petals withered and faded. I lean down and try to read one of the notes attached, but the rain has washed away the ink. I stand up and turn. I can see my house from here. It seems strange seeing it from this far away. It's almost alien. My beautiful big house built with gorgeous Peak District stone in a picturesque village in one of the most desirable and exquisite counties in the country. I bet I could have stood on this spot a hundred years ago and the view wouldn't have been much different.

Nanook starts walking, leaving me no option but to follow.

I breathe in the cold air and fill my lungs. I've genuinely missed this. When I first started out writing, the plan was always to buy a house in the countryside and have a dog or two. I imagined having a Range Rover and I'd put the dogs in the back and drive somewhere in the Dales, let them run free, stop off at a quaint village where I'd buy lunch from an artisan café. I had no idea, at the time, that my dream home would become my prison and, once the door was closed, it would stay closed and locked for five years.

I hope today isn't simply day release. I hope it's the beginning of a new chapter in my life. If I can go for a long walk and return home without incident, it could open up the world for me. I could pop into the village for fresh vegetables, buy a car and go on a day trip with Nanook, maybe even to the coast. Nanook has never seen the sea; he'd love it, I'm sure.

I'm smiling, and there's a spring in my step. I can't help myself. My head is full of plans which will hopefully become a reality.

There's a bench up ahead by a dry-stone wall. I sit down. I'm out of breath. This is the most exercise I've done in years. Nanook sits beside me, tongue lolling, panting hard. I should have brought a drink for us both.

'This is fun, isn't it?' I ask, my arm around Nanook, rubbing him hard. 'We should do this more often.'

'Good morning!'

I jump. I have no idea where the voice has come from. Nanook jumps up at the wall behind us. I turn and see a man in the field. It's the farmer I've seen often through my telescope. We've walked further than I realised.

'Oh. Good morning,' I say. This feels very strange. I'm about to have a conversation with someone I don't know.

The farmer approaches and immediately goes to stroke Nanook, who laps up the attention. 'Beautiful dog.'

'Thanks.'

'I've got three myself. They're getting on a bit now, mind.'

Through the telescope, I haven't been able to judge how old the farmer is. The way he holds himself and moves seems young, but up close his face is lined and his wiry hair is grey at the temples.

'One of them's almost blind and another's got arthritis in her back legs. Good company, though. I wouldn't swap them for the world.'

'Neither would I.'

'Not seen you round here before. Just moved here?'

I laugh. 'No. I've been here about five years. I live in Gallows View House.'

The farmer turns and looks over his shoulder. 'Ah, you're the writer?'

I'm suddenly very nervous. I feel exposed. 'You know about me?'

'The whole village knows about you. A world-famous writer who never leaves his house. I've heard plenty of stories about you in the pub.'

I frown. 'Oh dear. Nothing bad, I hope.'

'All fanciful.' He smiles and shows a set of crooked teeth. 'If people don't know, they make stuff up. Bill Cox, the landlord, he thinks you're in the witness protection programme. His wife reckons you're one of those ghost writers writing for someone famous and you're paid to live in isolation, so you won't talk.'

'Nothing so dramatic, I'm afraid,' I say, laughing anxiously.

'Is it true there was a fire the other week?'

'That's right.'

'Nobody hurt, I hope.'

'No.'

A gust of wind whips up from nowhere and I shudder.

'Do you want to come in for a coffee? The wife bakes for the shop in the village, but she always leaves plenty for us to eat.'

'Your wife?' I ask. I've never seen anyone else on the farm.

'Yes. Julie. Sorry, I haven't introduced myself – Robert Morrison.' He holds out his large, calloused hand.

Reluctantly, I shake it. 'Aidan Cullen. This is Nanook.'

'Come round, meet the wife,' he says with a smile.

'I can't. Sorry. I need to be getting back. I've got a deadline.'

'Oh. Well, you know where we are. Pop in any time. We're always here.'

'I will. Thank you.'

I step back from the wall and make my way down the road. I look back over my shoulder and Robert Morrison raises his right arm to wave.

'Just a regular couple, Nanook,' I say. 'A farmer and his wife living their lives in their own way. Nothing special. Nothing exciting. Simply existing.'

Chapter Forty-Three

Nanook comes charging into the conservatory without warning. I think there is someone out there, someone spooking my dog. I turn to look out of the window and see no one. But huge fat drops of rain are falling. Despite enjoying the snow and jumping into rivers when out with Luke, Nanook hates the rain.

I sit down and snuggle my dog.

'You're supposed to be a guard dog and you're frightened of a bit of rain,' I say. I stand up and lock the door, securing the Patlock over the handles. I'm about to enter the main house when the doorbell rings.

I freeze.

I can't get used to someone simply walking up to the front door and ringing the bell. It's going to be a long ten weeks until the iron gates are ready. I hoped they aren't delayed in any way.

The doorbell rings again and Nanook barks before dashing off through the kitchen and into the hallway.

I'll have to answer the door. Whoever is calling will know I'm in. I hope it's not that farmer or his wife coming round with fresh-baked goods. I don't want to start a friendship where we pop over to each other's houses uninvited for coffee. Has my impromptu excursion opened a can of worms?

Nanook steps to one side as I approach the door. I close one eye and look through the spyhole. It's DS Katherine Marshall. I sigh. Relieved. Even so, I would prefer one night alone with a book and a drink without having to talk about a killer on the loose.

I remove the jammer, unlock the door and take a deep breath before pulling it open. I shiver in the cold. DS Marshall is soaked. Her hair is flat to her head and rainwater is dripping down her face.

'Come on in,' I say, quickly moving out of the way and allowing her to enter. I close and lock the door behind her. 'I was in the conservatory; I didn't hear you pull up.'

'That's OK,' she says, wiping her feet on the mat and carefully removing her coat. 'The rain just started without warning. One minute it was dry, the next it was a deluge.'

'Let me take that. I'll put it in front of the Aga. Help yourself to a towel in the bathroom. Would you like a drink?'

'I'd love a coffee,' she says as she heads for the downstairs toilet. It's almost like she's a regular visitor now and comfortable with making herself at home.

Me and Nanook go into the kitchen. A few minutes later, DS Marshall follows. She remains in the doorway, a perplexed look on her face.

'Something's different,' she says.

'Sorry?'

'Something about you. You seem different.'

I smile. 'I went out today.'

'Really?' she asks, sitting on one of the stools.

'I was at my desk, and, I don't know, I wasn't really in the mood to write. I looked out of the window, and I just thought "I'm going for a walk." Before I could talk myself out of it, I put Nanook on his lead and we went out.'

DS Marshall matches my beaming smile. 'How was it?'

I think for a moment while I make our coffees. 'It was good,' I say. 'I enjoyed it.'

'That's good. I'm so pleased for you, Aidan. Where did you go?'

'We went up to the crossroads, turned left, went up the Leigh Road and to the farm and back. I even chatted with the farmer – something I wouldn't have done a week ago.' I set the coffees down on the countertop and sit on the stool opposite.

'It sounds like you've turned a corner.'

'Well, not quite, but I've reached the corner, which is the main thing.'

'Will you go out again tomorrow?'

I chuckle. 'I don't know about that. We'll see. Maybe in a few days.'

'I bet Nanook enjoyed it.'

'He did. He usually only goes out when Luke's home.'

Her face drops.

'Is something wrong?' I ask.

'It was Luke that I wanted to talk to you about. I've tried calling him – I've left a few messages – but he's not got back to me. Is he here?'

'No. He's in Newcastle.'

She looks uncomfortable. 'I'm not sure how to say this … but does Luke live here full-time?'

I frown. 'Yes. You know he does.'

'He doesn't have another address?'

'No.'

'Does he have his post delivered here?'

I'm confused by the question and where this is heading. 'Yes,' I reply, tentatively. 'Well, we don't get much post. Things like bank statements and bills are all by email nowadays.'

'So, he doesn't get any post?'

'Why are you asking about post?'

'Luke Jackson isn't registered on the electoral roll at this address.'

I raise an eyebrow. 'Isn't he?'

'No. But you are.'

'Huh! I've never thought about it before. I get a postal vote, you see, so I never wondered how Luke votes.'

'There's no vehicle registered to this address, either. You said Luke has a van.'

'Yes, he does.'

'Do you have the documentation for it?'

'Well, I don't, obviously. Luke will. Somewhere. What's all this about?'

Katherine can't make eye contact with me. She's clearly uncomfortable with the conversation. 'I'm wondering how much you really know about Luke Jackson.'

It's a while before I say anything. 'Are you trying to tell me he's been leading a double life or something?' I ask. 'Does he have a wife and children up in Newcastle?'

'Aidan, how sure are you that Luke Jackson is Luke's real name?'

My eyes widen in shock and I'm sure my mouth has dropped open. 'What?'

'I can't find any presence of him on social media. He's not registered with HMRC as being self-employed. He's not on the electoral register and he's not listed at any GP surgeries in the county.'

'I … I don't understand.' I climb down from the stool and go over to the conservatory. The sound of the rain hammering on the glass roof is deafening. I sit down on the edge of the sofa. Nanook comes up to me and places his head on my lap. He can sense I'm upset about something.

'How long have you known Luke?' DS Marshall asks, standing in the doorway. She has to raise her voice over the sound of the rain.

'Since university. More than twenty years.'

She comes over to me, crouches beside me. 'Think very carefully, Aidan. Do you remember anyone else ever calling him Luke, or by another name?'

'What? Of course other people called him Luke. His name is Luke. Luke Jackson. What are you getting at?'

I jump up from the sofa and storm into the kitchen, out into the hall and into the living room. I stand in front of the fire and warm my hands. They're shaking.

DS Marshall follows.

'Looking at the little evidence we have in this case, especially with the most recent murders copying a book that hadn't been released when they were committed, the list of potential suspects is limited. Coupled with the fact that we have to assume the killer is someone you know very well. Luke is the only person who fits that profile.'

'But … I don't understand. Why? Why would he set my house on fire? Why would he try to kill me?'

'He stands to inherit everything from you.'

'But he's known about my will for years. Why now?'

'Because you're worth a great deal of money now.'

'I'm not. I receive an advance on my books, which, when you break it down, comes to about … well, I don't know exactly, but it's not millions. Outside of the crime fiction reading community, I doubt you'll find many who have heard of me.'

'There's this house.'

'Oh, come on, you're clutching at straws. I've lived here for five years. If Luke is really doing this, why would he have set fire to it if he wanted the house? I need a drink.'

I go over to the oak table where I keep my various bottles of Irish whiskey and reach for my favourite. I wave the Bushmills at DS Marshall, but she declines the offer. I pour a healthy measure and slug it back in one gulp. I don't like what she is saying at all.

Things are slotting into place in a very ugly way. I pour another and go to sit down.

'When is Luke next due back home?' DS Marshall asks.

'I don't know. He comes and goes as he pleases, as he has every right to do.' I'm feeling very defensive. She can sense my tone but doesn't back down. After a moment's silence she examines me carefully before speaking again.

'Tell me about the night of the stabbing.'

The hair on the back of my neck stands up. Why is she bringing that up? I look at her. 'Why?'

'Is that what's kept you together all these years? He saved you, didn't he? I mean, that's bound to bond people together, isn't it? But sometimes, people think that if they've saved a life then they need to keep saving it, or that they're responsible for it.'

I shake my head. 'Are you saying Luke really isn't my friend? That he saved me once and now he's sticking around because he feels obliged to?'

'No. I'm trying to work out what the bond is between you.'

'Why? We're just friends. Mates. Does there have to be any deep meaning for it to exist? Aren't you friends with people from university still?'

'No, actually, I'm not.'

'Then surely that says more about you than it does about me,' I say, raising my voice. 'I'm able to maintain a long friendship while you're not. Why are you saying these things to me?' My hand shakes as I have another drink.

'I'm not trying to hurt you, Aidan.'

'Well, I'd hate to see you when you *are* trying to.' I go back to the table and refill my glass.

'All the clues point to Luke.'

'You said you have very little evidence.'

DS Marshall lets out a heavy sigh and runs her fingers through her damp hair. 'I really don't want it to be Luke, but I need you to explain to me why it isn't.'

I remain at the drinks table. My head is down, looking deep into the golden liquid in my glass. 'I can't,' I say quietly without turning around.

'Can't or won't? What aren't you telling me, Aidan?'

I don't reply.

'Is it about you being stabbed? Does all this go back to the night you were stabbed?'

Why does she keep talking about that night? What does she know about it? That was the night my whole life fell apart. I suddenly feel freezing cold and start to shake at the memories.

I hear tyres on gravel and Nanook barks. 'Oh my God,' I say, peeling back the curtain and looking out into the night. 'Luke's back.'

'I didn't hear anything.'

I turn around to face DS Marshall. I can feel the tears pricking my eyes and my hands shaking. 'Please. Don't say anything. Please. I'm begging you. There's something I haven't told you.'

Chapter Forty-Four

I should have known. Right from the beginning, I should have known something like this would happen. Everything always ends in tragedy for me.

I come round in a daze. I have no recollection of what's happened, but I immediately know it's something bad. I look around my stark kitchen. It's always so clean, so tidy, so bright. Now all I can see is red. There is blood everywhere. So much blood. Whose blood is it?

I'm not in any pain. Maybe I'm in shock. I look down and see my right hand clamped tight against my stomach, trying to stop the blood from flowing. It's not working. I can see it seeping out between my fingers. Surprisingly, I feel calm. Maybe it's the thought of life ebbing away from me. Maybe it's a good thing I'm dying. Maybe it's a good thing it will all be over soon.

Nanook comes into the kitchen. The sound of his nails on the slate tiles echoes around the room. His white fur is stained with blood. He's walking in it. His ears are down. He's as confused as I am and wants me to look after him. I can't even look after myself. I don't know where Luke has gone. I hope he's not coming back.

I've no idea where my mobile is. I need to call for help.

On the floor, lying against the island, DS Marshall is in an uncomfortable position. There's a smear of blood on the granite worktop where she held on for dear life before the energy drained out of her and she fell to the floor. She looked at me, pain, horror, fear in her eyes and gently closed them. She hasn't opened them since.

'DS Marshall? Katherine?' I ask quietly. I need her to wake up. She's a detective, for crying out loud, she needs to take charge here.

'Katherine. Please. Tell me what I have to do.'

I ease myself to the floor. I feel pain for the first time and blood continues to ooze out of my stomach. I feel light-headed.

I put my hand in DS Marshall's pocket, feel around for her phone and take it out. I unlock it, using her fingerprint. I scroll through the contacts trying to find a familiar name. What was the name of the DC who came with her that first time? The one who marvelled at my kitchen? I'm scrolling through the huge list of contacts but can't remember her name at all. I scroll back up, see the word 'Boss' and assume this is the best person to call.

A man answers. 'Katherine, what can I do for you?'

I try to speak, but no words come out. I can taste blood.

'Katherine? Is everything all right?'

'It's not Katherine. I'm using DS Marshall's phone. Something's happened.'

'Who is this?'

'My name is Aidan Cullen. Can you send an ambulance to my house, please?'

'Where's Katherine?' He sounds panicked.

'She's here. She's with me. I can't wake her up.'

'What's happened?'

'We've been stabbed. We've both been stabbed. Please. Help us. There's so much blood.'

'Shit. OK. I'll get help to you. I need you to stay on the line, Aidan. My name's Victor Finch. I'm Katherine's boss.' I can hear movement in the background and assume he's assembling his team. 'Now, explain to me everything that happened. Who stabbed you?'

I can feel the tears rolling down my face. I don't want to say his name, but I have little choice. It's gone too far. 'Luke,' I say, my voice barely audible.

'I'm sorry?'

'Luke. Luke Jackson.'

'Why did he stab you?'

'DS Marshall. Katherine. She was asking him questions.' I'm finding it difficult to breathe. 'She wanted to arrest him. For the murders. No alibi. There's … my kitchen … so much blood.'

'Aidan, I have an ambulance on the way. I need you to stay with me. Is Luke in the house now?'

'No. He left.'

Did he?

'How long ago?'

I don't answer. I can hear his voice, but it seems so far away. I'm not sure if he's talking to me or someone else.

'Aidan, are you there?'

'Yes. I'm sorry. I'm dying, aren't I?'

'Aidan, we're on our way to you now.'

'Please … will you look after my dog for me?'

'Aidan…'

'He's all I've got.'

Wake up.

I open my eyes.

There are people looking down at me. Their faces are pale, and expressions horrified. They're both wearing identical clothing, white paper forensic suits I've written about so many times. What's going on?

'Aidan?'

A man crouches down in front of me. Despite him wearing a face mask, I can smell the strong coffee on his breath when he talks.

'Aidan, I'm Brian. I'm a paramedic. We're going to patch you up then take you to hospital.'

'No.' I'm awake now. 'No. I'm not going to a hospital.'

'Aidan, you've lost a great deal of blood.'

'I'm not going. I'm sorry. No. I can't. I can't go. I can't.'

'He's in shock.'

'He's a recluse,' I hear a female voice say. A woman enters my eyeline. It's the same one who liked my kitchen. 'He never leaves the house. He told us he hasn't been out for five years.'

'I'm not going. I can't. I'm sorry, I can't.' My breathing is ragged. It hurts.

'We're going to have to sedate him.'

'No. Please. No. I can't go to hospital. Please. I need to stay here. Nanook? Please. Don't take me outside.'

Chapter Forty-Five

I open my eyes and close them again. It's too bright. I saw the room for less than a second, but I know it's not my bedroom, or any room in my house. Where am I?

I open my eyes again. There's a window to my right with a Venetian blind. The slats are half open and the blinding sunlight is streaming through. The walls are white. There's a door to my left. It's ajar and I can see a toilet. There's no carpet on the floor. It's tiles. I don't have tiles in my bedroom. I have carpet, grey carpet.

I look down at the bed. It's a hospital bed. I've got a canula in the back of my hand running to a machine at the side of my bed. There's an oxygen monitor attached to the forefinger of my right hand. I try to sit up, but it causes me so much pain that I scream out.

I'm hot. It's so hot in here.

I'm thirsty.

Where's Nanook?

The door opens and a nurse in a light-blue uniform walks in. Her hair is tied in a loose ponytail; strands are dangling around her face. She looks tired.

'You're awake,' she says with a hint of a smile. 'How do you feel?'

I try to speak but I can't. My mouth is too dry. I clear my throat, but it hurts.

'Where am I?' I croak.

'Chesterfield Royal Hospital.'

'Why?'

She looks at me with a heavy frown while she messes about with the machine next to me. 'You've been stabbed. Don't you remember?'

Now it's my turn to frown. 'I … don't know what… Stabbed?'

'It'll all come back to you in time. Try and get some rest.' She turns and heads for the door.

'Nanook,' I call out.

'Sorry?'

'Nanook.'

'I don't know what you're saying.'

I can feel the tears rising up inside me. I really need my dog.

'Nanook.'

'A doctor will come in and see you later. Go back to sleep.'

She leaves.

I run my hand through my hair, but there's nothing there. All I can feel is bristle.

I lean back on the bed. I don't know where I am or how long I've been here. I need to go home. I need Nanook.

When I open my eyes again, there's a doctor in a suit looming over me. He's a huge man with neat grey hair, broken capillaries on his nose, and I can see where he missed shaving this morning. He smells of a very tangy aftershave that's making me want to sneeze, but I know it'll hurt if I do so.

'Mr Cullen, you're with us. Welcome back to the land of the living. How are you feeling?'

'I don't know.'

'Slight confusion following anaesthetic isn't uncommon. Try to relax. It'll all come back to you.'

'What happened?'

'You've been stabbed, Mr Cullen,' he says in a cheery voice, as if this is an everyday occurrence for him. Maybe it is. 'When you were brought in, we thought it would be a simple repair of the stomach wall. No such luck, unfortunately. The tip of the knife had broken off inside you and it seemed reluctant to come out. A tricky little bugger. There was severe rupturing of your stomach wall and you've had a blood transfusion. It's healing nicely, though, now. Your oxygen levels are still low, but they're improving every day.'

'When can I go home?'

'It'll be a while before that can happen. Don't worry, we won't keep you here a moment longer than necessary. I've already got a list of people waiting for your bed.' He smiles a gap-toothed grin. 'Plenty of rest. I'll come and see you again tomorrow.'

Plenty of rest. That seems to be everyone's answer for everything.

The doctor leaves, taking a nurse with him, and leaving behind his smell.

I look around the room at the bland walls. It's too bright in here, and too hot. How can I rest when I'm sweating and uncomfortable?

I'm worried about Nanook. Where is he? He's going to be missing me so much.

I sigh. So, I've been stabbed. Again. History is repeating itself.

Chapter Forty-Six

Time is a lost concept in a hospital. There's nothing to do. I can't get up and go for a walk because I'm in too much pain and still hooked up to a noisy machine. I feel drained and shattered, but I can't sleep. I'm uncomfortable in this bed; the sheets could do with changing and I'd really love to have a shower. I've nothing to read and I haven't written anything for … well, I don't know how long. How long have I been here? Two days? Three? A week? A month? The world could have ended beyond the confines of these four walls and I wouldn't know about it. And where the fuck is my dog?

There's a light knock on the door and it opens. It's the doctor again with his gap-toothed smile. The aftershave comes in before he does.

'How are you feeling today, Mr Cullen?'

'The same as yesterday,' I say.

'Are you up to answering some questions from the police?'

'Of course.'

He fully opens the door and steps inside, followed by two people who look familiar, but whose names escape me.

'Hello Aidan, remember me? DC Gemma Graves.' She smiles.

Yes, I remember her. She liked my kitchen.

I give her a weak smile. 'Where's Nanook?'

'He's fine. He's at the station in kennels.'

'Kennels? He'll hate that.' I can feel the emotion rising up my throat.

'Honestly, he's fine. I've been to see him a few times. He's eating his food and his tail's wagging. He's perfectly fine.'

I really want to cry. I miss Nanook so much.

'He likes a Bonio in the afternoons. About two o'clock.'

'I'll see what I can do. Aidan, this is my boss, Detective Inspector Victor Finch.'

He says hello and sits down, unbuttoning his jacket as he does so to reveal a once white shirt that has been through the wash so many times it's practically grey.

'Aidan, we'd like to ask you some questions about the night DS Marshall came to your home. Do you feel up to it?'

I nod. I try to make myself comfortable on the bed, but movement hurts. I manage to shuffle myself into a sitting position.

'Aidan, any time you feel ill, or tired, let me know,' the doctor reassures me with a fake, saccharine voice. I still don't know his name.

'I'm fine.'

The doctor goes over to the window and sits beneath it. All eyes are on me.

'When DS Marshall, Katherine, came to your house, was Luke already there?' Finch asks slowly.

I think for a moment. 'No. It was raining heavily. I was pouring us both a drink and I saw lights through the gap in the curtains. I pulled them back and saw his van pull into the driveway.'

'OK. What happened that led to you and Katherine being stabbed?'

I take a deep breath and try to swallow, but my mouth is too dry. I reach out for the plastic beaker of water, but it hurts when I move. My doctor leaps into action. He pours me a drink and hands it to me. I take a lingering sip. It's room temperature and stale, but right now it tastes like a fine single malt.

'DS Marshall was asking me about Luke and the fact that there wasn't any record of him on the electoral register or with HMRC. I didn't realise. It was all news to me. That's when he came in. I think we both sort of ganged up on him. I suddenly had all these questions for him. DS Marshall wanted to know whether Luke had alibis for the times of each of the killings. She didn't accuse him as such, but it was obvious what she was getting at.'

'What were his alibis?' Gemma asks.

'He didn't have any.'

'He didn't have a single alibi for any of the murders?' Victor asks, incredulously.

'No. He said he was in Newcastle, but he's been staying in an empty building. There are no neighbours to witness his comings and goings.'

'Did he admit to the murders?' Victor again.

'No. He … he told me to tell DS Marshall that he wasn't the killer. He said I knew him better than anyone and that he wasn't capable of that.'

'What did you say?'

'I didn't help matters, I'm afraid. I can't remember what I actually said but he suddenly snapped. He started shouting. He screamed at me to tell DS Marshall that it wasn't him, but … I couldn't. I can't be sure it's not him.' I reach over to the bedside locker for a tissue to wipe my eyes. The tears are in full flow. I can picture it all. The look of horror on Luke's face. I've never seen him like that before.

'Aidan,' Victor begins. 'Do you think Luke committed those murders?'

I steady my emotions and take a deep, shaking breath. 'I really want to say no.'

'But?'

'But the evidence suggests otherwise, doesn't it? He has no alibi, he has a motive and now we've seen he's capable. I can't believe he's done this.'

Victor Finch shifts in his seat and looks at his colleague, Gemma.

'Are you all right, Aidan?' the doctor asks.

'I'm fine.'

I'm not.

'Aidan, do you have a photograph of Luke?' Victor asks. He seems to be getting desperate for answers now. He's getting louder.

I'm getting a headache. 'I don't think so.'

'You don't have any photos of your friend?'

I feel sick. 'You take photos when you're out and about and having fun, don't you? Or when you're on holiday. I don't really have a reason to take a photo.'

'What about before you stopped going out?' Gemma asks. Her voice is still as calm as when she entered. 'There must have been photos of you and Luke hanging out together. You've known each other since university: you must have had your photograph taken at some point.'

I shrug. 'I don't know. There are some albums in the basement, I think. You could look through those.'

Victor and Gemma exchange looks, and Gemma quickly jots something down in her notebook.

'Aidan, we've been through your phone—'

'My phone? Why would you do that?' I interrupt. I'm getting light-headed. It's like I'm not here.

'It's what we do when we're investigating a murder and we have a person of interest we need to speak to,' he almost barks. 'The number you have listed for Luke doesn't work.'

'What does that mean?'

'It means it's no longer switched on. It was a pay-as-you-go number and is no longer in use.'

I look from Victor to Gemma and back again. I'm trying to read their faces, but I can't.

'Look, I'm getting the impression there's something you're trying to tell me. Normally, I'm good at reading between the lines, but I have a massive headache and I'm in a lot of pain. You're going to have to spell it out to me.'

Victor swallows hard. His Adam's apple bobs beneath the collar of his shirt and pops back up again. 'We believe Luke committed the murders in order to frame you so he could get his hands on your house and money.'

'He wouldn't have done that. He had no reason to do that. You're ... no. I...' I'm trying to get my words out, but I can't. I'm gasping for air. I see the doctor jump out of his seat and rush over to me. He grabs an oxygen mask from somewhere and places it over my mouth.

'I think we should leave the questioning there for now,' he says. He's right next to me, but he sounds echoey. 'Aidan, take slow, deep breaths. You're fine. You're safe. Calm down.'

'We have more questions,' I hear Victor say. 'We need a statement.'

'You both need to leave. Now.'

I can hear shuffling and moving about, but I've no idea what's going on. I hear the doctor ask for one milligram of Lorazepam.

I suddenly feel very tired, and everything around me blurs. I close my eyes and drift off into an unnatural sleep.

I've no idea how long DC Gemma Graves has been sitting by my bed. She's slouched in the chair, and she looks bored to tears, so I'm guessing it's a long time. I look past her, into the distance and through the slats in the blind at the window. It's dark outside. How long have I been asleep?

'You're awake,' she says. Her voice is croaky and her smile is tired.

I try to sit up.

'Is … is DS Marshall all right?' I ask.

I sit up slowly. Every millimetre of movement hurts.

'DS Marshall died, Aidan,' she says, softly.

I want to cry, but I don't think I have the energy.

'I'm so sorry,' I say.

Gemma nods. She's struggling to maintain her emotions.

'I liked her,' I say.

'So did I. Aidan, are you up to giving me your statement?'

I'm not, but I don't think I can really say no.

'What do you want to know?'

'Everything,' she says, more firmly. 'I want to know everything. We need to go right back to the beginning. I want to know about the night you were stabbed in the pub car park, to you moving into the house in Gallowsfield and right up to the moment my colleague – my friend – was murdered in your kitchen.'

I swallow. It hurts.

'That's a long story.'

'I've got plenty of time.'

Chapter Forty-Seven

I 'm awake.

The room is more silent than usual. The noisy machine by my bed has gone. My bladder is full, so I throw back the sheets and swing my legs over the side. It's the most movement I've done in … I don't know how long, and the pain from the stab wound is intense. I almost cry out in pain.

I lift up the hospital gown I'm wearing and look down at the huge padding taped to my stomach.

I walk tentatively into the en suite. I feel like I'm learning to walk all over again and have to hold onto the wall to keep from falling.

I pull the cord and the light comes on. It's bright and I wince, squeezing my eyes shut against the glare from the brilliant white strip-lighting above the sink.

I sit down to pee. My legs won't keep me upright for long. I go over to the sink and look at myself in the mirror for the first time in years. The sight is shocking. I don't recognise myself. This isn't me, surely. When I think of how I look, I think about my author photo. I remember having it taken. I remember going to have my hair cut at an expensive place in the centre of Liverpool, treating myself to a wet shave with a cutthroat razor. I remember looking at those photos and seeing myself looking dapper in a dark-grey suit, my dark hair neat and swept back, an enigmatic smile on my lips, the hint of wrinkles in the corners of my smiling eyes. That's how I've pictured myself. But I'm old. I'm drawn. I'm sad. I'm ugly. I don't recognise myself at all. Who is this man looking back at me? The light above reveals every crease and wrinkle in my face. My hair has been shaved. I'm so thin, gaunt almost.

'Who *are* you?'

Back in the room, I don't go straight back to bed. I walk, slowly, over to the window. I'd like to see what kind of view I have. There's a padded seat at the window. I sit on it and turn to look out. I see the grounds of the hospital, the bare trees, swaying slightly in the winter breeze, the brilliant blue sky and a low, dull sun. To my left is a driveway and, standing by an Astra, is Detective Inspector Finch talking to a man I don't recognise in a pin-striped suit. They're having what looks to be an intense conversation.

What are they talking about?

Finch looks my way and stops talking. The man in the pin-striped suit turns around and follow's Finch's gaze. They're both looking at me. They exchange a few more words and then walk away from each other.

They were talking about you.

They were talking about me. I know it.

There's a knock on my door. It opens to reveal a young man in a white polo shirt with the hospital logo on the left breast, and black trousers. He has short, curly blond hair, pale skin and bright blue eyes. There's a sickly smile on his lips that I instantly take a dislike to. He has a clipboard under his arm. I know he's not here to take my temperature, so I guess he's come to talk to me. But about what?

'Mr Cullen. My name is Stephen Bartholomew. I've come to have a chat, see how you're doing.'

Oh God, he's a bloody therapist.

I'm sitting up in bed. I'm not doing anything. I've no book to read, no pad and pen to write with, I'm simply counting down the minutes in my head until a doctor comes in to discharge me and I can go home to my dog and lock the door on the world. I'm definitely going to have to move now. I don't think I'll ever be able to go into my kitchen again without seeing all that blood.

'Are you a nurse?' I ask after I've cleared my throat. My mouth is permanently dry in here. I wish they'd turn the sodding heating down.

'I'm a mental health nurse.'

'Why do you want to talk to me?'

He steps fully into the room and closes the door behind him. 'You've been through a great trauma, and not the first one, I understand. Events like these can affect us in all kinds of ways.' He hitches up his trousers and sits down. 'That's why I've come to talk to you, to see how you're coping.' He smiles. But the smile doesn't reach his eyes. I don't trust him.

'I'm fine. Well, I will be once I get home and get my dog back.'

'Nanook,' he says, looking down at his clipboard. I wonder what else he has written on there about me.

'That's right.'

'Named after Nanook of the North?'

'Yes.'

'What breed is he?'

So he doesn't have everything written on his clipboard, then.

'He's a German Shepherd.'

'Ah. I've got a Springer Spaniel. He's five and completely bonkers. I've never known a dog to have so much energy.'

'Nanook's the same. He knows when to sit in his bed and relax while I'm working, but when he's in the garden and I throw his ball, he could fetch it and bring it back all day long and not get tired.'

'They're great companions, aren't they?'

'They really are.' I smile. I picture Nanook out in the garden, bounding about in the snow. I miss him so much. I really need him right now.

'Aidan. Sorry, do you mind if I call you Aidan?'

'No.'

'How are you feeling after being stabbed? I don't mean physically, I mean mentally.'

I take a deep breath before answering. 'I'm upset by what's happened. I feel betrayed.'

'By Luke?'

I nod. 'I thought I knew him. I thought we were friends.'

'Tell me about him.'

'What do you want to know?'

'What's he like as a person?'

I'm not sure how to reply to that. 'What I know, or what I think I know about Luke, doesn't match with the events that happened. I always thought Luke was a kind, happy person, but now I'm struggling to… I can't…' I shake my head.

'It's OK. I understand how conflicted you must feel.' He looks down at his clipboard again, then back up at me. 'Aidan, when you're discharged, will you return to your home?'

'That's the plan.'

'Do you think you'll be OK in that house after everything that's happened in it?'

'When I get Nanook back, we'll be fine.'

Stephen stands up. He approaches the bed and sits down on the end of it. I don't like him being so close.

338

'You look scared,' he says, softly.

'Sorry. It's nothing to do with you. I'm just not comfortable with people being so close.'

He stands up and goes over to the window, where he sits on the padded seat. 'That's OK. Personal space is important. There was a fire at your house recently, wasn't there? Were you hurt?'

'No.'

'Aidan, my job is to assess whether you pose a threat to yourself or others once you're discharged—'

'You think I'll try to kill myself?' I interrupted. 'Why would I do that?'

'You don't feel suicidal?'

'No.'

'Have you ever felt suicidal?'

I don't answer straight away. I've felt suicidal many times over the past twenty years. 'Occasionally.'

'I have a list here of the medication you're taking. You're on a very strong antidepressant and you take Lithium,' he says.

'Yes.'

'Do you ever miss a dose?'

'No.'

Liar.

'Do you ever take more than the prescribed dose?'

'No.'

LIAR.

'That's good.' He smiles again. He really shouldn't. It's not a friendly smile. 'Your home is important to you, isn't it?'

'Yes,' I answer straight away.

'Does it bother you that police and forensic officers have had access to it while you're not there?'

'Of course it does. But I know that, once I'm back home and I've given it a thorough clean, I'll be fine,' I say.

Lies, lies and more lies. They're all lies.

'Aidan, you were stabbed before, weren't you? About six years ago,' he says.

'Yes.'

'I'm guessing this has brought back bad memories for you.'

'It has.'

'Do you want to talk about it?'

'No.'

'Traumas can have unexpected effects on us. We think we're handling them, but we're not. Sometimes, our mind feeds us false information, to protect us from what happened,' he says.

'OK.'

Where is he going with this?

'When you were stabbed in the car park of the Bucket of Blood pub, whereabouts were you stabbed?'

I swallow hard. 'In the stomach. Twice. And once in the back.'

'Wow. It's lucky you survived.'

'Yes. Luke … came back to save me.'

'Luke saved you?'

'Yes.'

'Do you remember things from that night clearly?'

'Yes.'

'Even though it was six years ago?'

'Yes.'

I can feel a headache coming on, probably brought on by the heaviness of the frown on my forehead.

'OK.' He stands up. 'Well, I'm going to have a chat with my colleague, confer, if you will, and I'll come back and see you in a day or two.'

'When can I go home?' I ask.

'That's not my decision to make.'

'Then whose decision is it? Can I talk to them?'

'I'll need to talk to my boss, Professor Gillespie, who will need to talk to your consultant, and we'll go from there.'

'How long is all this going to take?'

'You're keen to get home?'

'Wouldn't you be? I hate this room. I hate how hot it is. I hate the fact that those sodding windows don't open. I hate the food. And I want my fucking dog back,' I say. I know I'm coming across as hysterical, but I don't care anymore.

'Leave it with me.'

He leaves, closing the door quietly behind him.

I sit back on the bed, but something is bothering me about the conversation we've just had. Why was he asking me about being stabbed six years ago? That's got nothing to do with this. It was a random mugging gone wrong. Unless... Do the police think Luke stabbed me six years ago? He did seem to turn up suddenly. And I know he's capable of hurting me. I know he's capable of murder. Is that why he's been looking after me all this time? Guilt. He's been driven by guilt. And now he's sick of looking after me, bored of having to pick up the pieces of my broken life. I realise I never really knew Luke, and the tears start to fall. He was my only friend in the world, and I never really knew him.

Chapter Forty-Eight

The man in the pin-striped suit turns out to be Stephen Bartholomew's boss, Professor Brendan Gillespie. He comes to visit me a couple of days after Stephen's visit. He's still wearing the same suit, or maybe he has a few of the same one. I can't judge him for that; I own several of the same hoodie at home.

He has a thick, stylish mound of dark grey hair, but his face looks young, which makes me think he's gone grey prematurely. Is it in his genetic make-up, I wonder, or has he had a stressful life? He's wearing a shiny, thick band on the third finger of his left hand. It looks new, as if he hasn't been wearing it for long. Newly married. Second or third marriage? Or maybe it's his first and he married late. So many possibilities. You can't get everything about a person from just looking at them, no matter what Sherlock Holmes thinks.

'You're a writer,' he says as he sits down on one of the plastic chairs. I'm not sure if he's asking me or telling me.

'Yes.'

'Thrillers,' he says, giving the word unnecessary intensity.

'That's right.'

'You must have to do a lot of research, especially into the psyche of the human mind and what makes people tick?'

'Not really. I have a lot of textbooks and there's a great deal on the internet.'

He crosses his legs. 'What do you know of the criminal mind?'

'Why are you asking me that?'

'I want to know your level of expertise.'

'I'm not an expert. I haven't studied psychology or criminology. I get what I need to know from the net and practically forget about it when I've finished.'

'Ah, you see, that's what I find fascinating. The thing is, we don't forget anything. It's all stored, up here.' He taps his temple. 'Our very own hard drive with unlimited space.'

He's not come here for a friendly chat. I get the feeling I'm going to have to be careful how I answer his questions. He's not listening to what I'm saying; he's more interested in what I'm not saying.

'Stephen tells me you're eager to go home,' he says.

'I am.'

'You have a dog.'

'Yes.'

'Would you like to go home now?'

It's a trap.

'Now?' I say.

'Yes.'

'As in right now?'

'Well, as soon as you've changed your clothes, yes.'

'I haven't had my stitches out.'

'I've spoken to your consultant, and we think it would aid in your recovery if you were able to pop home for an hour or two, see your dog.'

'I can see Nanook?' I can feel myself smiling.

'Yes.'

'But I'll need to come back here?'

'Yes. We know how important your home is to you, so we thought, if you were to go home, see what state the police have left it in, play with your dog for a while, it might help you. Your clothes are in your locker. Shall I come back in half an hour for you?'

He stands up and, without waiting for me to answer, he leaves.

I remain sitting up in bed. I don't like this. Something is wrong. Why are they doing this? Surely, they simply want to take my stitches out and discharge me. They're not interested in my mental well-being. But, on the plus side, I get to see Nanook. I'm also keen to see what the police have been doing in my house. If they've touched anything in my office and messed up my files, I will not be happy.

I climb out of bed and open the locker. My jeans and hoodie are in there, neatly folded. I can feel a warmth building up inside me. I'm going home. I'm going to see Nanook again.

Chapter Forty-Nine

I'm being driven home. I'm in the back of a very stylish Range Rover. Professor Brendan Gillespie is driving, with Stephen Bartholomew in the front passenger seat. Neither of them is talking. I get the impression they said everything they needed to say to each other before they came into my room to collect me.

This is definitely a trap. I'm assuming the police have been unable to find Luke and they're getting desperate. One of their own has been killed. They'll move heaven and earth to secure a conviction. Add to that the series of murders happening around Derbyshire in the past few months and the attention of the nation's press will be on them, too. Has there been another murder? No. They'd have already told me about that, especially if it copied one of my books. No. Something else is happening here.

It's a long drive, made even longer by the heaviness of the silence. I sit in the back, relaxing in the heated seats as I watch the landscape go by. The Derbyshire countryside in winter is beautiful. With the leaves off the trees, you can see far and wide. It looks cold, and a lingering frost is dancing in the sunlight. I love where I live. I love my surroundings. It's calming to live somewhere vast where there are very few people around.

I couldn't live in a city again. Whenever I think back to my student days in Liverpool, all I remember is the people and the wall of noise. How did I ever cope?

I see a sign saying 'Welcome to the village of Gallowsfield'.

My house comes into view. We turn off the smooth tarmac of the road and down my gravel driveway. I smile.

Hello, old friend.

I'm home.

Professor Gillespie pulls up beside a car and a police van. There are no people in the vehicles so I'm guessing they're already in my house. I feel like a visitor to my own house.

I open the car door and step out into the cold air. It's been so long since I've been outside that I'd forgotten how exposing it is. I shiver and pull my hoodie tighter around me.

'Are you all right?' Stephen asks.

'I'm fine. Whose cars are these?'

'I don't know.'

He's lying.

'Shall we go inside?' Brendan asks, like it's his home and he's welcoming me to it.

I fish my keys out of my jeans pocket, but the front door opens before I reach it. DC Gemma Graves greets me with a smile.

'Good morning, Aidan. You're looking well.'

'What's going on?' I ask. I look past her, but I can't see anything in the shadows.

'Nanook's in the back garden waiting for you.' She avoids my question.

I look at her face, trying to read the expression. There's angst in her eyes.

I push past her, ignore DI Finch in the kitchen making himself a cup of tea using my tea, my milk and my mugs, and head out into the back garden through the conservatory.

Nanook spots me straight away. He comes pounding down the garden, tongue lolling, eyes bright, ears pricked. I squat to my knees, and he ploughs into me, almost knocking me over. He fusses and licks and barks and yelps, and I grab him and cuddle him and stroke him. He looks thinner and his coat isn't as shiny. There's a strange smell to him, too. I know the police aren't looking after him how I do. I can't expect them to, really. The sooner we're back home together, the better.

'Mr Cullen, we need to talk,' DI Finch says from the doorway of the conservatory.

I look back at him. I really don't like him. What gives him the right to make himself comfortable in my home without my permission? I'm going to need all new locks when they finally leave me alone.

With Nanook by my side, we walk, slowly, into the living room. The kitchen has been cleaned, thank goodness. The last time I saw it, there was blood everywhere. Some of it mine. I'm pleased the police had the good grace to have it professionally cleaned before I came back. I'm not sure how I would have coped with seeing that.

Finch follows me. In the living room, a fire has been lit. I may have to write a letter to the chief constable of Derbyshire Police. I don't like the liberty his officers are taking with my home. Professor Gillespie and Stephen Bartholomew are sitting on one sofa. Stephen looks very grave. I can't read Brendan's face. DC Graves is on the other sofa. Finch tells me to sit down. I don't need his permission to sit in my own living room. I hesitate. I don't want to sit next to Gemma. I've nothing against her, I'd just prefer to sit by myself. But there's no alternative, so I sit down. Nanook remains by my side, and I place my hand on his head. It's good to have him back.

I look at them all in turn. Why do I feel so nervous?

'Aidan,' Finch begins, 'this has been one of the most complex investigations I've ever been involved in. And, even though I believe I know everything that's happened, I still have so many unanswered questions.'

'Have you found Luke?' I ask.

'We've found him.'

'Is he still alive?'

Finch doesn't answer. I look at Gemma, but she's playing with her fingers. Stephen isn't looking at me, but Brendan is. His stare is burning a hole right through me.

'Where is he?' I ask.

'Aidan, what do you know about dissociative identity disorder?' Brendan asks, leaning forward.

'Absolutely nothing. What is it?'

'It used to be called Multiple Personality Disorder. It's a complex psychological condition that is caused by many factors, including severe trauma. These traumas usually take place in childhood. But I have known of a couple of cases of it affecting adults.'

'I don't understand.' I look around, but all I see are blank faces. I hold on tighter to Nanook. I don't like where this is going.

'It's a severe form of dissociation, a mental process which produces a lack of connection in a person's thoughts, feelings, actions. It's a kind of coping mechanism. A person literally shuts themselves off from a situation or experience that's too violent or traumatic for that person to deal with.'

'And you think Luke has this dissociative disorder?'

Brendan looks at Finch.

'Aidan, Luke is dead,' Finch says.

'Dead?' I feel sick. It all makes sense, I suppose. He killed all those people, and he killed a detective. There would be no coming back from that. The only way out would be to commit suicide. 'How? When?'

'Gemma,' Finch instructs.

'Luke Jackson was fatally stabbed six years ago, outside the Bucket of Blood pub.'

Chapter One

The wind had picked up while he'd been in the Bucket of Blood. The back door almost slammed back in his face as he pushed it open. He made his way over to the VW Polo, head down, dragging his feet on the broken tarmac, his head full of dark thoughts.

He placed the box on the roof of the car, struggled to get his keys out of his trouser pocket and unlocked the boot.

'Aidan!'

Aidan jumped at the sound of his name being called. He looked up and saw Luke walking towards him. He ignored him, put the box of unwanted books in the boot and slammed it closed.

'Aidan, wait,' Luke said, running up to the car. 'Floella's just told me what this evening was all about. I'm sorry, OK? I didn't know.'

'You weren't supposed to know. It was a surprise. I told you all it was a surprise. If you'd have known what I was going to say, it wouldn't have been a surprise.'

'I know. I'm a dick, what can I say?'

Aidan looked at him, saw the smile, the blue eyes lighting up and twinkling in the moonlight.

'I'm not laughing, Luke. You know how long I've wanted to be published. You know how much this means to me and you couldn't let me have just one night, could you?'

'Look, I'm sorry. I didn't think. I genuinely forgot you said you had something to announce. I went out with Daisy today and things just developed. I honestly, hand on heart, did not intentionally mean to steal your thunder. You know I wouldn't do anything like that. Look, come to the Indian with us. We'll have a double celebration. Bring your books.'

'No, thank you. I'm not in the mood to celebrate.'

'Come on, don't be like this, Aidan. We can still celebrate. We can still have a good night out, a few too many drinks, a good laugh.'

Aidan sighed. 'You know, I went into that pub tonight with my head high, thinking I was going to impress all my mates. I thought everyone would be over the moon for me, lots of back-slapping and cheering and hugs and handshakes. I didn't get any of that. I got blank looks and awkwardness. None of them are my friends, Luke, not a single one. I know Clare and Martin had a housewarming party in the summer. I know everyone in that pub tonight went. Where was my invitation?'

'Ah,' he said, looking down at the ground.

'Exactly.' Aidan smiled. 'They're not my friends and tonight confirmed that. I don't know what I've done to be pushed out like this.'

'Aidan, I didn't know you hadn't been invited to the housewarming. I expected you to be there.'

'Did anyone ask where I was?'

'Erm…'

'Did you?'

'I…'

'No. I didn't think so. You might have expected me to be there, but you didn't actually do anything when you realised I wasn't. Enjoy your Indian, Luke.' Aidan pulled open the driver's door and was about to climb into the car when Luke grabbed him and pulled him out.

'Aidan, don't, please. I feel bad. I wanted to say something about the housewarming, but I didn't want you to feel uncomfortable. I mentioned to Clare that you should be there.'

'And what did she say?'

He looked away, his face reddening slightly.

'She doesn't like me. I know she doesn't. I don't know why. When I sent her the text about tonight and I didn't hear back from her, I knew. I wanted to rub her nose in my success and had to bribe her here with free champagne. And I saw Floella look at her watch before she even sat down. They're not my friends, Luke, and neither are you.'

'Jesus Christ,' Luke said under his breath. 'You're loving this, aren't you? That's really why you organised tonight, isn't it? If you knew how Clare felt about you, why invite her at all? Why not just invite me and Floella and Grey, and let the news of your success get back to her that way? No, the reason you wanted her here is so you could pick apart this evening later, to show how much of a victim you are.'

'What?'

'You're a victim, Aidan. You always have been. You wallow in self-pity all the time. Why don't people like me? Why is Clare such a bitch to me? I tell you what, Aid, don't bother coming to the Indian with us. You go home to your shitty little flat, and tomorrow you can make a list of all the reasons people don't like you. I'm sure you'll enjoy that.'

Aidan was physically shaking with rage. He watched Luke turn ugly as he spat the truth he'd been holding onto for months. He stepped back, almost falling against the car. His eyes blurred as the anger rose up inside him and clenched at his heart. He had to feel his way into the driver's seat. He slammed the door closed. His breathing was short and sharp. Through the windscreen, he watched as Luke walked away.

Aidan opened the glove box and scrambled around inside it. He knew it was here somewhere. He knew it was illegal to carry a weapon around with him, but it was for his own protection. He'd never use it for anything other than self-defence. Never. His fingers touched the cold stainless-steel handle. He pulled out the flick knife and held it in his hand. It felt heavy. He pressed the button and the blade flicked out at a frightening speed. He smiled. Who was the victim now?

The next few seconds were a blur. Aidan had no recollection of getting out of the car, of storming towards his best friend, of calling his name, of grabbing him by the shoulder, spinning him around and sinking the blade into him over and over and over again until every last ounce of breath was stabbed out of him. But that's what happened. That's how Luke Jackson died.

Chapter Fifty

The fire crackles in the silence of the room. I look from the police officers to the doctors and then down at my hands. DI Finch finally speaks.

'You weren't stabbed six years ago, Aidan. Besides the stab wound you received a couple of weeks ago in your kitchen, you have no other stab wounds anywhere on you. The flick knife used to stab DS Marshall, and you, was the same knife used to stab Luke Jackson to death. That knife was never found, but we have looked through the records and evidence gathered from the case, and the blade of the knife matches the fatal wounds inflicted on Luke. We've also spoken to a couple of friends of yours. One of them...' He takes a notebook out of his coat pocket and begins to flick through it.

'Floella Montrose,' Gemma reminds him.

'That's right. When we couldn't find Luke, we put out an appeal for anyone with any information about him to come forward. Ms Montrose called us. She said she couldn't understand why we were looking for him when he was dead. She told us everything that happened that night. You were surprising everyone with the launch of your literary career. Then Luke arrived, late, with his girlfriend, and announced to the whole room he was engaged. The spotlight was taken from you. He stole your thunder, and everyone decided to go for a curry to celebrate, but you didn't.'

'That's right. I left the pub and was attacked in the car park,' I say.

'No. You weren't. Gemma?'

For the first time, DC Gemma Graves turns to face me. She can't meet my eyes, though. 'It wasn't until everyone was at the Indian restaurant that the reason for the night was revealed to Luke. Feeling guilty, he decided to go back for you. He found you in the car park, getting into your car to go home. There are no witnesses, but we can only assume you got into an argument. Maybe years of resentment came to the surface, and you snapped.'

'No. No, I didn't. You're wrong.'

'Luke Jackson was stabbed eleven times. It was a frenzied attack. Floella Montrose told us that you took his death very hard. You blamed yourself because you'd arranged the evening in the first place. You pushed everyone away. But she says they always suspected that you were involved somehow.'

Brendan says, 'The trauma of what you did to Luke, to your best friend, was too much for you to cope with.'

'I was stabbed,' I say, softly. I feel a tear roll down my left cheek. I don't wipe it away.

'When you moved to Derbyshire, you used the story of being stabbed to protect yourself from what you'd really done. You couldn't deny a stabbing had taken place, but you could change the victim.'

'But I've seen Luke. Recently. He lives here,' I say.

'In your head, Luke was still living, and you kept him alive by creating a whole new person, a Luke you wanted to have around,' Brendan says. 'You explained his absence by him constantly working away. You brought him back when you wanted some company around you, but all of the conversations were one-sided.'

'I don't know what you're all trying to do to me, but Luke is alive. He's a living, flesh-and-bone person. He takes Nanook for walks, for crying out loud.' I'm getting agitated now. This is actually very scary. Upon hearing his name, Nanook sits up. I hold onto him just that little bit tighter.

From her folder, Gemma takes out a glossy black-and-white photograph. She hands it to me. 'This was taken from a CCTV camera above the Golden Swan pub in Gallowsfield the day after Melanie Burton's body was found.'

I know straight away what I'm looking at. It's a very grainy image, but it's zoomed in on a man walking along the side of the road with a dog on a lead. Even though I'm dressed in layers and a big winter coat with the hood up to protect myself against the cold, it's obvious it's me and that the dog is Nanook.

'But how could I? I hadn't left the house for years. Last week was the first time I was able to leave.'

I'm so scared. How is this happening?

'The thing with dissociative identity disorder,' Brendan begins, 'is that, when a task needs doing, one of the personalities that is more suited or better able comes to the front. You said Luke has been taking Nanook for walks. But the thing is, Aidan, Luke is dead. It is you who has been embodying Luke's persona. Look closer at the photo,' he says.

I look down at the picture in my shaking hands.

He continues. 'You have the hood of your coat up, but it's still easy to tell that you have a shaved head. You've turned yourself into Luke, even copying his hairstyle. When you're Aidan, you wear a wig. I knew straight away there was something wrong when your wig came off in the hospital. There had to be a legitimate reason why a man with no sign of baldness was wearing a wig.'

This is too much to take in.

357

'Luke's dead.' I say in a quiet voice.

'Yes,' Brendan replies.

'I killed him?'

'You did,' Finch answers.

'But, hang on, if I had this dissociative thing, then wouldn't my therapist have picked up on it? I've been talking to her for years.'

Gemma clears her throat. 'Aidan, the fire in the house knocked out the phone lines. You haven't had an internet connection for weeks, yet you've ticked off Skype calls with your therapist in your diary.'

I open my mouth to say something, but nothing comes out.

Gemma takes another photo out of her folder and holds it up to me. 'Who is this person?'

'That's my therapist,' I say.

'No. This is your mother. We've searched everywhere for a Charlotte Wood and been unable to find a registered therapist with that name. When we googled the name, we found a Charlotte Cullen née Wood, who was killed in a car accident in Dublin. You don't have a therapist. You've never had a therapist. You've been talking with your mother all these years.'

'I'm guessing your mum wanted the best for you,' Brendan says, his voice soft, leaning forward, elbows on knees. 'Your mother looked out for you, just like Luke did, and she's been taking on the role of therapist ever since you moved here, to talk through your problems.'

I want to cry. When Mum died, when the police came to see me in the hospital in Dublin and said she couldn't be saved, I had to be sedated. I was inconsolable. I loved her, I cherished her, and she was gone. Luke took care of me. He helped me to organise the funeral. He stayed with me through my grief.

The room falls silent. I can hear the distant hum from the fridge in the kitchen. My head feels heavy as I try to make sense of it all.

'But, in my statement I gave to you,' I say to Gemma, 'I told you everything. I told you how Luke saved me when I fell asleep in the bath. I'd have drowned if he hadn't come home. He can't be...' I trail off.

'A story you invented to feel someone was looking out for you, caring for you,' Brendan says gently. 'Luke took care of you following your mother's death, and he has been doing so ever since.'

I can't take any of this in. But there is a burning question that has risen up to the front of my mind. I'm afraid of the answer, but the truth must be known.

'But ... the mirror. Where did it come from? Who put it there?'

Gemma pulled up an old photo album from the side of the sofa. She opened it to a marked page and handed it to me, pointing at a picture of my gran sitting in an armchair in her house in Ireland, smiling to the camera, the wooden mirror on the wall behind her.

'You brought it with you here when you moved from Liverpool. Your basement is full of boxes full of items belonging to your grandmother and mother,' she said.

I don't say anything. I don't know what to say. This is too much.

'So, who killed Melanie Burton and the others?' I eventually ask.

'You did,' Finch says.

'What?' I look up. 'No. No. I couldn't. I ... couldn't do anything like that. I'm not a killer. I'm... What happened to those people was disturbing. I'm not capable of that. I might be able to get my head around killing Luke in a moment of madness, but there is no way, no chance... No.'

'Would you like a drink of water?' Stephen asks.

'Gemma,' Finch instructs his DC again.

'A hair was found at the scene of Melanie's murder and at the campsite at Monyash. The DNA is identical at each crime scene. It's Nanook's,' Gemma says.

I look down at my dog. I don't believe any of this. It's lies. It's pure fiction. I hold my dog tighter.

'I … I don't have any memory of this. You're all lying. I'd know. If I killed all those people, I'd know about it.'

'Luke killed them,' Brendan says. 'You killed them as Luke.'

'You're seriously fucking crazy if you expect me to believe any of this shit. Why? Why would I do any of this? I'm living the life I've always wanted. I have a nice home, a good career. Why would I want to ruin it?'

'There is an argument for the self-destructive side of your personality to want to put all of it in jeopardy. You did it before, very successfully, in killing your best friend, Luke Jackson. You literally got away with murder. You're a crime writer at the very top of your field. Your books all sell incredibly well, here and around the world. According to your agent, there's even a film adaptation of *Out of Darkness* in early development. What better way to test your success than to make your work come alive?'

The room falls silent.

This isn't real.

'But surely, if I had this dissociative … what is it?'

'Dissociative identity disorder,' Stephen fills in for me.

'If I did have that, I'd know about it. I'd know that I was killing these people, even if I was pretending to be Luke.'

'Not necessarily,' Brendan says, sitting back on the sofa and crossing his legs at the knee. 'Switching between personalities can be consensual, forced or triggered. Consensual is if one identity has the capacity to do something that the other doesn't, as we saw when Luke was walking Nanook.'

'And what about the triggered or forced switches?' I ask.

'If something happens to frighten you, a flashback or a reminder of a past trauma, you could switch to Luke in order to cope with it until you've calmed down. He's the stronger of the two, both mentally and physically. A switch that is forced is one that isn't wanted by one of the alter egos involved.'

'So, Luke could appear when Aidan doesn't want him to?' Gemma asks.

'Yes.'

I look, mouth open, between the two.

'My home was set on fire. I could have died. Are you saying I did that?' I ask, looking at everyone in the room in turn for a sensible answer.

'Yes,' Brendan answers simply. 'Luke looks after you. He's been doing it since university, when your mum died. When these murders started happening, you thought someone was targeting you, so you needed Luke to save you. What better way than putting yourself in serious jeopardy?'

'I have no memory of any of this. I'd know. Surely?'

Nobody looks at me. They all think I'm guilty.

'DI Finch,' Brendan says, 'it's time.'

'What are you talking about?' I ask.

I look at Finch as he steps towards me. He clears his throat.

'Aidan Cullen, I'm arresting you for the murder of Luke Jackson, Melanie Burton, James and Millicent Hargreaves...' He grabs my arm to pull me up from the sofa.

I lunge at him. I wrap my hands around his throat and we both fall to the floor.

'Don't you fucking touch him!' I scream at him in a Liverpudlian accent.

'Luke, calm down!' Brendan Gillespie shouts and grabs my hands. As he pulls me away from Finch, he turns to Gemma and says, 'A forced switch.'

Chapter Fifty-One

I'm sitting on the padded seat by the window, looking out at the grey, depressing landscape in front of me. It's not inspiring at all.

The sky is a brilliant blue and the sun is beating down, but its rays aren't hot. It's still bitterly cold out there, not that I've been out for a while. There was a hard frost overnight. I can see it on the tops of the cars in the car park.

I finished reading a book last night. I have three more on my bedside table to read, but I need to pace myself. I've almost run out of new books, and I don't know when I'll be getting any more.

'Good morning, Aidan.'

I turn and there's Professor Gillespie standing in my doorway wearing the same pin-striped suit he wears every single bloody day. I don't say good morning back. I really don't like him. He's messed with my head and made me into something I'm not.

'How are you feeling? Did you sleep well?'

He's trying to be friendly. I know his game.

'I slept very well. Thank you,' I say with a faux smile. If he wants to play games, then we can play games.

'I've been told you missed your group therapy session yesterday.'

'I was busy.'

'Oh?' he asks, stepping further into the room. 'Doing what?'

'Writing. Obviously. I have a deadline.'

He hitches up his trousers and sits down on the wooden chair by the door. It creaks under his weight. I turn back to look out of the window.

'Aidan, we've been over this many times before. You're not a writer anymore. That part of your life is over. You need to accept that. How do you expect to get better if you can't accept your reality?'

I look back at him. He has a smugness about him I don't like. He might be clever and have letters after his name, but he has no idea how to talk to people.

I don't reply to him. I do what I always do when I don't want to talk: I turn to look out of the window. It's not long before I hear him lift himself up off the chair and leave the room. His highly polished shoes click-clack on the tiled floor as he goes down the corridor.

I look down and see Nanook by my feet. He looks up at me. I pat the seat next to me and he jumps up. He places his head on my lap, and I stroke him.

'I'm so glad you're with me, Nanook. I don't think I could do this on my own. I had a new idea for a book last night. I've been thinking it over this morning and I'm liking the sound of it. It's a sort of meta-thriller. I'm going to put myself in it. And you, too, obviously. Anthony Horowitz did it with *The Word is Murder* and Joseph Knox did it with *True Crime Story*. I reckon I could pull it off.

'Obviously, with how things stand at the moment, I'd have to write it under a pseudonym and just use myself as a character. What do you think?'

Nanook looks up at me and yawns.

'Wow, you're a tough audience, Nanook. Now, I was thinking, for my pen name, I'd use my mum's maiden name and my dad's first name. It would be a little nod to them.'

I stroke Nanook and turn back to looking out of the window. I feel myself smiling. It's good to have a plan and a goal. And, as long as I have my dog, I'm perfectly fine.

I look down, but Nanook's not there anymore. I'm not too worried. He'll be back. He always comes back. And as for me, I'm fine. I'm always fine.

Acknowledgments

Writers will tell you that writing a novel is hard. And they're correct. It's incredibly challenging to think of a story from scratch and spend a large part of a year crafting it from inception to the final page. We spend so much time on our own that some days it can be a struggle to sit down in front of the computer. However, with *Chapter One*, I had so much fun writing it. The idea has been in my head for years and when I finally found the time to sit down and create Aidan and Luke's world and the individual first chapters for Aidan's books, I loved every minute of it.

Of course, many people helped in crafting the book you're reading or listening to, and I would like to thank Imogen Papworth and Josephine Lane at Audible and Stephen Hogan and Lucy Paterson for dramatizing the novel for audio.

Thanks to everyone at One More Chapter and HarperCollins who has worked with me on this book including my gifted editor, Jennie Rothwell, and Kara Daniel, and CJ Harter for the copyedits and Simon Fox for the proofread.

My agent, Jamie Cowen at Ampersand, is a great support and you wouldn't be reading this book without him championing me and my work.

To Philip Lumb, Simon Browes, Andrew Barrett and "Mr Tidd" for all their technical support.

To my mum, Chris, Kevin, and Jonas for being at the end of a phone to keep me motivated and on the cusp of sanity.

Finally, a huge thank you to all the readers, booksellers and bloggers who keep spreading the word about my books. Thank you so so much for all you do. I appreciate it more than I can ever say.

The author and One More Chapter would like to thank everyone who contributed to the publication of this story...

Analytics
James Brackin
Abigail Fryer

Audio
Fionnuala Barrett
Ciara Briggs

Contracts
Laura Amos
Laura Evans

Design
Lucy Bennett
Fiona Greenway
Liane Payne
Dean Russell

Digital Sales
Laura Daley
Lydia Grainge
Hannah Lismore

eCommerce
Laura Carpenter
Madeline ODonovan
Charlotte Stevens
Christina Storey
Jo Surman
Rachel Ward

Editorial
Kara Daniel
Simon Fox
CJ Harter
Charlotte Ledger
Ajebowale Roberts
Jennie Rothwell
Helen Williams

Harper360
Jennifer Dee
Emily Gerbner
Ariana Juarez
Jean Marie Kelly
emma sullivan
Sophia Wilhelm

International Sales
Peter Borcsok
Ruth Burrow
Colleen Simpson
Ben Wright

Inventory
Sarah Callaghan
Kirsty Norman

Marketing & Publicity
Chloe Cummings
Grace Edwards
Emma Petfield

Operations
Melissa Okusanya
Hannah Stamp

Production
Denis Manson
Simon Moore
Francesca Tuzzeo

Rights
Helena Font Brillas
Ashton Mucha
Zoe Shine
Aisling Smyth
Lucy Vanderbilt

Trade Marketing
Ben Hurd
Eleanor Slater

**The HarperCollins
Distribution Team**

**The HarperCollins
Finance & Royalties
Team**

**The HarperCollins
Legal Team**

**The HarperCollins
Technology Team**

UK Sales
Isabel Coburn
Jay Cochrane
Sabina Lewis
Holly Martin
Harriet Williams
Leah Woods

**And every other
essential link in the
chain from delivery
drivers to booksellers
to librarians and
beyond!**

DCI Matilda Darke Series

Have you discovered the DCI Matilda Darke Thrillers?

A DCI MATILDA DARKE THRILLER

MICHAEL WOOD

Two murders.
Twenty years.
Now the killer is
back for more...

FOR Reasons Unknown

A DCI MATILDA DARKE THRILLER

MICHAEL WOOD

Two perfect families.
Two broken marriages.
And a killer who needs
to be stopped…

Outside Looking In

'She is the perfect heroine' ELLY GRIFFITHS

A DCI MATILDA DARKE THRILLER

MICHAEL WOOD

Eight killers.
One house.
And the almost
perfect murder…

A Room Full of Killers

'Tightly delivered and played at exhilarating pace'
PAUL FINCH

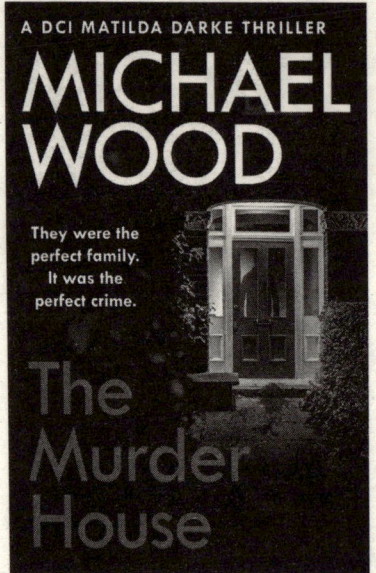

ONE MORE CHAPTER

One More Chapter is an
award-winning global
division of HarperCollins.

Subscribe to our newsletter to get our
latest eBook deals and stay up to date
with all our new releases!

signup.harpercollins.co.uk/
join/signup-omc

Meet the team at
www.onemorechapter.com

Follow us!

 @OneMoreChapter_

 @onemorechapterhc

 @onemorechapterhc

 @onemorechapterhc

Do you write unputdownable fiction?
We love to hear from new voices.
Find out how to submit your novel at
www.onemorechapter.com/submissions